Dear Reader,

It's one thing for a man to marry and gradually acquire a family. It's quite another for a man who's never owned much more than he could carry to suddenly find himself in charge of two twelve-year-olds—girls at that. But that's exactly what happened to me. I was charged with giving them a stable environment and becoming a steadying influence on them, neither of which I, a footloose cowboy, felt I was equipped to do. I won't say the task wasn't frightening and daunting at times, but the girls taught me things about myself I hadn't known before.

They also brought Laurie into my life and thereby hangs a tale.

I hope you'll find our story as much fun as living it was.

George Whittaker

Please address questions and book requests to: Harlequin Reader Service
U.S.: 3010 Walden Ave., P.O. Box 1325, Buffalo, NY 14269
Canadian: P.O. Box 609, Fort Erie, Ont. L2A 5X3

BARBARA KAYE

RAMBLIN' MAN

Harlequin Books

TORONTO • NEW YORK • LONDON
AMSTERDAM • PARIS • SYDNEY • HAMBURG
STOCKHOLM • ATHENS • TOKYO • MILAN
MADRID • WARSAW • BUDAPEST • AUCKLAND

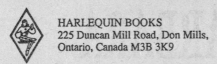

HARLEQUIN BOOKS
225 Duncan Mill Road, Don Mills,
Ontario, Canada M3B 3K9

ISBN 0-373-88513-X

RAMBLIN' MAN

PROLOGUE

IT COSTS MONEY just to get out of bed in the morning, Laurie Tyler thought glumly as she sat at the kitchen table and completed the hated monthly chore of paying the household bills. Considering their modest life-style, there seemed to be an excessive amount of them.

She was only minutes into the task when it became apparent that there wouldn't be any extra money that month, either. Laurie always hoped there would be, although she couldn't imagine why she did. Just a stubborn streak of optimism, she supposed. Sighing, she unfolded the electric bill and began writing yet another check. Here it was November, and Christmas was just around the corner. Fortunately her brother and sister never asked for anything and always acted thrilled with whatever she was able to give them. Andy and Jill were only too aware that their schoolteacher sister, the woman who had been in sole charge of them for nine years, existed in a perpetual financial bind.

As she sat finishing the chore the only sound was the ticking of the old-fashioned clock on the kitchen wall. The big house was very quiet. Jill wasn't home yet, and Andy no longer lived there, having graduated from college and taken a job in San Antonio last summer. Next May, Jill would complete her sophomore year. They were good kids, the best. There had been many dire predictions about what would happen to teenagers who were raised by an older sister, but Laurie hadn't experienced more than minor, normal problems with her siblings. Now they were adults, and in two years Jill would be out of the nest. Laurie was

beginning to see the faintest glimmering of light at the end
of the tunnel.

Once all the bills had been paid and each envelope
stamped, she stood, went to the sink and looked out the
window above it. Autumn had come to the High Country
of West Texas, and the countryside was breathtaking. Un-
precedented rains that year had the area's ranchers jumping with joy, but weather conditions had no effect on
Laurie's financial circumstances. Though everyone in the
Davis Mountains referred to her property as the Tyler
Ranch, it had been years since any livestock had grazed
there. She recalled the herds of white-faced, cinnamon-
colored Herefords her father had raised, and wondered if
the place would ever again qualify as a working ranch. One
did not stock two-hundred acres with livestock and hire
workers to tend them on a schoolteacher's salary.

Laurie also wondered if she cared any longer. She was
thirty-two and would be thirty-four when Jill graduated
from college. Would she want to start up the ranch from
scratch or just sell the place and do something else entirely? She didn't know, but it was a moot question, anyway. For the next two years she would do exactly what she
was doing now—teaching school, paying the bills and just
hanging on.

Ten years ago if someone had tried to tell her that was the
way she would be spending the thirty-second year of her
life, she would have laughed. Ever since she'd been old
enough to think about such things, she had been sure she'd
live her life differently than most High Country folk, and
in some other place. She'd had vague plans of getting her
Master's degree, then teaching in a big university, or possibly a small prestigious one. And she had imagined herself married, with a family by now. That apparently wasn't
meant to be, Laurie thought sadly.

At that moment she heard the sound of an approaching
vehicle. Leaving the kitchen, she walked to the dining room
window and peered out. The pickup coming toward the
house belonged to the DO, her good friend Cassie Mait-

land's ranch, so Laurie naturally assumed Cassie was paying her a visit. She opened the front door and went out onto the porch in time to see not Cassie, but George Whittaker, the DO's foreman, climbing out of the cab. She would have known that lean frame and the rakish set of his Stetson anywhere.

Her heart gave an involuntary leap, something that annoyed her no end. Her foolish attraction to George was one of long standing and was totally one-sided. He knew she was alive, and that was about it. He devoted one day a week to the Tyler Ranch—at Cassie's insistence, Laurie was sure—at which time he cleared brush, mended fence, and made general repairs, then hung around long enough for a convivial cup of coffee or can of beer. Laurie had always begrudged the hours she'd had to spend in the classroom on "George's day." It was the one day of the week when not even the most unruly student in her sixth-period class needed to fear being kept after school.

It was pitiful, really, she thought now, that an hour or so around the kitchen table with this particular man was the most exciting aspect of her life. She couldn't honestly say she remembered much that they'd ever talked about, since George never used two words if one would do. He was utterly polite and almost painfully shy around women. Worse, he was a footloose cowboy, a man who cherished his freedom. While it wouldn't have been entirely fair to characterize him as a drifter—he'd worked for Cassie for four years—he had that look in his eye, as though his mind always was focused on some distant horizon. In short, he was a bad sort to fall for. George could break a woman's heart and never know he was doing it. All he had to do was flash that nice smile and focus his blue eyes on her, and her insides melted.

Laurie wondered why he was there. It wasn't "his day." Briefly she entertained the pleasant notion that he might have come to visit for no reason at all. "Well, good afternoon," she said, brushing her honey-colored hair away from her face, then shading her eyes with her hand. "Did you get your days mixed up?"

"Hi, Laurie. No, I know what day it is. I..." George stopped at the foot of the steps and looked up. He was the picture of seriousness. "Actually, I came to say goodbye."

Laurie's hand dropped, and she steadied herself. Outwardly her composure was intact, but inside she felt something die. A dream, she supposed. A foolish dream, not rooted in anything approaching reality. "Oh? Going anywhere in particular?"

"To Oklahoma to see my family for a while, and then...I don't know. Thataway." He pointed west.

"I see." She drew a deep breath. The announcement was unexpected but not particularly surprising. Men like George never had any reason to stay in one place. They made sure of that. "Good luck."

"Thanks."

"It was nice of you to take the time to say goodbye."

"Don't mention it."

"And thanks for all your help around here."

His eyes swept his surroundings. "Wish I could have done more. What you really need is a full-time man on the place, someone who can help out on a day-to-day basis, not just every once in a while."

Laurie uttered a dry, mirthless laugh. "Yes, I guess I do. I surely could use one of those."

George kicked at the ground with the toe of his boot, then looked at her. "Laurie...uh, there's something I've always wanted to ask you, but I figured it was none of my business. Still isn't, I reckon."

"That's okay. Ask whatever you like."

"How come a pretty woman like you never got married?"

There was a tense moment of silence. Since they'd never discussed much of a personal nature, Laurie had never told him about the fiancé who had disappeared shortly after her parents' deaths. Nor had she mentioned that with teaching school and raising two teenagers she'd had no time for fun and meeting people her own age. "Oh, obligations, duties, people who needed me. All those things you've been running away from." Her gaze did not falter.

George looked as though she'd stabbed him with a knife. She honestly hadn't meant to sound so accusing, but the words were out and there was no way to retract them. She noticed that he tried to smile, but apparently he couldn't. He just nodded. "Yeah. Guess you've got me pegged, all right. Well...so long." He touched the brim of his hat and turned away from the intenseness of her eyes.

"George, wait a minute. There's one more thing."

Taking a deep breath, Laurie descended the steps. She walked up to him, and stood very close. Later she would wonder where she had found the nerve. "I hope I'm not entirely out of line, but..." She raised her face to his and placed a light, melting kiss on his very startled mouth. "Goodbye. Have a safe journey. I hope you find whatever it is you're looking for in the next place. Send me a postcard." Then, summoning up every drop of poise she possessed, she smiled, turned and went up the steps. Once on the porch she quickly crossed it and disappeared behind the front door.

When she was safely behind the closed door, she shed a tear or two. Not many and not from heartbreak. Rather, the sadness came from suffering yet another disappointment, from realizing the finality of the goodbye, from knowing she would miss him. She'd never see George again, but she would survive. The Laurie Tylers of the world always did.

CHAPTER ONE

Four months later

THE ELEGANT two-story brick house stood on a quiet, tree-shaded Oklahoma City street and reminded George of anything but a renowned psychiatric clinic. He paused on the sidewalk to study the grand entrance. Then he crossed the walk, climbed the steps and rang the bell. His ring was met with a buzzing sound, indicating that the door was open to his touch.

He stepped into an impressive foyer, the tiled floor of which was polished to a dazzling shine. Ahead of him, a sweeping staircase rose to the second floor. From somewhere in the building came the muted sound of a telephone ringing; otherwise, all was hushed. George removed the big Stetson from his head, momentarily wondering if he had come to the wrong place. He thought he'd followed directions precisely, but many of the fine old homes in the neighborhood had been converted to professional offices.

Just then he heard some kind of movement at the top of the stairs. Lifting his eyes, he saw a plump, silver-haired woman standing on the landing. "Mr. Whittaker?" she inquired softly.

"Yes, ma'am."

"Please come up. I'm Dr. Frances Ames."

If ever George had doubted the wisdom of this consultation it was at that moment, but he obediently climbed the stairs and followed Dr. Ames into a large room that looked more like a society matron's fashionable parlor than a psychiatrist's office. It was furnished with a print sofa upon which was strewn an assortment of needlepoint pillows. Matching wing chairs flanked a fireplace, and a silk flower arrangement adorned a coffee table. There was a large cluttered desk in front of a draperied window, but Dr. Ames did not take a seat behind it. Instead she picked up a folder that was lying open on it and sat in one of the wing chairs, indicating the other with a sweep of her hand.

"Please have a seat, Mr. Whittaker. I understand you are Mrs. Greene's brother, is that correct?"

"Yes, ma'am, er, Doctor." George found it almost impossible to believe that the grandmotherly woman was one of the country's leading psychiatrists. He took a seat and placed his hat in his lap, unconsciously fingering it as if it were a sort of security blanket. He'd never felt more uncomfortable in his life. It had been his contention that he was the last person in the world who should have come here, but who else was there to do it? His stepmother, Anna? Hardly. Neither he nor his sister had ever felt very close to her. His father? Jonas Whittaker was so bewildered by his daughter's actions that his early sympathy had given way to anger.

Dr. Ames slipped on a pair of eyeglasses and smiled at him compassionately, seemingly able to read his thoughts, certainly able to sense his discomfort. "Please try to relax. This is one place where you can say whatever you like. I'm here to help you."

"Doctor, I don't think I'm the one who needs help."

"Perhaps I should put it another way. I'm here to help you understand and deal with your sister's condition. According to her primary-care physician, she's a very sick woman."

"She tried to kill herself," George said dully. He had thought that saying it aloud might make it seem more real to him, but it didn't. "Some of the doctors have tried to be kind by saying it could have been an accident, but I don't buy that for a second. If that neighbor hadn't stopped by when she did..."

"Don't be too quick to judge your sister's actions. In-ability to concentrate or to remember is a common sign of mental disorder. Ellen simply might have forgotten she'd already taken medication."

"Come on, Doctor. She took enough pills to fell a stal-lion. Is that stupid or sick?"

"What do you think?" Dr. Ames asked. "It isn't nor-mal behavior. It's mental illness."

"Well, you're right to think I don't understand why El-len is doing this to herself, to all of us."

"Us?" Dr. Ames prompted.

"Me, my dad, her kids. Not that I think Stacy and DeeAnn are old enough to have any real idea of what's go-ing on."

"How old are they?"

"Twelve. They're twins."

This time the doctor's smile was rather sad. "Don't be too sure they aren't aware of what's going on, Mr. Whit-taker. Twelve-year-olds are often much more astute than we think. And, of course, they are the most unfortunate vic-tims of situations like this. How are the girls taking it?"

"Oh ... surprisingly well, I think. They miss their mom, of course. They don't like being at the farm. They stick to me like glue, and I spend as much time with them as I pos-sibly can. As long as they're with me, they seem to do all right. But they have to be confused."

Dr. Ames nodded, and her eyes dipped briefly as she studied the contents of the folder in her lap. "I understand that Ellen's sickness began right after her husband left her."

"Yes. Leaving would have been bad enough, but he left her for another woman."

"How long had they been married?"

"Almost fourteen years."

"How long has it been since her husband left?"

George shifted in the chair. In all the thirty-three years of his life he had never been forced into the position of re-vealing personal details to a stranger, and he'd never imag-ined he would do so. Only the persistent badgering of Joe

Lindsay, his family's physician, had prompted him to see Dr. Ames. Still, he would have gladly given all he owned to be able to stand, thank the good doctor for her time and forget his sister's dilemma, his father's anger, and the twins' confusion—forget everything. But, of course, his conscience would never allow that. "I came home for a visit in Mid-November. It happened shortly after that. Apparently the, er, alliance with the other woman had been going on for some time. My dad suspected it, Ellen denied it, and since I was away, I didn't know anything about it."

Dr. Ames frowned thoughtfully. "Four months ago. Then your brother-in-law left his family shortly before the holidays?"

"Yes. A real prince, huh? I'll tell you right off, Doctor, that I never cared much for my brother-in-law, and the feeling was mutual. But when he left, Ellen went to pieces, and everything's been royally scr—messed up—ever since."

"How is the rest of the family reacting to Ellen's crisis?"

"My stepmother never had any kids of her own, so she's at a loss over it. My dad isn't a young man, and Ellen's suicide attempt hit him so hard that he's resorting to anger. The girls . . . well, what would young girls think? Suddenly their daddy's gone and their mother cries all the time. Frankly, Doctor, I'd like to give my sister a good shake. . . or a spanking. And I'll spare you a description of what I'd like to do to Steve."

Dr. Ames digested what he said without a flicker of expression. "Are you married, Mr. Whittaker?"

"No, thank God! Never have been."

The doctor closed the folder, leaned forward and spoke earnestly, sympathetically. "I'm going to try to explain to you what happens to some people when a beloved spouse leaves, particularly when a new lover is in the picture." She paused, as if trying to choose her words carefully. "You might say that the world falls off its axis. Everything stable in life vanishes, or seems to. Self-esteem collapses. Security gives way to fear. The future becomes meaningless.

There are no consoling words or thoughts. Relatives, friends, pastors—all those people we normally turn to in time of distress—do no good. If one word can adequately describe the experience, I suppose that word would have to be panic."

Wearily, George rubbed a hand over his eyes. He had spent so many sleepless nights worrying about this that he was almost numb. "How long does this panic last?"

"Who can predict? For some it's a transitory thing that soon gives way to anger, then acceptance. Others withdraw so completely that they require years of counseling. Left untreated, some die by their own hand. Tell me something about Ellen's marriage."

George thought a minute. "Well, Doctor, I've been away from home for most of the last fourteen years, but when I was around Steve and Ellen..." He paused, hesitant about voicing his thoughts, partly because he wasn't sure how to put them into words. "She's crazy about the guy, always has been. I never understood it, but that was the way it was. It was like Steve was the sun and Ellen just orbited around him."

"Hmm. Predictable. We find that people who rely too heavily on others for their well-being are prime candidates for depression. That isn't the healthiest relationship a man and woman can share."

"Probably not, but it seemed to work okay for fourteen years."

"Were they good parents?"

"Never having been a parent, I hate to judge, but they have good kids. At least, they had good kids."

"But now there are problems?"

"Oh, nothing serious so far. Just acting up, bids for attention, that sort of thing. They get on Dad's nerves something fierce."

"What about their father, Mr. Whittaker? Hasn't he offered to step in at this difficult time?"

George made a scoffing sound. "We don't have the slightest idea where he is. You see, he accepted a job somewhere in South America. He's a geologist. So is the other woman. They left together. Steve doesn't know about any of this."

"Did he leave without making any sort of financial arrangements for his daughters?"

"No, the bank sends a check every month."

"Then possibly someone at the bank could get in touch with him."

"I thought of that, but no one there knows anything of Steve's whereabouts. He opened a new account and instructed the bank to mail a check on the last day of every month. Apparently he doesn't want to be found. He'd better hope I never find him."

Dr. Ames scribbled something in the folder. Then she closed it, crossed her hands over it and looked directly at George. "I suppose you know that Ellen's been diagnosed as being in a severe depression and is considered a threat to herself and the children."

George's shoulders sagged. "Yes."

"I've visited her several times, and both your family physician and I believe she should be hospitalized."

"Dr. Lindsay told me as much. Frankly, it scares the hell out of me."

"You wouldn't be normal if it didn't."

"I don't mean about Ellen's going into a mental hospital," George said quickly. "I guess she belongs with people who know how to take care of her. I'm afraid for the kids. What's going to happen to them? I've worried about it until I can't handle it anymore."

"But they have family," Dr. Ames said. "Their grandfather, for instance."

George frowned. "I'd really prefer that Dad not have to take on that responsibility. He was over forty when I was born, so he's kinda old to have twelve-year-old grandkids. And, too, he's not as sympathetic to Ellen's problems as he was in the beginning. He says she's just trying to make everybody as miserable as she is. And, if you'll pardon me for saying so, he says psychiatry is hogwash."

Dr. Ames just smiled. "Well, then, there's you. You seem to be a stable individual, and you obviously care for the girls very much."

"I'm not sure I'd be a better choice for guardian. I don't even have a home. I make my living as a cowboy, working from place to place. If this business with Ellen hadn't happened, I'd be long gone by now."

"Mr. Whittaker, I think you'll agree that the girls' welfare is of paramount importance right now. Their father can't be found, and their mother won't be coming home for many months, maybe longer. Unfortunately, in times of emotional upheaval, children sometimes picture themselves as being at fault. Those girls need a stable environment. If neither you nor your father is prepared to take care of them, they'll simply have to be placed in a foster home."

George's eyes widened. "No! There's no way Stacy and DeeAnn are going to live with people we don't even know." The thought was so alarming that he could feel himself shake all over.

The doctor sighed, and again her smile was full of compassion and sympathy. "Life has such a way of throwing us curves, doesn't it? Well, Mr. Whittaker, if you won't consider a foster home, I'm afraid you'll have to accept the fact that, for the time being, your wandering days are over."

THE DRIVE from Oklahoma City to the cotton farm where he had spent so much of his childhood took two hours, giving George plenty of time to think, to brood, to worry. How quickly life could change. Four months ago his plans had been firm. He'd spend the holidays with his family, then head on west, to Montana or Idaho, someplace he'd never been. That was the pattern his adult life had taken. His calling was not compatible with settling down. Since the age of nineteen when he'd left Oklahoma State University to hire on at a ranch in the Panhandle, he had been wandering. He kept his possessions few and simple, and he formed no attachments, neither to people nor to places.

When things got too comfortable and predictable, he moved on.

Yet, when he was being completely honest with himself, he admitted that saying goodbye had become harder as he'd gotten older. Last November, when he'd left the Davis Mountains after working there for four years, he'd discovered that he hated to go. There had been people he hadn't wanted to say goodbye to: Cassie Maitland, for one, the best boss he'd ever worked for, bar none; Homer "Shot" Barnes, for another, the best drinking buddy he'd ever had; and Laurie Tyler, who, quite simply, was the classiest woman he'd ever met. And, despite the turmoil attendant on Ellen's emotional troubles, he'd thought of them all many times during the last four months.

And despite his wandering ways, George did believe in marriage, home and family. He guessed he'd always known he would settle down eventually, if only to prevent his ending up a saddle-weary cowpoke reduced to doing odd jobs around some ranch. And, realistically, he'd supposed that a wife and kids would go along with settling down. But he hadn't wanted to settle here—not on an Oklahoma cotton farm. And not now! And a wife was supposed to come before kids. Dammit, he wasn't ready!

Then the faces of Stacy and DeeAnn flashed through his mind, along with Dr. Ames's words: *Those girls need a stable environment.* He wondered if he could do it. *Dear God*, he thought. Just contemplating being responsible for two young kids sent a wave of fear rushing through him. And the thought of being stuck here, in the place he'd so happily fled at nineteen, was worse. Ellen did not have a monopoly on panic and depression. He felt as though someone was closing the cell door behind him.

George slowed the truck and turned off the two-lane blacktop onto a well-traveled dirt road that sliced through ironing-board-flat plains. The fields on either side stretched seemingly into infinity. Within weeks the plows would be out, and another year's crop would go in the ground. He had returned to the farm in November in time to help his father with the harvest, but he'd sure planned to be gone before planting season. One thing George could say for cotton: it was just about the prettiest crop there was. But that was the sum total of things he could say for it.

Parking the truck at the side of the frame farmhouse, he went in search of his father, and found him in the barn tinkering with his tractor. Jonas looked up when the door creaked open.

"You're back. So, what did that fancy shrink have to say?"

George propped one booted foot on the tractor's running board. "Ellen's going into that place, and she might be there for a spell."

Jonas digested that, then acknowledged it with some obscure sound, but he said nothing. However, George could tell by his father's expression that he thought it all was nothing but so much nonsense. And, being a fair man, George understood the way Jonas felt. His dad and Anna were simple people of the soil who didn't much care what happened outside their limited universe. Hardship was a way of life. "Unable to cope" was not a phrase in their vocabulary.

"I guess we ought to get the nitty-gritty over with first," George went on. "How're we going to pay for it?"

"Steve's insurance," Jonas said. "I checked. She's still his wife."

"Good. Now for the biggest problem. The kids. The doctor says they need a stable environment."

"They can stay here," Jonas said.

"Hell, Dad, you and Anna have all you can do to run the farm, and those girls have enough collective energy to propel a rocket."

"Got any better suggestions?"

George took a deep breath. "Me."

Jonas's head came up with a jerk. "You? Ridin' herd on a couple of kids is gonna kinda cramp your style, isn't it, son?"

"I'll manage. I don't know what else I can do."

"Are you tryin' to tell me you're thinkin' about stayin' here?"

"The doctor started making noises about a foster home. I don't think any of us wants that."

"You won't like it. Coupl'a months from now you'll be chewin' the furniture."

"Maybe," George said with a grim set to his mouth. "Admittedly, I'd prefer ranching, but I'll do what I have to do. Right now, I have to think about Stacy and DeeAnn. Maybe the three of us can live in Ellen's house."

"The payments are too high. It ought to be sold. And where the devil do you plan to find work in town?"

"I don't know!" George all but shouted. "Wherever I have to. I'll pump gas, sack groceries, something." The minute those words were out he could have sworn he heard the cell door being bolted.

"Where've you been, son? These days folks pump their own gas and sack their own groceries."

"Forget that for now. What I want to know is, do I have to do something to make this legal? See a lawyer or anything?"

"What for? The daddy's gone, and the mother's in a funny farm, so family takes care of the girls. That's you and me. Who's gonna complain?"

"Guess you're right."

"You'd better give this some serious thought, son."

"I've had two hours to do nothing but think about it. Are the girls home from school yet?"

Jonas nodded and cocked his head in the direction of the house. "The bus dropped 'em off about fifteen minutes ago."

GEORGE FOUND his nieces in the upstairs bedroom they shared when they were at the farm, which was all the time now. They were a couple of cute, dark-haired scamps who looked so much alike it was almost funny. But once you got to know them you learned that Stacy was a little taller, had a rounder face and definitely was the leader of the duo.

DeeAnn had a sweet, amiable disposition and was much quieter than her sister. The door to the room was ajar, but he knocked on it to get their attention.

"Uncle George!" Stacy squealed and bounded off the bed. "Where've you been?"

"I had to go to the city on business. If you two ladies have a minute or two, I'd like to talk to you." He took a seat beside DeeAnn on the other bed and rumpled her hair. She just smiled up at him adoringly.

"What's up?" Stacy asked as she sat back down on her own bed.

George had never had any trouble talking to the girls, which he found somewhat surprising since he in no way fancied himself especially good with kids. He hadn't known what else to do, so he'd always talked to them as though they were adults, even when they were very young, and unwittingly had established a rapport with them. The twins, in turn, regarded their uncle as a dashing, romantic figure who lived his life unhampered by the conventions that governed other adults. All the things that seemed to drive their parents crazy just rolled off him. In short, Uncle George was fun.

Now he got right to the point. "Your mom is going to have to stay in the hospital for quite a while."

The girls exchanged glances. Then Stacy said, "We figured as much."

"So, how would you like to live with me until she's better?"

It took a minute for that to sink in. When it finally did, Stacy jumped to her feet and joined her uncle and sister on the other bed. "Oh, boy! Did you hear that, Dee? We're going to Montana!"

George laughed. "No, not Montana. I wouldn't do that to you. Maybe I'll just move into your house with you."

"You're going to stay here?" Stacy asked, wrinkling her nose. "Mom says you never stay anywhere long. She says you were born with itchy feet."

"Daddy said you're nothing but a no-count drifter," DeeAnn chimed in. She didn't talk much, but when she had something to say, she didn't mince words or worry about hurting feelings.

"Oh, he did, did he? Well, it could be that I've just never found any reason to stay in one place. But if my two best girls need me, I'm staying."

The last thing George expected was what followed. Stacy looked around him at her sister, then lifted her eyes. "We don't want to stay. We want to go far, far away."

"What?"

"Everybody at school knows what happened," Stacy explained in a wistful voice. "They know Daddy left, and they know Mom took those pills. The kids whisper behind our backs, and the teachers try too hard to be nice to us. It's awful. We want to go away. Please take us to Montana. We'll be the best kids you ever saw. We know how to iron our own clothes, and we even know how to cook...a little. Do you like grilled cheese sandwiches?"

"I love them." It seemed to George that his heart suddenly weighed fifty pounds. He drew both girls closer to him, one under each arm, and he kissed the top of their heads. "Well, dad-gummed if you haven't thrown me a fast one. I...can't take you two all the way to Montana."

"Why not?" DeeAnn asked solemnly.

"It's...too far. And I don't have any place to live in Montana. I just figured I'd hire on at a ranch and live in its bunkhouse. You two need...a stable environment, and cowboying isn't stable. I've got to find something else to do."

"You won't like it," Stacy predicted. Then something occurred to her, and she looked at him fearfully. "Uncle George, you wouldn't leave us here at the farm, would you? We hate it here. There's nothing to do."

He could certainly sympathize with that. "No. No, I can promise you that. I won't leave you here on the farm." George sighed. It had been a long, trying day, and he'd had a lot to contend with all at once. He hadn't had time to de-

cide what he was going to do; he only had accepted the fact
that the two girls were his responsibility until Ellen got well.
When he thought about it, that was quite a lot for a roaming cowboy who'd never had anyone but himself to look
after. "I'm not sure exactly what we'll do," he told the
girls. "Guess I'll have to study on it a bit. But the minute I
make up my mind, you two will be the first to know,
okay?"

Stacy and DeeAnn nodded in happy unison. They felt
much better. Uncle George had come to their rescue, and
neither of them cared a whit where the three of them went,
as long as it was away.

George got to his feet. "I'll see you two at supper. I've
got some thinking to do." He crossed the room, but when
he got to the door Stacy's voice stopped him.

"Uncle George?"

He turned. "Yes, hon."

"Maybe you can tell us something. We wonder why
Daddy left, but mostly we wonder why Mom took those
pills. She still had us. Why weren't we enough?"

George swallowed thickly, and his eyes stung. "I don't
know, sweetheart. I wish I did." He did know he was going to be the best damned surrogate daddy that any two
kids ever had....

AFTER SUPPER, the twins had homework to do and went to
their room. George didn't feel like watching television with
his dad, so he went to his room, stretched out on the bed
and propped his head on a pillow. The panic that had assaulted him during the drive back from the city was gone;
now he stared hard reality in the face. Was he crazy to be
considering taking on responsibility for the twins? He was
probably the least qualified person in the world for the job
of guardian. He was sure there were at least three dozen
things about being in charge of two young girls that hadn't
occurred to him—*and that might be a good thing*, he
thought ruefully. The ones that had crossed his mind scared
the living hell out of him. In the first place, the kids were

girls. What the devil did he know about girls? For sure you couldn't give their butts a smack or their ears a boxing if they misbehaved.

Suddenly he thought of Laurie Tyler and wished with all his heart that she was around. Laurie had been through something like this—she'd raised her sister and brother—and she would probably be able to give him some guidelines to follow. She could at least help him avoid some of the pitfalls that surely were associated with the care and feeding of twelve-year-olds. Gentle Laurie was so perfect in so many ways that she usually made him feel gauche, but she had a kind heart. And since George considered Laurie the last word in graciousness, poise, good breeding, and just about every other admirable quality, he would have taken her advice as the gospel. But she was hundreds of miles away and couldn't help him at all.

As suddenly and simply as that, the idea formed, then took hold and wouldn't let go. *Why not?* he finally asked himself. *Why not? We have to be somewhere.* He thought, then thought some more. Finally he swung his legs off the bed, left the room and crossed the hall to the twins' bedroom. "You ladies have a minute?"

Stacy and DeeAnn both looked up and smiled. "Sure."

"How would you like to go to Texas?"

Their faces fell. "Shoot, Uncle George," Stacy said. "We've been to Texas a million times."

George smiled. A dozen or so would have been more like it. "I'm not talking about just over the state line. I'm talking about way down deep in Texas, maybe five hundred miles from here."

To the girls, five hundred miles was almost galactic. "Oh, boy!"

George took a deep breath. "Okay. Then that's where we're going."

"When?"

"Soon. A week or so. Whenever we can get all the loose ends tied up. But I want you to promise me something. If you decide you don't like it—if you're ever unhappy with

our arrangement—I want you to tell me. Don't brood about
it. Okay?"

"Okay," Stacey said, smiling broadly. "We promise."

"Then I'll see you in the morning."

"Thanks, Uncle George."

Thanks. He hoped they'd still be thanking him a month
from now. He hoped he wouldn't want to kick his own butt
a hundred times. *Whittaker, you damned well better make
this good.*

CHAPTER TWO

Two weeks later

LAURIE STARED at her sister in disbelief. "Jill, you can't be serious!"

"I am, Laurie. Very serious."

"Married? It's unthinkable! I won't allow it. You can't possibly be thinking straight. You're little more than a child."

A wry smile tugged at the corners of Jill's pretty mouth. "I'm going to be twenty next month. I'm not a child anymore, as much as you'd like me to be one."

Laurie ignored that last remark. "Well, twenty is much too young to be thinking about marriage."

"Do you want me to wait around like you did, wait until I'm an old ma—" The words died on Jill's lips.

"Old maid? What a quaint expression. An old maid like me, is that what you were going to say?"

"No, I... Oh, Laurie, I know what it's been like for you, having to take care of Grandpa and raise Andy and me when the folks were killed. I know it hasn't been easy. Andy and I used to talk about it a lot, about how lucky we were to have you. If it hadn't been for you, we'd probably have ended up in a foster home or something. But we were always sorry that you never had time for fun." Jill jumped to her feet and rushed to give her sister a hug. "When Tony and I are married, you'll be free at last! I should think you would welcome this."

"Welcome it?" Laurie cried. "Listen to me, young lady. I've taught school all these years and kept this miserable

excuse for a ranch so that you and Andy would have some
kind of permanence. The only thing I've ever really wanted
is for both of you to graduate from college. Andy came
through, and you're going to do the same. That's my final
word on the subject! I don't want to discuss it further!'' She
stalked out of the room.

Five minutes later she was back. ''Jill, honey, we have to
talk about this.''

Jill hadn't been the least perturbed over Laurie's outburst, for she knew her big sister well. When it came to her
two young siblings, Laurie was a real pushover. Jill couldn't
recall a single time that she or Andy had asked for anything within reason and their sister hadn't managed to get
it for them, though in some cases only the Lord and Laurie knew how. ''Tony graduates in May,'' Jill said. ''His
dad is opening a store in Albuquerque, and he wants Tony
to run it. I'll finish school there. I know how much it means
to you. I promise I'll finish.''

''Oh, Jill, I...'' Laurie's shoulders rose and fell deject-
edly. This had hit her like a thunderbolt, even though she'd
known for some time that Jill and Tony were very serious
about each other. She had been home from work maybe
fifteen minutes, and had been ready to savor a peaceful
Friday afternoon with the long weekend ahead, when Jill
had sprung this on her. The worst part was knowing she
couldn't forbid the marriage. Jill might seem terribly young
to her, but she was too old to have to get her big sister's
permission to marry. And now Laurie was experiencing a
profound sense of loss. It came to her with something of a
start that she didn't want to let go. Andy and Jill had been
at the very center of her life for such a long time.

Anyone who knew Laurie would have understood her
state of mind at that moment. For nine years she had been
head of the family, and she was only thirty-two. Jill had
been ten and Andy twelve when their parents had died in an
automobile accident, and their aged grandfather had been
living with them. In the blink of an eye, Laurie had gone
from being a carefree young teacher who was happily

planning her own wedding to being breadwinner, nurse-maid and parent. Even so, she hadn't been able to foresee just how many radical changes would take place in her life.

Len McFarland, a professor at nearby Sul Ross State and the man to whom she was engaged, had faded from the picture with remarkable speed. However, Laurie's bitter-ness toward her ex-fiancé had long since evaporated. She was, above all, a pragmatic woman, and in all honesty she didn't blame Len for his disappearing act. He'd only been twenty-six at the time. Had she been a twenty-six-year-old man in the same position, she seriously doubted she would have been interested in a bride who came equipped with two young siblings and an elderly, ailing grandfather.

Those nine years had not been easy, filled as they were with responsibilities, worries and never enough money, but they had been full and busy. Now she felt more maternal than sisterly toward Andy and Jill, particularly Jill, who was the baby of the family.

"Honey," Laurie said with a sigh, "I know you're in love, which is normal, and I like Tony, I really do. He's a fine young man with a good head on his shoulders, but when one marries at twenty—well, you're going to be mar-ried an awfully long time. At least, you should be. I just...want you to think about this long and hard. Mar-riage is not all fun and games."

"I know that, and I have thought about it," Jill said so-berly. She looked away for a moment, then back at Lau-rie. "I love Tony, and I've invested two years in him. I'm not going to let him go off and have some other woman prey on his loneliness. I'm not going to let him go to Al-buquerque without me."

Hard-headed, Laurie thought. *She's always been that way.* Laurie could usually reason with Andy, but not with Jill, not once her sister had made up her mind about some-thing. So there it was. Laurie looked at Jill and saw what she had deliberately avoided seeing before—a woman. An unsophisticated, inexperienced one, but a woman, never-theless. Someone capable of making a decision. "I see."

She sighed again. "Well, I—I'll give you the nicest wedding I can possibly afford, but I won't go into debt over it."

Jill's face broke into a radiant smile, and this time she hugged her sister ferociously. "Oh, Laurie, I knew, I just knew you'd be great about this. I told Tony you would. He's going to have a fit because I told you when he wasn't around, but I just couldn't hold it in any longer, and he has a biology lab this afternoon. Listen, when you've had a chance to get used to this, you can start making your own plans. Maybe you'll want to talk to that man at the bank some more, the one who asked if you'd be interested in selling this place."

Laurie had all but forgotten the tentative inquiry. She had thought she wouldn't be interested in selling her property for at least two years, when Jill had graduated from school. But now.... "I don't know, honey. I just don't know."

"Yeah, it's probably too soon. Sure would be nice to have all that money, though."

"I'm not sure it's all that much. I wasn't interested enough to ask any questions."

"Whatever it is would be a nice nest egg. Say, Laurie, may I ask Tony to supper tonight? He gets so tired of dorm food."

"Of course."

"The three of us can start making plans, okay?"

"Sure."

Jill was dancing around the room like a Mexican jumping bean. "I'm supposed to meet him on the campus at four-thirty, so I'd better get going. Oh, I'm so excited!" She calmed down long enough to look at Laurie seriously. "And you have to be relieved. After all these years, you'll have time to think about no one but yourself, to do what you want to do instead of what you have to do." Slipping into a denim jacket and grabbing her billfold and keys from a nearby table, she gave a jaunty little wave and sailed out the front door.

Laurie stood in the center of the room for several long minutes after Jill left, grappling with a dismal, melancholy feeling. Losing Jill was inevitable, natural, even if it had come sooner than she had expected, so she didn't understand all the doom and gloom. How many times had she longed for freedom from responsibilities? When Andy had graduated and taken that job in San Antonio only last summer, she had been able to let go without a whimper. But, she conceded, that had been different, because she'd still had Jill, who needed her.

So now she really would be free to do whatever she wanted. Trouble was, she didn't have the slightest idea what it was she wanted. Perhaps that was the crux of the problem: she'd been so busy just holding things together that she hadn't planned for her own future. Now the future had arrived, and she just felt . . . empty and alone.

Wandering into the kitchen, she put on water for a cup of instant coffee. While waiting for it to boil, she opened a drawer and withdrew a packet of brochures. She had sent off for the literature well over a year ago and hadn't looked at it in months. The cover of the packet showed a handsome, suntanned couple on the deck of a cruise ship, smiling and waving, and across the picture, in bold red letters, were the words ''Cruise the South Pacific.'' Laurie opened the packet and idly thumbed through the brochures she had read dozens of times. The place names seemed the epitome of adventure and romance: Hawaii, Tahiti, Samoa, Sydney, Auckland. Fourteen days at sea; the trip would gobble up the best part of a month. She'd vaguely planned to go in April, during the Southern Hemisphere's autumn. It had been such fun to dream about, but she'd always known it was nothing but a dream. She'd be lucky to save enough money for the round-trip airfare to Los Angeles, let alone enough for the cruise. She slipped the packet back into the drawer and closed it.

Several minutes later she sat at the big wooden table, sipping her coffee and watching the faucet drip. It needed a new washer, which was one chore she could take care of

herself. She actually was fairly handy around the house.
She had to be. The ranch house was old and always needed
attention, more attention than Laurie had either time or
money to give it. Still, it was the only home she had ever
known, and in a curious way, even its glaring imperfections were a comfort to her.

The house had been old when her parents had bought it
shortly after their marriage in 1954. It had been built,
Laurie seemed to recall, by a man who had come to the
Davis Mountains during the Depression of the 1930s in order to escape the harsh economic conditions of the indus-
trial east. Her father had put it through several renovations,
adding a dishwasher, a new stove and refrigerator, a second bathroom and another bedroom. His final improvement had been to build a caretaker's cottage behind the
main house. The ranch was prospering in those days, and
her father had planned to hire a couple to help him run it.
The cottage had proved to be a blessing; Laurie had managed to keep it rented off and on through the years, though
currently it was vacant. The Tylers had never been wealthy
or even very well off, but the house had always looked nice
when her parents had been alive. Now it just looked forlorn and neglected, even though it was spotlessly clean on
the inside.

Standing and carrying the cup with her, Laurie went to
the sink and looked out the window just in time to see a
streak of orange dash past. That was Princess, a big, floppy
tabby who supposedly belonged to the Millers down the
road but who spent as much time at Laurie's house as she
did there. That reminded her to check the bowl of cat nib-
bles she kept on the back porch. Once it had been filled, she
straightened and let her eyes sweep the scene before her. It
was March, and the landscape was bleak, the sky gray, but
spring was just around the corner, and soon the sad condition of the yard would again be apparent. Only four
months ago she had harbored hopes that this spring would
be the one that finally saw some outward improvement in
her property. George had told her—

Abruptly her thoughts braked, and she went back into the house. George! She still missed him, dammit, and that was the one foolish aspect of her exceedingly sensible life. What was to miss? A man who used to spend one day a week here, playing the role of general handyman, and the only reason he'd done that was because her best friend and George's boss, Cassie Maitland, had asked—probably ordered—him to. That was the sum total of their "relationship."

Laurie uttered an impatient sound of self-derision. She and George Whittaker had shared maybe three dozen cups of coffee, a few beers and some conversation. She knew only the most basic facts about him. He'd never said one word of a personal nature to her or even indicated that he thought of her as a woman, desirable or otherwise. Certainly he'd never touched her. Then one day, with very little more than a "So long, Laurie," he was gone, off to unknown parts, following the time-honored tradition of footloose, fancy-free cowboys. Laurie seriously doubted he had thought of her once since his departure, so she didn't know why she persisted in thinking about him. Her attraction to him was one of the most frustrating experiences of her life, and she was much too old to moon over the nicest smile this side of paradise and a pair of blue, blue eyes.

A woman could end up with a damned inferiority complex if she dwelled too long on the fact that the two men she had most cared for had been able to walk away from her with a noticeable lack of regret. One of these days, she reasoned, she was going to stumble onto the right kind of man, someone warm and caring who didn't blanch at the thought of hearth, home and responsibilities—someone who not only didn't mind settling down, but expected to...someone she could lean on a little. She thought that might be nice—leaning instead of being leaned on. And when she found that superlative individual, he was going to wonder what had hit him. She had no intention of living alone forever.

That prompted her thoughts to return to Jill. *Albuquerque! And Andy's in San Antonio. I haven't seen him in six months. Lord, if Jill goes through with this marriage, I really will be living alone!* A hodgepodge of emotions assaulted her. She wouldn't have been human if one of those emotions hadn't been, as Jill had suggested, a certain sense of relief. Events of the last nine years came to her in a rush: Len's hasty exit, the inherited debts she'd had to pay off, her grandfather's death, and all those stern encounters with Andy's high school principal who had claimed her brother was "obstreperous." Then there was the night she'd had to rush Jill to the hospital for an emergency appendectomy, and the agony she had suffered when Andy learned to drive. And always there had been the money crunch.

But there had been high points, too: watching both Andy and Jill graduate from high school, then Andy from college. Laurie supposed the highest point, the greatest sense of satisfaction came from knowing she had held things together.

The telephone's shrill ring interrupted her thoughts. She reached for the instrument on the wall. "Hello."

"Laurie?" said a familiar feminine voice. "Cassie."

"Hi, Cassie. How're things?"

"Great. If they were any better I couldn't stand it."

Laurie smiled. Cassie had been Mrs. Scott Maitland for a little over four months, so her friend was still sailing a foot off the ground. "That's good. Give Scott my regards."

"I'll do that. Anything new in your life?"

Cassie's tone implied that she expected the answer to be in the affirmative, which puzzled Laurie. There was no way her friend could know about Jill already...was there? "Jill wants to marry Tony when he graduates this year."

Laurie heard a low whistle on the other end of the line. "Well, I can't say I didn't expect it. I remember how lovesick she was last summer when Tony was away. How are you feeling about it?"

"Oh . . . disappointed, I guess. I certainly don't have anything against Tony, and I know he can provide for her. His father owns a growing business, and I'm sure Tony will be running it someday. They have a lot going for them. But I did so hope Jill would get her degree."

"I know." There was a pause, then Cassie asked, "Is that it? All the news?"

Laurie frowned. "Yes. Isn't that enough?"

"You haven't had an unexpected visitor, have you?"

"No. Cassie, what is this?"

"I didn't call just to pass the time of day. I have some news of my own. Guess who came to see me this afternoon."

Laurie laughed. "Tom Cruise?"

"Nope."

"Paul Newman, then?"

"Not even close."

"Prince Charles?"

"Now you're getting warm. Does the name George Whittaker ring a bell?"

Laurie tensed. "G-George? Here? You're kidding!"

"I am not. He's here, all right, big as life. I couldn't believe my eyes."

There was no need for Laurie to waste effort pretending with Cassie. She was the only other soul on the face of the earth who knew of Laurie's interest in George, and Laurie wanted to keep it that way. *He's back!* She was overcome by some complex sensations, most of them unpleasant. "He's just passing through, I presume. Men like George are always just passing through on their way to somewhere else."

"No, he came to see me because he wanted a job. I asked him what had brought him back, and he said he missed the High Country, the mountains."

Laurie snorted. "Didn't you once tell me he mentioned going to Montana? There are mountains in Montana."

"Not these mountains," Cassie said pointedly. "Besides, I don't think this place was what lured him back.

George was happy here, I could tell. You know, last November when he told me he was leaving, I had the strangest feeling that he didn't really want to go. Now he's back. Maybe his roaming days are over. Maybe the lure was a woman.''

"You're clutching at straws, Cassie. If George had any interest in me he would have shown it long before now."

"Maybe. I suspect he was more aware of you than he wanted to admit or knew how to show. Some men just fight it so, and George is one of them."

"I swear, since you got married you've become a blinking expert on men. Did...did you hire him?"

"Of course I hired him. He was the best foreman I've ever had, and I've been looking for someone. He starts Monday. He has some things he has to do, which brings me to the rest of the news concerning our friend George. You're not going to believe this, but...oh, hang on just a minute, will you, Laurie? There's some commotion outside."

Laurie waited. Cassie picked up the phone again in a minute or two and sounded breathless. "Sorry, but there's a minor emergency I have to tend to. Listen, Laurie, I'm sure George will be by to see you soon."

I hope not, Laurie thought. *I have enough on my mind without having to cope with those blue eyes.* She guessed that the only reason she knew George well—or as well as anyone knew him—was that he had worked for her best friend. But, she thought tartly, she wouldn't hold that against Cassie. The two women were close and had been for a long time. Their personalities seemed to mesh, and for years they had been the only women who attended the local ranchers' association meetings. But Cassie and Scott Maitland owned the fabled DO Ranch, by far the largest spread in the High Country, so saying Laurie and Cassie both were ranchers was akin to saying Limpia Creek and the Pacific Ocean both were bodies of water.

"I want to warn you that there's been a major change in George's life," Cassie went on, sounding amused.

"Change? What kind of change?"

"Laurie, I'd love to be able to chat with you about it, but I've really got to go. Just be prepared for a surprise, a real surprise. I'll talk to you later. 'Bye."

Laurie hung up the phone, completely puzzled. Oh, God, George, of all people! Well, this time she was going to stay away from him. The one thing she positively wasn't going to do was ever think of George, or any man remotely like him, in any romantic sense. If he showed up on her doorstep…well, she'd be pleasant, but distant. He wouldn't stay around long. Whatever that strange call was that made cowboys want to move on, it would come over him again one of these days. She didn't know why she was attracted to him, but she seemed to be, so the best thing she could do was just stay away from him.

Still, she was aware of a curious sensation building inside her. Apprehension? Dread? If George was back in the area, she couldn't avoid running into him, especially if he would be working for Cassie. That prospect shouldn't have been so alarming, but it was. He was the only man she'd ever met, and that included Len, who could completely destroy her equilibrium just by smiling at her. It was something she didn't understand, and she'd stopped trying to. The best she could do was cope with it.

Shaking off all thoughts of that wandering cowboy, she turned her attention to dinner. Tony always ate like a starving young horse and did not have a discerning palate, so anything she put on the table would please him. After giving it some thought, she took two packages of cube steaks out of the freezer and laid them out to thaw. That was probably too much food, but she'd eat the leftovers tomorrow. There was one thing a cook could count on: if a dinner guest was male and had grown up in Texas, chicken-fried steak with a small ocean of cream gravy would be a hit.

She took care of a few preliminaries and was on her way upstairs to change clothes when she heard the crunch of tires in the gravel driveway that led from the house to the

main road. Stopping, she went to the living room window
and peeked through the blinds. An unfamiliar red pickup
was pulling to a halt in front of the house. She squinted,
trying to see who the driver was. A man wearing a Stetson.
He turned in the seat. She couldn't see him distinctly
through the windshield, but she didn't need to. The angle
of the hat, the vaguest glimpse of the profile was enough.
Laurie would have sworn her heart actually stopped beating for a few seconds. Pressing a hand to her forehead, she
closed her eyes. *Why did he have to come? I'm just not
ready for this. Damn him! Some peaceful Friday this has
turned out to be.*

IT HAD ALWAYS BEEN George's belief that no one ever saw
anything interesting or got a decent meal while traveling on
interstate highways, since they'd homogenized America.
For that reason, he used state highways whenever possible
and had this time. Last night he and the girls had stopped
in a ranching town and stayed in a place called the Loveless Motel. The name had struck him as being hilarious. But
the Loveless had been clean, and its coffee shop had served
up ham, eggs and hash browns he could have written a
poem about. That breakfast easily would have done him
until supper, but he hadn't reckoned with the appetites of
twelve-year-olds. Promptly at noon their inner alarm clocks
had gone off. However, he was finally at their destination,
running two hours behind schedule, although why he felt
the need for a schedule he couldn't imagine.

George switched off the truck's engine. The vehicle,
purchased only two days ago, was the first he'd owned in a
number of years, but reliable transportation had seemed a
must now that he had the girls. He glanced over at his pas-
sengers. "Okay, I've got a job, so now the next thing we
have to do is find a place to live. But a motel will do for a
couple of days. First I want to see the lady who lives here.
Sit tight while I see if she's home."

"We're hungry," Stacy complained.

George rolled his eyes. "You can't possibly be hungry again."

"Yes, we are."

"Lord, you're either hungry or you have to go to the bathroom. Well, we'll eat in a bit. Wait here."

He got out of the truck and for a moment simply stood in the dirt yard and looked around. The house still needed painting. In fact, there was a lot that still needed doing. Some time and unlimited finances would have done wonders. As sorry looking as the Tyler place was, it had a lot of potential.

He climbed the porch steps, stopping at the top one and kicking it gingerly. He had repaired that step last October and was pleased to see it had stayed fixed. Crossing the porch, he raised his hand and knocked on the door.

The door opened, and George's eyes drank in the sight of Laurie. She still was dressed for the classroom, wearing a slim blue skirt and a matching sweater, the sleeves of which were pushed midway up her arm. A couple of gold chains hung from her neck, and more gold twinkled from her earlobes. Her honey-colored hair stopped just short of her shoulders and curled under softly. Laurie always looked well put together, no matter what the occasion, no matter what she was wearing. That could have been a studied talent, something acquired from years of standing at the front of a classroom under the super-critical eyes of youngsters, but George didn't think so. Some women simply had a knack for throwing on any old thing and looking great in it, and Laurie was one of them. It was one of the first things he'd noticed about her.

But her eyes were what he remembered most of all—warm and brown, though just plain "brown" did them an injustice. They glittered with gold flecks and were without a doubt the prettiest, most unusual eyes he had ever seen. And she had the manners of a patrician lady, which had the effect of rendering him a bit tongue-tied in her presence. Not that he was ever exactly glib, but with Laurie his dam-

nable shyness seemed more pronounced. "Hello, Laurie,"
he said.

Laurie, with deceptive calm, offered him a small smile.
She had had so much practice studying him without seem-
ing to that she did so effortlessly now. He wore the usual
garb, topped with a denim jacket, and his hat sat low on his
forehead. He wasn't a tall man, not even six feet, but he
carried himself so ramrod straight that he gave the impression of height. His eyes were as blue as eyes could be, and
underneath the big Stetson there was a thick shock of dark
brown hair that tended to curl at the nape and temples. He
was trim and hard, as cowboys were wont to be. But his
most outstanding feature was his smile. When turned on
full force it could melt a glacier. Lord, she was glad Cassie
had warned her! If she hadn't, Laurie knew she never
would have been able to handle the shock of throwing open
the door and finding him standing there. She might have
thrown herself into his arms, and wouldn't that have given
the cowboy a start! Even with the warning, she felt curi-
ously off balance.

Her outward control, however, amazed her. "Well,
George. It's nice to see you again."

Though his expression didn't betray it, George was
slightly taken aback by her lack of surprise at finding him
on her front porch. One would think she had last seen him
four days instead of four months ago. "Thanks. It's good
to see you, too."

"What brings you back to this neck of the woods?"

"You'll never guess. How've you been?"

"Fine."

"And Jill?"

"She's fine, too. Wants to get married this summer."

George's brows lifted slightly. "Oh? Same guy, I guess."

"Yes, Tony. And they'll move to Albuquerque."

"You'll . . . miss her."

"Yes, I will."

The conversation was stiff, awkward. And Laurie wasn't
all that interested in helping it along. She was sincere about

not being interested in a man like George. He was, in the argot of the country music she loved so much, a ramblin' man, and she didn't think for a minute that he was back in the High Country for good. Maybe she couldn't help being attracted to him, but she certainly could help what she did about it. If she had a particle of good sense she'd tell him she was just leaving, that she had to be...somewhere, anywhere. Just thank him for stopping by and then split. That was the way to handle this.

But then he asked, "Have you got a minute?"

"Well, yes, I guess so."

Turning, he waved toward the truck. Laurie's gaze followed the gesture, and before her astonished eyes, the door on the passenger side opened, and two jeans-clad girls got out and rushed toward them. When they reached George, they stood on either side of him, each clutching one of his arms. Open-mouthed, Laurie stared at him.

"These are my nieces," he explained. "This is Stacy and this is DeeAnn."

"Well..." Laurie couldn't have been more startled. "I'm...very happy to meet you, girls."

"This is Miss Tyler," George said, and the girls mumbled acknowledgments.

"George, what on earth...?"

"It's a long story."

"We're going to live with Uncle George," Stacy said proudly.

Laurie's eyes widened further. "You *are*?"

"Like I said—" George smiled weakly "—it's a long story, and if you can give me a few minutes, I...need to talk to you, Laurie."

She'd give him a few hours if that's what it took. She was alive with curiosity. A minute ago she was trying to think of a way to get rid of him. Now there was no way she would let him leave without hearing his "long story." It promised to be interesting. Stepping back, she held the door wider. "Please come in...all of you."

CHAPTER THREE

GEORGE HAD ALWAYS felt at ease in Laurie's house. It reminded him of the farmhouse in Oklahoma—homey, comfortable, clean and completely unpretentious. It was the kind of house that invited sitting and visiting. Laurie's house, he now realized, was one of the things he had missed most about the mountains.

He turned to find her staring at the girls in wonder, a small smile on her face. "Could I get you girls something to drink or to snack on?"

"Gee, thanks," Stacy said without hesitation. "We're starving."

"You had a hamburger and fries three hours ago," George reminded them quickly, lest Laurie think he was treating them badly. "It's impossible for you to be starving." He looked at Laurie. "Do all kids want to eat all the time?"

She smiled. "They must be going through a growth period. Tell you what, I just stocked the freezer with ice cream bars because Jill loves them so. How does that sound?"

"Mmm," the girls chorused.

"Is that all right?" Laurie asked George. "It won't spoil their supper, will it?"

"Nothing spoils their supper or any other meal."

"Then follow me."

George and the girls followed Laurie through the living room and dining room and into the kitchen, the room he remembered most of all. He and Laurie had shared many a cup of coffee at the round wooden table, and he recalled that the room had always smelled wonderful. For a working woman, Laurie seemed to do an awful lot of cooking. He'd never sampled any of it, but it had been his experience that when food smelled good it usually tasted good, too.

Once the girls each had an ice cream bar in hand, George said, "How about taking those things outside to eat them? I want to talk to Laurie. Besides, you need to walk around after being in the car all day."

Laurie was relieved that they didn't protest. She couldn't keep her curiosity in check much longer. George with two little girls in tow just didn't ring true. Once the back door banged behind Stacy and DeeAnn, she turned to him. "Have a seat. How about a beer?"

He pulled out a chair at the table and sat down, setting his hat on the table. "Thanks. It's been a long day."

Laurie opened two bottles of beer, placed one in front of him, then sat down across from him. She had entirely forgotten that she didn't want him there, didn't want to look at him. Her mind raced with questions, but she would let him explain things in his own good time. "George, those girls are adorable," was all she said.

"Yeah. We're getting along pretty good, but I sure wish they could synchronize their bladders. I must have made thirty stops between the Oklahoma state line and here."

Laurie smiled. "That's one of the problems when you travel with kids."

George took a hefty swallow of beer and set the bottle down. "I'm going to be working at the DO again."

Laurie came within a whisker of saying "I know," but caught herself just in time. She certainly didn't want him to know that his return was of such monumental importance that Cassie had rushed to call and tell her about it. "I guess . . . Cassie was glad to see you."

"She seemed to be. It was nice to feel welcomed back." George searched Laurie's face for some sign that she, too, was glad to see him. He found nothing. He'd had no reason to think she would fall all over herself with delight over his return, but he guessed he had expected her to treat him the way she had before, with easy camaraderie. Maybe he was keeping her from something. That was a dispiriting thought. He was more glad to see her than he wanted to be.

"How are you feeling about Jill getting married?" he asked. That seemed a safe topic of conversation.

Her eyelashes dipped briefly. "Oh...disappointed, mainly," she said. "And a little sad. They're both so young."

"But you like the guy okay?"

"Yes, I like Tony fine."

"Well, that's a plus. I never was very crazy about the man my sister married, and, unfortunately, I turned out to be right about him. Which brings me to the reason I have the girls with me. I guess you're curious."

"Wildly."

Folding her hands in front of her, Laurie gave him her rapt attention while the story poured forth. When he concluded it, George said, "I sure had planned to be far from here by this time, but this business with the girls threw a monkey wrench in my plans. Of course, when Ellen's well again, I'll take them home, but in the meantime... Frankly, I'm at a loss. You're the main reason I decided to bring them back here."

"Me?"

"You're the only person I know who might give me some guidelines, tell me what to do. You've been through this. I don't know many people I'd admit this to, but those little people scare the hell out of me."

She understood. "I know," she said simply. "Believe me, I know. How old are the girls?"

"Twelve."

Laurie winced. "Andy was twelve when the folks died. It's a nice age, probably the best between five and twenty-one. Twelve-year-olds seem to accept their imperfections because they've learned that everybody else is imperfect, too. But there are some difficult years ahead."

George knew only the barest facts about Laurie's past, but he admired her tremendously for having had the gumption to keep the family together. She couldn't have been a whole lot older than Jill was now when she'd had to take over. He momentarily wondered why, with Jill wanting to get married, Laurie wasn't going limp with relief. Why the sad eyes?

He didn't wonder long, though. He'd always placed Laurie in the "steady as a rock" category. She was a woman who was accustomed to having others depend on her, and no one could be around her long without learning that she was absolutely crazy about her brother and sister. With Jill out of the nest, she might not feel needed any longer. For some people, responsibility was as necessary to life as air to breathe, and Laurie was probably one of them. Was it reasonable of him to hope she could instill some of that sense of responsibility in him? he asked himself. He had always been free as the wind.

Then, without warning, something she'd said to him the last time he saw her, when he'd come to say goodbye, echoed in his mind. He had asked her why she'd never married—not that it had been any of his business; he'd simply been curious. She hadn't taken offense, but she'd leveled a look on him he hadn't been able to forget and replied, "Obligations, duties, people who needed me. All those things you've been running away from." George hadn't considered that fair. He'd always been something of a loner, and it was true he had a bad case of wanderlust, but that didn't mean he had been running away, did it?

She'd said that just before she'd kissed him goodbye. The gesture had barely qualified as a kiss—it had been more of a brush of lips, but he hadn't been able to forget it, either.

"What are you going to do?" he asked.

"Do?"

"When Jill leaves."

Laurie studied her cup of coffee and frowned. "I don't know. I have some options. Ted Weeks at the bank called last week. Some man representing a company from the east is looking for about two-hundred acres around here. I can't imagine why. Ted wanted to know if I'd be interested in selling. At the time I told him I couldn't make any major changes in my life for two more years, when Jill graduated. Now, however, things are different. If the marriage really does take place—''

"If?" George interjected.

"Things happen."

"You're not counting on that, are you?"

There was a pause, then Laurie's shoulders slumped slightly. "No. Jill isn't flighty, and she and Tony have been going together a long time. Anyway, now I might go talk to Ted seriously."

"Sell? Does that mean you might leave?"

Did he really sound alarmed, or was that her imagination? Probably the latter. "I might." In some curious way, Laurie felt she had said that more for her benefit than his, that it was a statement of independence, an assertion of her freedom from entanglements. She wanted to let him know that the next time they reached a parting of the ways, as they inevitably would, she might be the first one to say goodbye. Never again would she build her hopes, even nebulous ones, around a man like George. "With the kids gone, there won't be one thing tying me to the High Country."

George looked down at his cup. "I guess not." Funny, he'd never considered the possibility that Laurie might want something other than what she had. She'd always seemed happy enough, content. But then, how hard had he looked? It wasn't until he'd said goodbye to her that he had realized how much he enjoyed being around her.

In spite of all her good intentions, Laurie couldn't help being aware of him, and that meant she was aware of those blue eyes and all those even white teeth and that thick dark hair that looked made for fingers to walk through. He was too good-looking. He made her want to revive old dreams. She wished he hadn't come here at all. Then she dismissed the thought, remembering the girls. He wanted her help and advice, and if there was one thing she was a sucker for it was twelve-year-olds, having taught that age group for ten years.

"George, what on earth made you take on the responsibility of those girls?"

"Someone had to do it, and I seemed to be the only one available."

"Do you have any idea what you're letting yourself in for?"

"Probably not. I was hoping you might enlighten me."

Laurie tried to think where to begin. "You'll never be able to walk out the door without making arrangements for their care. In fact, you'll never be able to do anything without thinking of them first. Kids get sick, and you have to leave work to take them to the doctor. If they're really sick, you have to stay home with them or hire someone to do it for you. When they're perfectly well you'll find yourself spending most of your free time chauffeuring them. You'll have to get up with the chickens and make sure they eat something nourishing before they go to school, and they'll need lunch money. Little girls want to dress as well as their friends, and that's expensive. Speaking of dresses, how are you at doing laundry? Kids generate piles of the stuff. What about this summer when school's out? What are they going to do while you're at work? You'll be working at the DO. What about fall roundup when you have to be gone for days? The girls might not be babies, but they're much too young to go unsupervised for long periods of time." She paused and took a deep breath. "George, I could go on and on. And I'll tell you something else. Being in charge of a couple of kids leaves you no time for a social life of your own. Take it from one who's been there."

"Damn," George muttered, shooting her a rueful smile. "Guess it's a good thing I didn't talk to you first, huh? I really would have been scared."

"I don't mean to sound so discouraging, but you ought to be prepared. You're getting ready to assume the hardest role in the world."

"What's that?"

"Working mother. And I'm going to tell you about another danger that's very real."

"Might as well give it to me all at once."

"Getting so attached to them that you'll suffer horribly when you have to give them up."

George digested that, then shook his head. "No, I won't have to worry on that score. They're cute kids, and right now this whole business is something of an adventure for all three of us, but...parenthood and I just aren't made for each other."

Of course, Laurie thought. No danger on that score. George would never get attached to anyone because he didn't want to. Knowing that, why was she so drawn to him?

Then something occurred to her, something that would be very difficult to discuss with him, but it was something he needed to be reminded of. "George, you know that twelve is the time in life when girls begin to, er, change."

It took a minute for that to sink in. When it did, he had the worst feeling that his cheeks were turning pink. "Oh, God!" he said aloud. No female had ever discussed *that* with him. He'd been with earthy women who would talk about sex all night long if he would, but that was never mentioned.

He was so embarrassed that Laurie was embarrassed for him. "You really should find out how much they know. It's important."

He nodded helplessly. "What if they don't know anything?"

"Well, I—I guess you could send them to me."

"Thanks." George decided then and there that he'd been an idiot to take on this job. He was completely out of his element, and it was the most impotent feeling in the world.

At that moment there was some noise in the front of the house. The door banged loudly, they heard voices, and the next minute Jill burst into the kitchen with the future bridegroom in tow, along with Stacy and DeeAnn. "Look what we found outside," she said, indicating the girls.

"They assure us they belong here, but—" She stopped dead in her tracks, and her eyes brightened. "George!" she squealed with delight. Now Laurie remembered that Jill had always been crazy about George in a purely platonic way. "What are you doing here? Good grief, are you their Uncle George?"

George got to his feet, grinning. "I plead guilty."

"Well, I'll be. I thought you'd split for greener pastures."

"Guess I just couldn't stay away."

"Fantastic. You've met Tony, haven't you?"

George held out his hand, and the young man stepped forward to take it. "Sure have. Nice to see you again, Tony."

"Thanks. Nice to see you, too." Tony was a tall, good-looking, affable young man who spent half his time gazing at Jill with unabashed affection, like a puppy. Thankfully, Laurie thought, Jill never seemed to take advantage of his undisguised devotion but treated him, in turn, with just the right amount of deference.

"Oh, Laurie," Jill enthused, "Tony has the greatest new tape. I just have to hear it, but we positively won't play it too loud, promise. We're going to take it up to my room to listen to. Come on, girls. You can listen, too. Oh, George, it's really great to see you again. You're all staying for supper, aren't you?"

Laurie's eyes widened and flew to the packages of meat on the counter. Three more mouths to feed. Automatically she moved toward the freezer and reached for another one. Thank heaven for microwave ovens with defrost cycles, although given the choice she would have preferred not having George stay for supper. He'd been in the house for perhaps half an hour, and already she could feel herself being swept under by the spell he innocently and effectively wove. At the moment she honestly wished she had never seen him again.

Oh, you're being silly, her inner voice chided. *Your guard is up—the armor's in place. You don't have to worry this time.*

True. Surely she could endure a few hours of his filling up the kitchen and her senses. "By all means, George, you and the girls stay for supper."

He glanced at Laurie uncertainly. "Aw, I don't want to impose."

"You won't." She took a deep breath. "Please stay and help us celebrate the impending nuptials. It's chicken-fried steak. You like it, don't you?"

He smiled his disarming smile. "Don't you know that heaven's a place where nobody ever makes you eat anything but chicken-fried steak, Mexican food and barbecue?"

Laurie pushed herself away from the table. "I'll ... get started. Then I'm going to change into some comfortable clothes. Just help yourself to the beer."

THE HARDEST THING in the world to do, Laurie discovered, was avoid looking at someone seated across a table from you. It seemed that every time she was forced to glance in George's direction, he was looking at her. Again, that was probably her imagination ... or perhaps a bit of wishful thinking. She supposed she should be glad she had made enough of an impression on him that he had sought her out for advice on the girls, but she wasn't glad at all.

Fortunately, Laurie found there was little need for her to make conversation. Jill and Tony took care of that since they both were great talkers. Laurie didn't think they'd suffer through many silent evenings during their marriage. Wedding plans were forging ahead, at least in Jill's and Tony's minds. As she listened to them, it occurred to her that what they were talking about didn't sound like a modest affair at all. There was a problem. They had lived in the Davis Mountains all their lives and knew everyone for miles around. They would either have to limit it to the immediate families or have a crowd. She had seen these things get completely out of hand, and that wasn't going to happen to her. She hadn't scrimped all these years to throw away her meager savings on a twenty-minute ceremony. Tomorrow she and Jill were going to have a serious talk.

Jill had finished regaling them with anecdotes about her philosophy professor, whose thick German accent she could imitate to perfection. She then turned to George. "Stacy and DeeAnn sorta filled us in on how they came to be living with you. So, I guess you'll be around awhile."

"That's the plan right now," he said. "I'll be working at the DO again starting Monday, so I guess I'll spend the weekend hunting for a place for us to live. Got any ideas where I should start looking? It'll have to be something adequate for the three of us."

Jill thought a moment, then her eyes brightened suddenly and she snapped her fingers. "The cottage! The caretaker's place out back—you know. How about that, Laurie? You've been hoping to rent it right away."

"It's vacant?" George asked with interest.

Laurie almost choked. "Would anyone like more steak? There's plenty. How about you, Stacy? DeeAnn?"

"What do you think, Laurie?" Jill repeated.

"Oh, George wouldn't be interested in that little place."

"Why not?" Jill asked innocently. "Seems to me it's better than just an old apartment somewhere. At least there's room for the girls to play."

Tony looked up from the food he was devouring ravenously. "Sounds like a great idea to me. I never have liked the thought of you two being out here all alone."

Laurie got up to refill the bowl of mashed potatoes, and tried to think of a gracious way to stop the conversation before things went too far. She realized that Jill's intentions were good. Her sister had no idea that she thought of George as anything but a casual friend, so Jill's suggestion was a natural one. But, dear God, she didn't want him living here, where she would see him every day. She simply couldn't have it.

"You remember the cottage, don't you, George?" Jill went on. "It's not plush, by any means, but it's neat and comfortable. Newer than this house, that's for sure. You know, once Tony and I are gone, I'd sure feel better if you were living out back. Every time we rent that place we have to worry about what kind of people the new tenants will be—oh, God, we had one couple living there who almost drove Laurie nuts—but, heck, we already know you."

From the stove Laurie tried to flash her sister a silent, warning signal with her eyes, but Jill was looking at George and was completely oblivious to Laurie's discomfort, as were Tony and George. Laurie filled the bowl and returned to the table. She knew she'd been defeated. But maybe it wasn't such a bad idea, after all. It would be nice to have another body on the property. "I'll...show it to you after supper," she managed to say. "More potatoes, anyone?"

Everyone swore they couldn't eat another bite. Jill jumped up and began clearing the table, and the men got to their feet. "Thanks a bunch, Laurie, for the two-hundredth time," Tony said.

"I'll add my thanks, too." This from George. "That might have been the best chicken-fry I've ever eaten. As a small repayment for the food, if you'll get me a washer I'll fix that for you."

"What?" Laurie asked.

He indicated the sink. "I'll fix that drip for you."

The faucet. She had forgotten all about it. Small wonder.

"I WARNED YOU not to expect too much," Laurie said as she moved through the rooms of the tiny abode, switching on lamps. "It was meant to be shelter from the elements and not much more."

George and his nieces made a quick inspection of the place. He thought she did the little house an injustice. True it was small, and true there was only the barest minimum in the way of furnishings, but he'd lived in bunkhouses and boarding house rooms most of his adult life, to say nothing of the times he'd slept in isolated line shacks or in a bedroll under the stars. This, to him, was almost luxurious. There were two bedrooms; one had a double bed and the other twins, so that was perfect. There was a nice bathroom, a living room and an efficiency kitchen hidden behind folding doors. Certainly it contained everything anyone needed—beds, dressers, a sofa, a couple of easy chairs, and a dinette set. Above all, it was scrupulously clean.

"It smells brand new," he commented.

"I repainted after the last renters moved out. They had a toddler who loved to draw on walls with crayons, but I couldn't see that he did any other damage. The furniture isn't much. Most of it is secondhand stuff, but one thing I didn't scrimp on is the beds. They're top of the line."

George shook his head and uttered a little laugh. "I sure never expected to get anything like this. What do you think, girls?"

"It's nice," Stacy said, and DeeAnn nodded in agreement.

"Good. We'll take it," George said. "I guess we ought to discuss money."

Laurie had never set a firm, take-it-or-leave-it price for the cottage. She asked three hundred-fifty if she thought the tenant could afford it, but she had taken less. The rent money wasn't necessary to their survival. Usually she stashed it away to pay for little extras for Andy and Jill. And she had to remember that George now had the two girls, who were going to be a far bigger drain on his pocketbook than he realized. "Two seventy-five," she said quickly before she had time to think about it. "Water's included, but you'll have to pay your own electric bill."

"That's not very much," George said with a frown. "A place like this is worth three and a quarter, at least."

"Two seventy-five," she repeated.

"A deposit?"

"No. If you had little children or if I didn't know you, I might ask for one, but in your case, no."

He grinned and reached in his hip pocket for his wallet. "You're on. Two seventy-five, it is."

"I only want half that. The month's half over. We'll start full rent the first of the month."

George counted out the money and pressed it into her hand. "I can see I'm going to have a very agreeable landlord. What about the rules?"

"Rules?"

"Seems to me all landlords have rules. Don't you have a list of no-nos for new tenants?"

There was a touch of humor in Laurie's voice when she said, "Well, I don't allow wild parties, for one thing."

She had relaxed a little, George noticed, which made him feel better. She had seemed so uptight all afternoon, but that might have been attributable to Jill's wedding plans. He hoped so. He didn't like to think he might have something to do with her tenseness. He'd always thought he and Laurie were friends—only casual friends, perhaps, but friends, nonetheless. "Fair enough. I won't give parties, wild or otherwise."

"And I always told single men I didn't want them entertaining women out here. Andy and Jill were around, you know, so I couldn't have that. However—" she glanced at Stacy and DeeAnn, who never strayed far from George's side "—I believe your style has been sufficiently cramped for that not to be a problem."

George's eyes twinkled merrily. "Ain't it the truth. Anything else?"

"No, nothing. You're too far away for us to be bothered by a loud radio or anything like that." Just not far enough, she silently amended. It was going to be damned hard on her to have him out here.

Laurie stared at the money for a moment before stuffing it into her shirt pocket. She guessed she would use it to start a wedding fund. She'd collect four more full rent checks before the grand event, and that would help. But taking

George's money gave her the most peculiar feeling. A week ago if anyone had told her George would be back in the High Country and she would rent the cottage to him she would have laughed in his or her face. It probably was the dumbest move of her life, but she'd found herself in a situation she hadn't known how to get out of gracefully. Even now if she could have thought of a way to renege, she would have, but she couldn't, so that was that.

What a day! First Jill wanted to get married at least two years ahead of schedule. Then George showed up on her doorstep when she would have bet all she owned that she'd never see him again. With two young kids! Restless, carefree George, of all people. Now he was going to live right under her nose. Wait until Cassie heard about this!

She glanced down at the girls. They looked dead on their feet. "Would you like to stay here tonight?" she asked George. "I can get you some linens and bedding and anything else you might need right away. The girls look ready to drop."

"Well . . ." George looked down at his two charges. "What say, you two? Want to stay in our new house tonight?"

Stacy nodded. "We're sleepy, Uncle George."

"Tell me something, sweetheart. How come you always know when DeeAnn's sleepy or hungry?"

"She tells me, of course."

"Then it's settled," Laurie said, her voice crisp and efficient. "You can park back here or in front—it doesn't matter. And as for the phone—" she gestured toward the instrument sitting on an end table "—that's an extension of the phone in the house, and there's a buzzer. If there's a call for you, I'll buzz twice. Of course, if you'd prefer to have your own line, you can always have it put in later."

"I'm sure this setup will be fine. I'll have to stay in touch with Dad, but if you'll let me know what I owe when the phone bill comes in. . . ."

"Sure." Laurie placed one hand on each of the girls' heads. "How am I supposed to tell you two apart?"

"I'm Stacy," one said. "I'm taller."

"By half an inch," George said, smiling.

"And Uncle George says my face is rounder."

Laurie studied them seriously. "Yes, I guess he's right. I'll try to remember that."

"You'll also notice that Stacy's the one who talks all the time," George added. Then he gave DeeAnn a nudge. "Cat got your tongue, punkin?"

The girl shook her head and moved closer to him. *They absolutely adore him,* Laurie thought in wonder. She was seeing a side of him she'd never seen before, and, unfortunately, it only made him more attractive to her.

"I'll bet you girls want to take a bath," she said, "so I'll run to the house and get some towels and some bedding. I doubt that your Uncle George carries things like that along with him."

"No, they've always been furnished me. I usually travel light."

"No encumbrances—not things or people." Laurie shook her head. "That was the way you wanted it. Lord, George, however are you going to manage?"

"Don't ask me, but I will because I have to. You ought to know that."

"Of course." For a minute their eyes met, and for the umpteenth time since meeting George four years ago she wondered what there was about him that beguiled her so. Yes, he was handsome, but she'd known any number of handsome men. She simply didn't understand the lure and never had. During the months he had been gone she hadn't been able to entirely evict him from her thoughts, but she'd made progress. She would remind herself that she actually didn't approve of a man who couldn't make commitments, and that worked to a point. However, she had to admit it worked better when she couldn't see him. "I'll be right back," she said, and left the house hurriedly.

George stared after her retreating figure until he felt DeeAnn tugging at his hand. Collecting himself, he said,

"Okay, gang, I'm going to go bring the truck around and start unloading."

"We'll go with you," Stacy said.

"Why don't you just wait here?"

"We don't even have a TV."

He glanced around. "We don't, do we? Well, I suppose I could buy one. Or rent one. That might be better." He wasn't going to start burdening himself with a lot of possessions. Once Ellen was pronounced fit, there was no telling what would happen or where he'd go.

George and the girls had finished unloading the truck by the time Laurie returned, this time with Jill and Tony. All three of them carried enormous piles of sheets, blankets, towels and pillows. Everyone turned to making beds and stocking the bathroom. When all was pronounced ready for habitation, Jill and Tony left, but Laurie lingered long enough to give George a key to the cottage. "You might want to put that with your car keys. A single key is so easy to misplace, even when it's on a ring."

"You're probably right." He took his car keys out of his pocket. They hung from a metal ring to which a leather strap was attached. He added the cottage's key to it and held it in the palm of his hand. It seemed strange to be carrying keys, not only to a vehicle but to a front door. He guessed he had to go back to the days when he'd lived on the farm to remember when last he'd carried a key to a front door. As a suggestion of a smile played at his mouth, he put the keys back in his pocket.

Laurie reached for the doorknob. "You and the girls can have breakfast with us in the morning since your kitchen isn't stocked. I have some dishes and things that I put out here when necessary, but they're in a big box in the attic. I'll fish them out in the morning."

"Laurie, I'll buy whatever we need, and as for breakfast, the girls and I can drive into town. I don't want you doing more than you already have."

"I'd like to give the girls breakfast, if you don't mind. Is eight all right? We've never been able to sleep late, not even on Saturdays."

"Eight is fine. Thanks . . . for everything."

"You're welcome. Good night."

"Good night."

As she crossed the moonlit stretch of yard separating the cottage from the big house, Laurie wasn't aware that George stood in the doorway watching until she reached the safety of the back porch. She had too much on her mind. *Cope, girl, cope. George doesn't qualify as a crisis or even as a very big problem. Certainly he doesn't belong in the same category with inheriting your father's debts or stretching a paycheck to the limits of possibility, and you've handled that.*

Maybe, she thought with a sigh, but considering the way she felt whenever she looked at him, she thought that having George living in her backyard might tax her ability to cope to the limit. If, even for a minute, he happened to think of her as more than a friend—and that was reaching deep down into her fantasy grab bag—what could become of it? He was a wanderer by nature, a wild goose, and a person's inherent nature didn't change. Once his sister had recovered, he'd most likely be off again. Her own life, on the other hand, had always been ordered and measured by responsibilities. Her wildest flight of fancy to date was dreaming of a cruise to the South Pacific, and in the unlikely event such a trip ever materialized, she would spend months in the planning. She and George were as different as two people could be, yet she had wasted an awful lot of time during the past four years daydreaming about him in the most intimate sense.

As she pushed open the back door and stepped into the kitchen, her inner voice began hissing unsympathetically. *Oh, you're making me tired, Laurie. You're twisting this all out of proportion. George is back. Big deal. Think back to all the tenants who've lived in the cottage over the years.*

You scarcely ever saw any of them. There's no need for George to be any different.

Maybe, Laurie thought, but something told her that keeping George at a distance was going to be next to impossible.

CHAPTER FOUR

GEORGE HUNG UP the phone and stared thoughtfully into space. The duty call to the farm had been made. Now his dad and Anna knew where they were and had the new phone number, and Jonas had promised to call if there was any change in Ellen's condition. However, he warned George not to expect anything soon. According to Jonas, Ellen had greeted the news of her daughters' departure with a noticeable lack of emotion. The doctors called it withdrawal from reality; to Jonas it was a simple case of a softening of the backbone.

Stretching his legs in front of him and folding his arms behind his neck, George heaved an uneasy sigh. Then he glanced around the small living room of the first house he had ever rented. It was a real house with a real kitchen. More incredibly, in the next room two young girls lay sleeping soundly. They, like the house, were his for the time being. Unaccountably he was gripped by uneasiness. Two weeks had passed since the fateful day he'd decided to take Stacy and DeeAnn, but they had been at the farm then, and everything had just seemed to go on as before. Even during the trip from Oklahoma, he hadn't given much thought to the task ahead, mainly because the trip had been such an adventure for the girls.

Now they were here, and he was on his own. On Monday the workaday world would be upon them; the "adventure" would be over. They would have to establish a routine, stick to some kind of schedule. Routines and schedules had never been concerns of his. Maybe the reality of his changed circumstances was only beginning to dawn on him fully, but the most peculiar feeling came over him. He wasn't sure he could give it a name. Was it a sense of inadequacy or just plain fear?

So this was how responsibility felt, he mused. He couldn't say he welcomed it with open arms.

Then he shook off that thought as being unworthy of him. From now on all his thoughts had to be on the upbeat side. Positive thinking—that would be the key phrase. Getting to his feet, he walked to one of the front windows and stared out into the black night. A person could feel very small and alone in the country at night. George had spent countless nights under the stars, forty miles from the nearest known human and with only a horse for company, and he'd always welcomed the solitude. It was different when one had a couple of kids to take care of, though. Everything was different.

His gaze strayed across the yard to the main house with its lone light shining from an upstairs window. Laurie's room? He didn't know. He wondered if she'd ever experienced the inadequacy and fear that assaulted him now. Had she ever felt so hemmed in she'd wanted to scream? Surely she had. She'd been a woman, much younger than he was, when she'd suddenly found herself in sole charge of two young kids, so it must have been scary as hell for her at times.

Dammit, if she'd done it, he could, too, and if the going got rough, he'd just ask her what to do. She'd know and understand. All at once, George felt better. He had been smart to come back. He didn't intend making a pest out of himself, but it was always nice to have an ally.

The uneasiness and fear subsided. At last he thought he could sleep.

And sleep he did, like a baby. The bed was the last word in comfort, the house was dark and quiet, and he was more tired than he'd realized. The next thing he knew, Stacy was shaking him. "Uncle George, I thought you said we were supposed to have breakfast at eight. It's seven-thirty now."

He awoke by degrees, stretching and yawning lustily. "Okay, okay, you guys get dressed. I'll be right with you."

"We are dressed."

He opened one eye and saw both of them standing by the bed, dressed in jeans and clean shirts, their hair combed. "So you are. You look downright beautiful, too. Okay, I'll shake a leg." He started to throw back the covers but remembered just in time that he was stark naked. Damn, there were a lot of considerations with females in the house. "You ladies are excused while I get dressed."

Stacy and DeeAnn giggled and scampered out of the room, closing the door behind them.

LAURIE'S PREMONITION about the difficulty of keeping her distance from George proved true that weekend. Beginning with breakfast Saturday morning, he never seemed to be out of sight. Jill was mostly to blame for that. Tony had gone home to tell his parents about the upcoming marriage, leaving her with two whole days on her hands. She decided that fixing up the twins' bedroom in the cottage would fill up the empty hours. That prompted an attic search that everyone took part in. Frilly yellow bedspreads, remnants of Jill's young teen years, were discovered, along with assorted kitchen utensils, knickknacks and the inevitable family photographs, which were always good for a laugh. To Laurie's dismay, Jill uncovered dozens of long-forgotten snapshots of her big sister. One in particular caught George's attention.

"Who's this?" he asked Laurie.

She looked over his shoulder and grimaced. Why hadn't she thrown that one away long ago? "Me."

"I know it's you. Who's the guy?"

"His name is Len McFarland."

"I mean, who is he?"

"At the time that was taken, he was my fiancé."

George stared at the photograph a minute. So she had once been engaged. Nice-looking guy. And Laurie looked very young and very happy. "Carefree" was the word. He put the picture back with the others, but later, when Jill and the twins were out of earshot, he asked, "What happened? Or is it none of my business?"

Laurie shrugged. "I don't mind. It was a long time ago. That picture was taken shortly before the folks died. Len . . . didn't stay around long." She looked at him to see if he understood the implication, and it seemed he did.

"He ran out on you just when you needed him the most."

"Len was only twenty-six," she added, though she couldn't imagine why she felt the need to defend Len's actions.

"But you didn't let it knock you for a loop."

"I had . . . a lot on my mind in those days. I don't really remember how I felt." She did, though. She had felt betrayed, and it had taken a long time to get over that.

"I was thinking about Ellen."

"I know."

"I suppose I'll never understand how a woman can let one man mean so much to her. Ignoring her own kids, for pete's sake!"

"Don't judge your sister too harshly, George. Len left because I represented more responsibility than he wanted at the time. Ellen's husband left her for another woman after a marriage of many years. I have to believe there's a world of difference."

"I guess you're right." But he didn't think that—not for a minute. George felt pretty much the same way his dad did. As far as he was concerned, Ellen had chosen to cop out rather than cope. Laurie, on the other hand, was a coper. He doubted that life could throw her anything she couldn't field. Admiring someone like Laurie was the easiest thing in the world.

"Has there ever been anyone special in your life?" Laurie couldn't resist asking that.

"Once."

Odd. Laurie would have bet her next paycheck that the answer would be negative. "Where was that? Oklahoma?"

"No, it was when I worked in Wyoming. And it never went as far as an official engagement."

Laurie was dying to ask what happened but wouldn't, and when she didn't, George volunteered the information. "She ended up marrying a man who owned a hardware store. The kind of life I've always liked to lead . . . well, it's not especially attractive to women. Women like houses and families."

Laurie nodded. *Thanks for reminding me,* she thought sadly.

At that moment Jill walked by carrying an enormous box, and the twins were hard on her heels. "We're off to the cottage. Wait until we get through. You won't recognize the place."

Stacy and DeeAnn looked as happy as George had ever seen them. He watched them leave the house and shook his head. "You and Jill have been lifesavers," he told Laurie. "If I'd gotten the girls down here and they'd been struck with a case of homesickness . . . well, I'm not sure what I would have done."

"You would have managed. We always seem to do whatever we have to do."

"What are you going to do today?"

"Everything I don't have time for during the week. A supermarket run, for openers."

George brightened. "Would you mind if I went with you? I've got to have food in the house for the girls, and I don't have the first idea what to buy."

What could she say? To think she had hoped to stay away from him. Try as she might to regard him merely as a friend, to treat him as casually as he treated her, she couldn't. She was acutely aware of him every minute he was near. When he and the girls had walked through the back door earlier, her treacherous heart had begun its familiar dance. He had the weirdest effect on her and had from the moment she'd first laid eyes on him four years earlier. And now they were going grocery shopping together, of all things! All the coziness was just too much for her.

Actually it was a good thing she went shopping with him, she decided later. George, not surprisingly, had never been introduced to the complexities of a modern supermarket. Lord knows what he would have bought if she hadn't been along to advise him. When they returned home with their purchases, she helped him stock his kitchen. Then Jill announced she was preparing lunch for everyone. And so the weekend went. Laurie seldom had welcomed anything as much as she welcomed Monday morning. Maybe a return to work would get her mind on something besides George.

WITH GEORGE NEEDING to report for work at the DO bright and early, it seemed only natural for Laurie to take the girls to school, get them enrolled and make sure they knew which bus to catch that afternoon. And since George had forgotten to supply them with lunch money, she came up with that, too. Poor George had a lot to learn. She'd noticed that he'd looked a little harried when he drove off that morning—the result, she had to think, of getting two girls through their morning routine. Wait until he had schoolwork to contend with. Yes, he had a lot of surprises in store for him.

For George, getting back to the DO was like receiving a shot of high-potency vitamins. First he made his courtesy call on Cassie, then one by one the old familiar faces filed past to welcome him back. Shot Barnes was last.

"Well, lookee here at who's back," Shot chortled. "Couldn't stay away, huh?"

"Hell, I got an emergency call from the boss asking me to come back and get you worthless bums in line. So the goldbrickin's over, Shot. From now on, you're gonna work!"

Within an hour it seemed to George he'd never been away. Lord, it felt good to be back working with the old gang, doing what he did best. He would have enjoyed

working again on any ranch, but the DO was special in that
it made few concessions to the twentieth century. There was
a minimum of fencing and a maximum of free, rugged
country to ride through on horseback. He was in his right-
ful element. The day fairly flew by. At quitting time, Shot
invited him to stop by his house to say hello to his wife,
Joan, and to have a beer, just as they'd done countless
times in the past. George happily accepted.

Why he and Shot Barnes had become such good friends
he couldn't imagine. Save for their mutual love for an ar-
chaic way of life, they had almost nothing in common. Shot
had lived in the High Country all his life and was something of a local legend, partly because of his hell-raising
reputation, but mostly because he had been able to per-
suade the prettiest girl in Brewster County to marry him
fifteen years earlier. Joan had once been second runner-up
in the Miss Texas pageant, and her alliance with the likes of
Shot had sent shock waves through the local community.
George's personal opinion was that Joan had attached
herself to Shot because he represented a challenge. She still
had a beauty contestant's figure and the face of a goddess,
but beneath that gorgeous exterior beat the heart of an
overzealous reformer. To date, however, her efforts to re-
form Shot had produced minimal results.

And she had a wife's inherent suspicion of her husband's single pals, so she wasn't exactly overjoyed about
George's reappearance. If Joan were to rate Shot's pals on
a scale of one to ten, George guessed he would be somewhere in the top half, mostly because he was more clean-cut
and had better manners than the other cowboys she knew.
Still, he lived without the sobering influence of a wife and
family, so in Joan's mind he couldn't be completely trusted.
She was convinced that all single men were only minutes
away from some sort of devilment and were committed to
corrupting their married buddies. The fact was, however,
that Shot was far more apt to corrupt George than the other
way around.

"Well, George, you're back," she observed guardedly when they arrived at the house.

"Don't fall all over yourself with happiness, Joanie." George grinned.

She didn't grin back. "You working at the DO again?"

"Yep."

"Hmm."

"What's that supposed to mean?"

"Nothing. Just ... hmm. I guess this means the Friday night poker games will be starting up again."

George looked at Shot in surprise. "Haven't the guys been playing?"

"The get-togethers ain't what they used to be. Everything's been kinda dead since you left, pal. Joanie, honey, how about gettin' us a coupl'a beers?"

Joan shot him a withering glance. "Do I look like somebody's maid to you?" she asked and swished out of the room.

George laughed and sat down. "Same sweet Joanie."

"Aw, don't mind her, pal. She's still steamed about flunkin' out of charm school. I'll get those beers."

The two friends had a lot of catching up to do. During working hours there was no time for idle chatter; George had yet to hear the local gossip, learn who had gone where and who was doing what. He was content to ask questions and just listen to Shot talk. As the minutes became an hour, his mood mellowed. They were on the third round when Joan came back into the room, this time in a better humor. George had always been amazed that the woman could change moods as easily as other people changed socks.

"You living back in the bunkhouse, George?" she asked idly.

"No, I'm renting Laurie Tyler's cottage."

"Really?" This arrested Joan's attention. "Laurie's one of Melissa Ann's teachers. She thinks Miss Tyler hung the moon, and I must say Laurie's done wonders with that kid of ours. She's such a nice woman. You just have to wonder why she never married.''

''Must not be interested,'' Shot said. ''I know more than one ol' boy who would give next month's paycheck if Laurie would look his way.''

Joan uttered a disgusted sound. ''I don't suppose this would ever occur to either of you fine gentlemen, but Laurie Tyler would never be interested in an ol' boy. When Laurie latches onto a man, he'll be someone of class and means.''

George couldn't understand why that remark caused such an odd feeling in the pit of his stomach. He agreed with Joan completely.

''Well, the kids'll be getting home soon, so I'm going to fix supper,'' Joan announced. ''Will you stay, George?''

''No, thanks, Joan, I...''

Something clicked in his brain. George's eyes widened, and his eyes flew to his watch. The kids! He jumped to his feet. ''Holy hell! The girls!''

Shot and Joan exchanged startled glances. ''Girls?'' they asked in unison. ''What girls?''

''My girls!'' George reached for his hat, jammed it on his head and made for the door. ''Damn, I can't believe I forgot all about them!''

''You have girls?'' Shot asked, bewildered. ''Hey, pal...''

''My nieces,'' George said over his shoulder. ''I'll tell you about it tomorrow. Thanks for the beer. I gotta go.''

His heart was beating so hard and fast he thought it was going to jump out of his chest. He drove home frantically, negotiating the bends and curves in the road at an alarming rate of speed, while the sun seemed to set an all-time record for disappearing behind the hills. Damn, damn, damn! Some daddy he'd turned out to be. The thought of Stacy and DeeAnn all alone in that cottage wondering where he was, maybe scared, made him sick to his stomach. That he had absolutely, totally forgotten them was unforgivable.

The pickup raced down the gravel driveway and rumbled to a stop in front of the cottage. George got out at a dead run, but the minute he opened the door he knew there was no one inside, even though a lamp in the living room was on. "Stacy! DeeAnn!" he called uselessly. Bounding off the porch, he ran across the yard and pounded on Laurie's back door. It opened, and Jill stood staring at him.

"Hey, no need to break down the door. A simple knock will suffice."

"Jill, I—" Then, over her shoulder, he saw the twins sitting at the kitchen table with Laurie. They were having supper. Sagging against the door frame, he wearily pulled his hat off his head.

Jill stood back and motioned for him to come in. "We started without you."

"Hi, Uncle George," Stacy said brightly. "Where've you been? We're having chicken."

Laurie got to her feet and carried a plate to the stove. From the moment the girls had showed up at the back door with the news that George wasn't home yet, she'd had a pretty good idea what had happened. First day back at work with the old gang, somebody mentions stopping by for a beer at quitting time, and suddenly the girls are forgotten. "Working late?" she asked with a knowing smile.

George was out of breath. "No, I—I got to visiting with an old friend, and, well, the time just got away from me. I'm sorry. I . . . didn't mean for you to have to feed all of us again."

Laurie put the plate, now piled with food, on the table. "Have something to eat, George. You look positively terrible."

He sat down. He felt terrible, too. And limp with relief, to say nothing of totally foolish and inept. But the girls, oblivious to his agitated state of mind, were having a wonderful time.

"You're going to have to help us with our homework, Uncle George," DeeAnn informed him.

"Okay," he said listlessly, wondering if he could. "How was school?" It seemed to him that was something parents always asked.

"Fine. And we've got to shampoo our hair, but we do that ourselves," Stacy said.

"Good."

"Do we have a blow-dryer?"

"Yes."

"I want to iron a blouse for tomorrow. Do we have an iron?"

"No."

"We do," Jill said, beginning to giggle.

"Please, ladies," George said. "You've done too much already. Can't you make it one more day, sweetheart? I'll buy an iron tomorrow."

"Buy an iron tomorrow, if you like, George," Jill said, "but tonight they can use ours."

When the meal was finished, Laurie and Jill automatically began clearing the table. George got to his feet and looked at his nieces. "Troops, how about running on and getting started with your homework? I'll be along in a bit. Jill, let me help Laurie. I . . . want to talk to her."

Jill shrugged. "Sure. Be my guest."

When they were alone, George turned to Laurie apologetically. "I'm really sorry about tonight. It won't happen again, I promise."

"It's all right. Relax."

"I can't believe it happened tonight. They just . . ."

"Slipped your mind?"

"Yeah."

Laurie turned off the water faucet and looked at him with sympathy. "Don't be too hard on yourself. Let me tell you a story. The first day I returned to work after the folks died, I came out of the building at three-thirty to find Len waiting for me. He wanted to go somewhere for coffee, then do some shopping. I said sure. But just as I was about to get in his car, it dawned on me. I couldn't. The woman who stayed with Granddad had to leave promptly at four-fifteen, which was about the time Jill and Andy got home from school. I couldn't go anywhere after school, not just that afternoon but for every afternoon in the foreseeable future. It's a shock, a real shock."

George wondered if she was telling him the truth or just trying to make him feel like less of a klutz. Probably the former. He didn't imagine that Laurie wasted much time making up stories. And, of course, just about the time the realization of her responsibilities hit her, it would have hit the man in her life, too. So that would have been the beginning of the end of the romance. "Thanks," he said. "And it won't happen again."

No, it probably wouldn't. He was truly alarmed, and that would make an impression. But Laurie wondered how long it would take before the parental role suffocated him completely. The twins now were sufficiently comfortable with her and Jill to talk, and before George's tardy arrival, they had talked about home. They had mentioned their mother, saying only that she was "sick." They'd talked more about Uncle George, who was like a knight on a white charger to them. And they'd had plenty to say about their grandfather's cotton farm, a place they disliked but the place they would have to stay if it weren't for George. Laurie simply couldn't imagine a free spirit like George settling down to the life of a surrogate father. She was afraid it wouldn't be long before those poor girls were on their way back to that dreaded farm, and that was a shame.

"It's all right, George."

"Well, I guess I'll go try to help with the homework. Talk about the blind leading the blind! And, thanks again. Good night."

"Good night."

George hurried across the expanse separating the big house from the cottage and walked through the front door. Instead of the scene of industrious study he expected, the girls were sitting on the living room floor, giggling and playing with...a cat!

"What's this?" he demanded.

Stacy looked up. "This is Princess. Laurie says she hangs around a lot and probably will more now that we're here, 'cause she likes kids real well. We have to remember to buy her some food for when she's here.''

Wonderful, George thought. Just what I need—another female in my life!

CHAPTER FIVE

JILL HAD NO afternoon classes on Tuesday and promised to be home when the school bus arrived, so Laurie, more out of curiosity than anything, stopped by the bank after work to talk to Ted Weeks.

The banker, who had known her almost all her life, greeted her effusively. "Laurie, dear, it's so good to see you. Is what I hear about Jill true?"

The local grapevine was working efficiently, Laurie noted. She had learned Jill's plans on Friday; here it was only Tuesday and the banker knew about them. "Yes, it is, Ted. This summer."

"Good grief! Seems like only yesterday she was just a little girl."

"I know. And Jill's plans are the reason I'm here. Now I'm thinking about selling the ranch, and I'd like to discuss the offer you've received."

"Oh, that, yes. Sit down, Laurie, and let me refresh my memory. I sort of put that on hold." Ted rifled around in one of his desk drawers and produced a folder, which he opened and placed in front of him. "Here it is…uh, hmm, well, I'm not at liberty at this time to divulge the name of the prospective buyer, but I can tell you that the tentative first offer was for seventy-five thousand."

"Dollars?" Laurie asked in astonishment.

Ted laughed. "Yes, dollars. It's a good solid offer."

Lord, Laurie could barely imagine that much money in a lump sum. "Why on earth would anyone want to pay that much money for that pitiful patch of land of mine?"

"I'm sorry, dear. I'm not allowed to tell you anything but the dollar amount of the offer."

"Is this buyer interested in ranching?"

"Again, I'm not at liberty to divulge that."

Laurie frowned. She hated secretive deals. "Peculiar."

"Perhaps. Some people are peculiar about these land deals."

"Would this buyer want immediate possession?"

"That's the impression I got, yes."

Laurie bit her lip. Well, that took care of making an on-the-spot decision. This certainly was no time to make a move, not with the wedding in the offing. And though she knew she shouldn't let George and the girls be a consideration—they could be gone next week or next month—they were. Right or wrong, they needed her. And maybe she needed them in her life right now, too. "Tell you what, Ted, I'm going to beg off making a decision until after Jill's wedding. I just have too much else on my mind. But I'll give you a definite yes or no sometime this summer, all right?"

"Of course, it's all right. It's your property. But remember, you're not apt to do better, not ever."

"I know. I'm not thinking of that. There are a lot of personal things that must be taken care of before I can consider a move."

Laurie tried to put the offer out of her mind until she was ready to make a decision, but she couldn't help doing a little daydreaming while she drove home. Seventy-five thousand! The things she could do! With seventy-five thousand in the bank drawing interest, she could live an entirely different life. A cruise to the South Pacific could become reality. She might move to a city, a place where things happened. She could have an elegant little apartment furnished with glass-topped tables, a long mauve sofa and a small forest of plants. She would still have to teach, of course—the money wasn't a king's ransom—but at night she could go to concerts and Jazzercise classes. She might finally get her Master's degree and teach at the college level.

That would mean a higher salary. She could dine in trendy restaurants, see all the latest films and buy cosmetics at a department store counter instead of off the rack in the supermarket. And never again would she have to settle for "slightly imperfect" panty hose.

It was fun to think about, and daydreaming cost nothing. But as she walked through the front door of her house—a door she had walked through virtually every afternoon of her life—she stopped and glanced around. Jill's radio was blaring, as usual. She wondered how the girl had made it to twenty with eardrums intact. Still, if Jill had been in the house without the radio on, Laurie would have immediately checked her temperature.

Stacy and DeeAnn were sprawled in the living room watching television. Their faces broke into wide grins when they saw her. "Hi, Laurie," Stacy said. "Jill said it was okay to watch TV since we've already done our homework."

DeeAnn looked over her shoulder. "We wanted to get it over with before Uncle George got home and wanted to help. He's not much help."

"Go easy on him, girls. I imagine it's been some time since your uncle was within hailing distance of a classroom."

Laughing, Laurie walked into the kitchen and was greeted by the smell of something wonderful. Jill, who was a pretty good cook, had started supper! Suddenly she was swamped by the feeling of home. Daydreaming might be fun, but she wondered if anyone, least of all Laurie Tyler, would truly enjoy such a drastic change in life.

George showed up not long after that to collect the girls, and as they were leaving he said, "Weather permitting, I'd like to start painting your house this weekend. That's something I meant to do last fall, but I just never got around to it."

"Oh, I hate for you to go to all that trouble." Particularly since only a short time ago she had been thinking about selling the place, and apparently the condition of the house hadn't dissuaded the prospective buyer one bit. But then, selling out didn't seem all that attractive at the moment.

"No, it's something I really want to do," he insisted.

"Well . . . thanks."

Such a feeling of home! But later that night, reality reared its head, as it invariably did. Everything might be wonderfully cozy now, but all of them—Jill, George, the twins—would be gone one of these days. She had to keep remembering that. Somehow she was going to have to learn to think about herself for a change. Andy was gone for good, and soon Jill would be. The girls belonged to someone else, their real home was somewhere else, and George. . . Lord, hadn't she learned that George was as dependable as the weather?

What she needed to think about was walking through that door to an absolutely empty house every afternoon. The isolated ranch was no place for a woman alone. She had to think about growing old in the High Country, about becoming that grimmest of all stereotypes—a spinster schoolteacher.

So she supposed she would sell out come summer. Nothing would be the same when she was all by herself.

Then why let George go to the trouble of painting the house? her inner voice asked.

I don't know, she answered. *Maybe I just don't want any of them to think about how temporary this arrangement really is. Maybe I just want to hang on to the illusion of family togetherness, as long as I can.*

I really thought you were more sensible than that, Laurie.

So did I. So did I.

LAURIE HAD BEEN expecting Cassie to stop by any day, bursting with curiosity about George, so she wasn't the least surprised to find a note in her box in the teachers' lounge Thursday afternoon. Cassie had called to ask her to dinner that night. It was very casual. The invitation was for six-thirty. Laurie thought it might be a nice respite from having to pass the time of day with George when he got home.

Laurie always suffered a mild cultural shock when she visited Cassie and Scott Maitland's home. The place screamed of elegance and was so far removed from her own homey surroundings that it was laughable. The house was located in an area of the DO known as Horseshoe Ranch, which boasted a picture-postcard setting of lush green fields, fences, outbuildings and fat cattle. It was the kind of place city-slickers thought of when they heard the word "ranch," but Laurie knew of very few ranchers who lived amid such luxury.

"Let's have a drink and gossip while we're waiting for the others," Cassie suggested as she ushered Laurie into the living room.

"Others?" Laurie asked.

"Well, just Scott, Dad and one of Dad's cronies."

The two old friends sat on the sofa, had cocktails and talked. "When George told me where he and the girls were living, I almost fell down," Cassie said.

"I'll bet."

"Has anything, er, interesting happened?"

"No. Nothing's happened, interesting or otherwise."

"What's it like having him around so much?" Cassie wanted to know.

"Disturbing," Laurie answered truthfully.

"I can imagine. But it's occurred to me that fate or Kismet or whatever, has had a hand in this. You've been given a second chance. Don't blow it this time, kiddo."

Laurie laughed. "Give me a break! If I ever knew how to make a man sit up and take notice, I've forgotten by now. And face it. George is George. He's not going to notice any woman until he wants to." Laurie was suddenly glad to be talking about the situation—and especially glad Cassie was around to talk to.

Some friendships developed slowly over years of sharing common interests or simply life's highs and lows, but for Laurie and Cassie, friendship had been instantaneous.

Something had clicked between them, and a bond had been formed.

It had begun many years ago at a meeting of the cattlemen's association. Although Laurie had known who Cassie was—everyone knew the Ferenbachs—she had never been formally introduced to her, and Laurie certainly had never attended a cattlemen's meeting before that night. But in those first months after her parents' deaths she had still harbored innocent hopes of keeping the Tyler Ranch in the cattle business; she'd never dreamed that her father's debts would necessitate selling off all the livestock and anything else worth buying.

She and Cassie had been the only women present that night, so naturally, they had gravitated toward one another. When the meeting broke up, Cassie invited Laurie to the DO for a late snack. Since the woman who stayed with her grandfather during the day had agreed to stay until ten that night, Laurie happily accepted. Getting away from the house for one evening was a pleasant respite.

And so was engaging in woman-to-woman conversation. They had sat in the DO's huge kitchen, eating cold cuts and potato salad and talking until Laurie positively had to go home. She told Cassie the story of her life, literally. And she learned about Cassie's marriage to Robert Tate and her subsequent widowhood, all about her son, Rob, and something of the Ferenbach history. It amazed them both that they had so much in common. They both were women in "man's country." Both were single, and both had been through traumatic experiences that had ripped at the very foundation of their lives. From that evening on they had been fast friends, sharing life's events both great and small. Laurie had been there from the inception of Cassie's romance with Scott Maitland, and it was Cassie who had first recognized Laurie's interest in George.

Looking back, Laurie thought it was almost funny the lengths her friend had gone to, trying to throw the two of them together. Though she had been touched by Cassie's interest, she had kept reminding her of what George was: a footloose wanderer who worked hard at not forming attachments. But Cassie hadn't been dissuaded, not until that November day when George had ridden off into the sunset. His return to the High Country apparently had aroused Cassie's matchmaking instincts all over again.

Once again Laurie tried to squelch them. "I'm not putting myself in the position I was in last November," she now said firmly. "Not ever again. George is back, and I'd be lying if I said the spark is completely dead, but I hope I'm a lot smarter now."

Cassie, however, had held great hopes for a romance between Laurie and George for so long that she refused to give up now. And as a newlywed she wanted everyone in the world to be in love. "But you have to be encouraged by the fact that you were the first person he looked up when he came back," she insisted. "Well, there was me, of course, but I don't count. He wanted a job. Then he beat a straight path to your door."

"Cassie, I'm a realist above all. George looked me up for one reason—those two girls. He's like a fish out of water, and he needed some expert advice. If it hadn't been for Stacy and DeeAnn, I never would have seen him again. I remind myself of that daily." It was so nice to be with someone who knew the whole story. Pretense could be exhausting.

Cassie laughed lightly. "George in charge of two young girls is not a picture that comes easily to mind. There's poetic justice in there somewhere. How is he with them?"

"Not too bad. Better than you might think. He's as nervous and unsure as a first-time mother, but that's to be expected."

"What are the girls like?"

"Adorable. I'm trying very hard not to get too attached to them. George's sister is going to be better one of these days, and they'll be gone." She glanced down at her hands, then added, "Which is as it should be."

"And Jill's wedding plans?" Cassie asked.

"I can't say we've done much, but we're definitely going to have to get busy soon. I dread it."

"What? The wedding or having Jill leave?"

"Both."

"I know."

Cassie had a son by her first marriage and soon would be "losing" him, too. Young Rob was entering the Air Force Academy in September, so Laurie knew her friend understood exactly how she felt.

A minute of thoughtful silence followed, then Cassie leaned forward and spoke earnestly. "Now that we've dispensed with the gossip, I have something important to talk to you about, Laurie. The offer on your property."

Laurie's eyes widened. "Good Lord, how did you find out about that?"

"Dad's on the board of directors at the bank."

"Ah, I forgot."

"The board met yesterday afternoon. Ted Weeks might not be at liberty to tell you who wants this place, but I don't have any qualms about it. The prospective buyer is a lawyer who represents a big development company in New York. They want to build fifty 'ranchettes,' complete with swimming pools and underground sprinkling systems, then sell them to city-slickers who want some cool mountain air and gorgeous scenery." Cassie paused to make a derisive sound. "Oh, the company would make a bundle off the development, no question about that. Buy your land for seventy-five thousand, then build fifty homes that would sell for twice that much each. I've talked to some of the other members of the ranchers association, and we're all alarmed about this. I'm sure I don't have to tell you that we need those ranchettes like we need a seven-year drought. The water table simply won't support them. I guess I'm here to beg, plead, beseech, whatever. You can't sell to those people, Laurie. You just can't!"

Damn, Laurie thought. She might have known there would be a catch. The offer had been too sweet, and if she'd taken the time to think it through, she might have known that no one who seriously wanted to work the property would have offered that much money for it. She wasn't without conscience or concern for her neighbors, and she agreed that such a development wouldn't benefit the High Country, only the developers. And she knew how passionately Cassie felt about such things. Her friend was a traditionalist in the truest sense of the word.

But then, Laurie thought pettishly, Cassie's situation was so different from her own. Her ranch had been in her family for generations, it had been bought and paid for long ago, and a spread like the DO was so big it could get along no matter what. But Laurie knew she'd never again get the chance at that much money. She heaved a sigh. Why couldn't decisions ever be easy? Why did other people always have to be considered? Not once in her life could she remember being able to do just what she wanted to do.

"Dammit, Cassie, it's easy for you to tell me not to sell. Who else is going to offer me that much?"

Cassie frowned. "Is the money that important?"

"Well, it certainly would be nice to have some for a change." Laurie hadn't meant that to come out as bitter as it did, but at the moment she felt no communion with her best friend. What would Cassie know about strained financial circumstances? Not only was she heir to the DO, she had married into one of the state's legendary oil families. She wouldn't begin to understand what seventy-five thousand dollars meant to Laurie. "And God knows, with Jill gone I won't need that place."

"Not even with George here?"

"Good grief, you're stubborn about that!" Laurie exclaimed. "He won't be here forever."

Cassie reached out and touched her hand. "Listen, I know there's a solution to this, something that will make everyone happy. So don't do anything right away, okay?"

"Oh, I won't. Not until after the wedding at the earliest."

"I'm going to ask around. There might be someone, or several someones who would just love to have your property. You wouldn't mind cutting it up, would you?"

Laurie couldn't understand her hesitation. Why did she care? What was the pull? It was just a piece of land and a house that was really nothing but a headache. "No," she said with a sigh. "I guess I wouldn't mind. Once I leave, what difference will it make?"

So that was the reason for tonight's invitation. And since Cassie's father was expected, Laurie guessed he would get in his two cents' worth. J.B. Ferenbach was a fourth generation, old-line rancher, and his friend probably was, too. Scott wouldn't say much. He was a Johnny-come-lately, not only to the High Country but to ranching in general, so he wasn't all caught up in that "land is sacred" stuff. But J.B. and his friend would be another matter entirely. She'd have to listen to their fervent pleas, all designed to make her feel as guilty as sin if she gave serious thought to accepting Ted Weeks's offer.

That was exactly what happened. It was hard for Laurie to believe that the five of them could sit amid the luxurious surroundings of the Maitland home and find nothing more interesting to talk about than the insignificant little patch of land known as the Tyler Ranch, a "ranch" that had not known the hoofbeat of so much as one cow in years. She could watch and listen almost dispassionately while Cassie, J.B. and the other man, a rancher named Amos Thompson, discussed the horrors that would befall the High Country if "those easterners" got possession of that land. She wondered how two hundred pitiful acres could make that much difference in country so vast it seemed endless.

Several times Laurie thought she saw Scott giving her sympathetic looks. When he had first arrived in the High Country, he and Cassie had been antagonists, with her disapproving of every move he made... until she'd fallen in love with him. Now they coexisted peacefully. Scott ran the Horseshoe, which was but a small part of the huge DO, and

Cassie ran the rest of the ranch. They had compromised because they loved each other. But that didn't mean Cassie approved of Scott's theories about modern ranching, just as it didn't mean Scott couldn't sympathize with Laurie.

She had always enjoyed being with Cassie, but she didn't particularly enjoy that evening. Who could enjoy being made to feel like a traitor? *Maybe I'm just in the wrong frame of mind tonight,* she thought. *Maybe I'd feel differently if I owned an enormous ranch that had been in my family for generations. I might feel passionately about its fate.*

As it was, however, all she wanted was to do the best she possibly could for herself and for the people she cared about most. And this time that was all she intended taking into consideration.

STACY AND DEEANN might have looked like two peas out of the same pod, but their temperaments were even more different than had been apparent at first. After studying them both at home and in her Language Arts class at school, Laurie thought she had them fairly well pegged. Stacy was gregarious and effervescent; DeeAnn was a thoughtful observer. Laurie got the impression that nothing much got by the gentler twin. Stacy was an above-average student, but DeeAnn showed signs of becoming an outstanding one. Stacy liked action and people, and if there was absolutely nothing to do, she contented herself with television because at least it moved. DeeAnn, on the other hand, could immerse herself in a book and become completely oblivious to everything going on around her. That was one reason she liked to sit at the kitchen table, reading while Laurie prepared supper, leaving her sister with Jill and Tony in the front of the house.

The twins had been staying in the cottage a little over a week when DeeAnn suddenly looked up from the book she was reading and said to Laurie, "Guess what I'm going to do when I grow up."

Laurie turned from the sink and smiled. "What?"

"I'm going to write books."

"Wonderful, DeeAnn. But why wait until you grow up? Why not start now?"

"Huh? I can't write a book yet!"

"Well, not a book maybe, but you could write stories."

"You think so?"

"You could try."

"But what can I write about?"

"Whatever you like. Something you know. Perhaps you could write a story about two young girls who live on their grandfather's farm."

"Yuk!"

"Hey, it was just a thought. Everybody's a critic."

The seed had been planted, however. From that moment on, during the times when the twins had to entertain themselves, DeeAnn could be found with pencil and tablet, scribbling away. "I hope I haven't created a monster," Laurie confessed to George.

"At least she's never at a loss for something to do."

The day came when DeeAnn decided it was time for Laurie to read the story she was writing. Laurie had expected a fairy tale about a handsome prince and beautiful princess, or a shy teenager with a crush on the best-looking boy in school. What she got was something else again. DeeAnn's story concerned a little girl whose father had left home. One sentence in particular fairly leapt off the page and hit Laurie right between the eyes. *When her daddy left, the little girl felt like her heart had sharp points.*

Laurie's hand went to her mouth, and she felt her eyes well with tears. The first minute she had alone with George she showed the story to him. His reaction to the sentence was much the same as her own had been. At that moment, she thought, George fully realized and accepted the enormity of the task he had taken on. He looked shaken to his toes. Laurie placed a light, consoling hand on his arm and tried to convey her willingness to help him in any way she could. "Well, damn," he said thickly, his own eyes moist. "I guess…I guess we're just going to have to find a way to smooth off those sharp points."

CHAPTER SIX

APRIL CAME and went. Laurie's life slipped into a smooth routine, and despite her intentions, George and the girls became almost as much a part of it as Jill was. Jill celebrated her twentieth birthday. The house got painted, and the difference that made was startling. In fact, on most weekends George could be found puttering around, repairing this or that. Laurie repeatedly reminded him that none of it was his responsibility, but he did the chores, anyway. She had to admit that a pair of strong, willing hands could work wonders.

And she couldn't very well allow him to do so much work on her place without pitching in. While he painted, she weeded flower beds that hadn't been touched in years and divided matted clumps of iris and day lilies. While he mended the fence, she stood by to hold the rails he nailed in place. Sometimes she didn't do much but hand him things and lend moral support. The result was that they spent far more time together than she had planned to in the beginning. But Laurie enjoyed every minute that he was near, and she wondered if he derived any pleasure, however small, from her company.

He did. In fact, it was dawning on George more and more that she was the easiest person in the world to be around. Loner that he was, he tended to find most people wearisome for long stretches of time, but not Laurie. That was surprising, considering that they had very little in common. She was well-educated and well-read, while he'd spent his adult life staring at the south ends of northbound cows. It was a great life for a man who cherished his freedom, but intellectually stimulating it wasn't. Yet there were never any long, awkward silences between them. Laurie could always think of something to talk about. He guessed that came from being a teacher. But she didn't chatter idly about nothing in particular. When she talked she usually had something amusing or interesting to say.

As he worked, she often talked about the ranch as it once had been. "Daddy kept a big old tractor in that barn," she told him once. "It was new then—the barn, not the tractor—and when I was a little girl I loved to sit high up in the seat with him and to go rumbling off across the fields. There were cattle and horses and chickens and bees. My dad made the best clover honey." George began to realize that the Tyler Ranch had been a very nice place at one time, and he found himself wishing he could have seen it then, though just why he wished that he couldn't imagine. He never got attached to places.

And he began to understand, from a word dropped here and there, that she existed in a permanent financial bind. Not a critical one; she paid her bills. But the bind was tight. He'd never had much money, but he'd never needed much since his wants and wishes were few. A little money would have been a godsend to Laurie. He wondered if she was still thinking about selling out once Jill was gone. He wondered a lot about what went on in her head, and that was something else new to him. Normally he wasn't particularly curious about people.

Above all, he was smart enough to realize how much she had helped him ease into his newfound role of parent. He could always count on Laurie for sound advice. George was pretty damned proud of the relationship he and the girls had established, and he had Laurie to thank. There had been only one really difficult time, and it had been mercifully brief. It was the night he'd mustered the courage to have "that talk" with them. Even now he winced when he thought about it.

He had sat them side by side on the sofa in the cottage and taken a seat across from them. Then, looking at their rapt faces, he'd tried his best to remember how Laurie had phrased it.

"Girls, I guess you know that you're at the age when your, er, bodies are starting to...ah, change."

Stacy and DeeAnn had looked at each other, then back at their uncle. "You mean we're going to start our periods pretty soon, right?" Stacy asked.

"Ah, yes, that's what I was referring to. I just wanted to be sure you...know what to expect."

"We saw a movie at school last year. What do you want to know about it, Uncle George?"

"Nothing! I, er, wondered if you had any questions."

The girls shook their heads. "We have a book. Do you want to read it?"

"No!" he had exclaimed, then reconsidered. "Well, maybe I should. But if you ever do have questions, you just...go ask Laurie, okay?"

"Okay."

It was a cop-out, but he was sure Laurie would forgive him for resorting to it. He didn't know what he would do without her.

George, without realizing it, was feeling the fragile beginnings of the first real adult friendship he had ever known. And Laurie, without wanting to, found herself gravitating toward him like a moth to a flame.

Wedding plans forged ahead, and as Laurie had feared, the affair showed signs of costing twice as much as she'd hoped. Jill's dress, for instance. It had seemed to Laurie that there were dozens of beautiful, less expensive gowns in the bridal shop, but Jill's wistful expression had melted her resistance, as usual. And there would have to be four bridal attendants, because Jill had four absolutely best friends, any one of whom would have been hurt over being excluded. But at least the house's new facelift meant she wouldn't be ashamed of holding the reception there, so that would help.

Stacy and DeeAnn appeared to be happy, well-adjusted girls, and the stories DeeAnn wrote gradually became cheerier. That, in Laurie's estimation, spoke volumes about George's influence on them. If they'd suffered emotionally from being separated from their parents, it wasn't apparent. They made friends at school, and Melissa Barnes, Shot and Joan's daughter, was their favorite. And they were fascinated by the green mountains and crystal clear creeks after living all their lives on flat, dry plains. When they were home, Stacy could spend hours scampering around the hills behind the cottage, collecting rocks and gathering wildflowers. DeeAnn on the other hand, was never far from her books, pencil and paper.

There was no good news from Oklahoma; Ellen had good days and bad days. George kept in close touch with Dr. Ames, the psychiatrist, and every month Jonas sent the child support check. Laurie knew that had to be welcome. George admitted he couldn't believe how much two girls could cost.

Laurie had plenty on her mind, but she conceded that, by and large, life was serene. If there was a disturbing aspect to her existence at all it was George himself, but that was her fault, not his. She wouldn't understand how she could be so fascinated by a man who treated her merely as a friend helping him through a difficult time... and not an especially close friend at that. He treated her with unfailing politeness, courtesy and a certain amount of deference, which she found impossible to overcome. George, she thought ruefully, had always been and remained the most frustrating man she'd ever known.

But she had to give him an 'A plus' for his handling of the girls. The transformation from footloose cowboy to ever-watchful guardian had been swift and complete. Not once since the night he'd stopped at Shot's house had he failed to come straight home from work and tuck them under his wing. If he still was inept in certain aspects of child care, it wasn't because he didn't try. It seemed to Laurie that he was making a genuine effort to get inside the girls' heads and find out what made them tick, something all too many adults never tried to do, and he was rewarded by their absolute devotion. A nod of approval from Uncle George meant the world and all to them.

Still, Laurie suspected he must have chafed at the bit occasionally. Any man would, and a former free spirit like George doubly would. Even the most devoted parent could get tired of huge doses of children. What on earth did he do on the nights he was holed up in the cottage with the twins? she wondered. Didn't he often gaze out over the hills and long to be on his way? He had no social life that she knew of. She didn't, either, but that was a way of life for her. Wouldn't it be different for a man? Sometimes she burned with curiosity but forcibly restrained herself from asking questions. It was none of her business.

But it wouldn't hurt to offer to take the girls some evening in order to give him a little diversion, and the next time she talked to him she did.

George didn't waste his breath pretending he wasn't grateful for the offer. Shot had greeted the news of his friend's guardianship of twelve-year-old twins with hoots of laughter and had spread the word far and wide. Ever since, George had taken more than his share of good-natured ribbing from his pals about turning into a homebody and never joining them on their nights out. It had become something of a sore point with him, so Laurie's offer was a tempting one. "Sure you don't mind?" he asked.

"Of course I don't mind," Laurie assured him. "I wouldn't have offered if I did."

"Friday night?"

"Friday night is fine." Why *Friday* night? she wondered.

"Thanks. I seem to say that a lot these days. I'm never going to catch up on the favors."

On Friday evening, while Stacy and DeeAnn were in the living room with Jill and Tony, waiting for supper, Laurie saw George get in his truck and drive off. She told herself she didn't in the least care what the occasion was, but that wasn't true. Did he have a date? She would have given anything to know where he was going and, more importantly, who he was going with.

THE "OCCASION" was a poker game in the DO's bunkhouse, so chosen by the married men because the bunkhouse didn't have a telephone; therefore their wives couldn't call. George never had understood why that was important, but it seemed to be.

He pulled up to the bunkhouse just as Shot was arriving. "Well, so Joanie let you off the leash tonight."

"Aw, Joanie doesn't have any idea where I am. Told her I had some shopping to do in town."

George shook his head. "Shot, why don't you just tell her where you're going?"

"Hell, that wouldn't be any fun. Thinkin' I'm gettin' away with somethin' is all part of the game, pal."

"I can't believe that Joanie really cares if you play poker with the guys once in a while."

"She doesn't. But she'll bitch about it, anyway. That, too, is part of the game."

George had never understood the Barnes's marriage, and he thought that a family psychologist would have a field day studying it. The first wonder was that Shot and Joanie had ever married each other to begin with. The second was that they'd had three kids and stayed married for fifteen years. Joanie still griped, and Shot still worked hard at doing what he wanted to do. Furthermore, George would have been willing to bet they'd still be operating like that fifteen years from now.

Three hours later George was still sitting around the big wooden table with the five other men present, wondering what there was about such evenings that he'd thought he'd missed. If they had ever been uproarious fun, they no longer were. He had long since folded his last hand, and had nursed two beers all evening. "Dinner" so far had been salted peanuts, so he was in dire danger of starving to death. And Shot was dead drunk, which mean he would have to be driven home. Frankly, George could hardly wait for the evening to end so he could go home, too.

It did, finally, when he stood, shoved his hat on his head and told his friend they were leaving. "Come on, Shot. I'll drive you home."

"I can drive myself."

"No, you can't. Don't you pay any attention to those public service announcements? Friends don't let drunk friends drive."

"I ain't drunk," Shot said belligerently.

"I know. And I'm the tooth fairy. Come on."

Twenty minutes later George pulled to a stop in front of the Barnes's house. "Here you are, safe and sound."

"Come on in and have one for the road," Shot said, reluctant as always for the night to end.

George shook his head. "I don't want one for the road, and you damned sure don't need one."

Shot didn't budge. "Well, come on in, anyway. If you don't, I ain't goin' in, either. Joanie won't say anything if you're with me."

He was wrong. Joan met them with an expression that looked like a thunderstorm about to break. "Where in the confounded devil have you been, Homer Barnes?" she bellowed.

Shot, none too steady on his feet, grinned. "Hon, it was the damnedest thing. You know Russ Nolan? Poor guy fell and broke his leg . . . just feels terrible . . . so George and I decided to stop by and visit with him, kinda help him take his mind off his woes."

Joan stared at him a couple of seconds before growling, "You miserable, lying polecat! I saw Russ Nolan this afternoon, and he looked fine to me. For sure he didn't look like he had a broken leg."

Shot's liquor-soaked mind tried to sort and analyze that. "Well, ah, what time did you see him, hon?"

"Around three. What difference does it make?"

"Well . . . I—I think ol' Russ broke his leg around four."

Joan's eyes narrowed. "Shot, I figure you tell me about five lies in an average week, but that's the biggest one you've ever come up with."

George did his best to keep a straight face since Joanie had turned her attention to him. Her expression clearly said that she found him only slightly less contemptible than her husband. Fastening him with an icy stare, she said in the unfathomable way of Joan Barnes, "We're having a cookout tomorrow night, with or without him." She jerked her head in Shot's direction. "I wasn't going to ask any of the single guys, but Shot says I have to invite you. Try to rustle up a date, will you? I don't want a bunch of stags hanging around, guzzling beer and making asses of themselves."

"What a gracious invitation, Joanie. How could I possibly refuse? Are we dressing?"

"Shove it, George." Joan turned and left the room, angrily flicking a dish towel.

The minute he and Shot were alone, George let the laughter bubble up from his chest. Shaking his head and wiping his eyes, he said, "Pal, I sure hope you never have to take up lying for a living. You're the worst I ever heard."

Shot's drunken grin just broadened. "George, I just want you to know you're the best ol' buddy a guy ever had. If Joanie kills me in my sleep tonight, it'll have been worth it. I had a great time."

GEORGE WAS STILL laughing over Russ Nolan's broken leg when he turned onto the gravel driveway. It came to him with something of a start that he was glad to be home. Lights were on all over the big house, and Tony's car was parked in front, so he decided to stop and check on the girls. At least that was the excuse he used. Laurie answered his light knock and seemed surprised to see him.

"You're in awfully early," she observed. She'd imagined he would be out until the wee hours. "Did you have a good time?"

"Do you want to know the truth? It wasn't so hot. Are the girls still up?"

"No, I put them to bed in Andy's old room about thirty minutes ago. Come on in."

Jill and Tony were on the sofa, watching television. George waved to them but followed Laurie into the dining room. Some sort of game was spread out all over the table. "Have you had supper?" Laurie asked.

"Yeah. Beer and peanuts."

She pulled a face. "The refrigerator is full of leftovers. Why don't you heat up something while I put this away?"

"I can get something at my house."

"Why do that when I have so much food?"

"Well, okay. I'm starved. How did the baby-sitting go?"

"Oh, I never have any trouble with Stacy and DeeAnn."

"Yeah, they're great kids, which makes me want to wring Ellen's neck."

George called his father every Sunday night without fail. Even if he hadn't mentioned the calls to her, Laurie would have known about them because of the phone bill, which he was scrupulous about paying. And every Sunday night it crossed her mind that this could be the day when the news would be good, that Ellen was recovering and asking about the girls. Laurie always experienced a twinge of something indefinable. She refused to think it might be fear; that would have been unconscionable. She would remind herself that she wanted Ellen to get better, that it was what should happen. The girls needed their mother. Still, Laurie knew she would suffer a tremendous sense of loss when they left. And she wouldn't let herself dwell on what George would do when that happened. She was sure she already knew.

She put the game away and joined him in the kitchen while he ate—ravenously, she noticed. It occurred to her that it had been some time since she'd really talked to him—not that George ever talked a lot. But he was freer with words now than he had been previously, and he was a lot less shy with her. The girls gave them something in common. But the deference remained and created a gap between them that she simply couldn't bridge.

Which was okay, she decided quickly. She had no desire to be George's best buddy. She simply couldn't think of him that way, so maybe it was a good thing the gap was there. It kept her from dreaming too much, wanting too much.

"What did all of you do tonight?" he suddenly asked.

"I graded papers, and Jill and Tony and the girls played Monopoly."

Probably a much better way to spend Friday night than in a bunkhouse poker game, George thought. Then a question occurred to him—one he'd wanted to ask her many times. "Laurie, what do you do for fun?"

"Fun?" Laurie asked as though the word were foreign to her. "I don't know... what's fun?"

"Recreation. Just... fun."

"Well, I guess nothing."

"That's terrible."

"Is it? I never think about it." True, her life was in a rut, but whose wasn't? Perhaps if she could spend several hours a day in the company of someone she cared for a great deal—meaning a man who, in turn, cared for her a great deal—perhaps then mundane activities would take on the aura of "fun." But alone, taking care of routine responsibilities and paying the bills—who had fun? Maybe there were ten people in the whole world who led fun-filled exciting lives, but Laurie doubted it. "Cassie and I used to do a few things together," she added, "but right now she's a newlywed. For some reason, I don't seem to be as interesting to her as a new husband. I can't imagine why."

There was a pause, then George said, "I was wondering if you'd care anything about going to a party with me tomorrow night." He said it as if he half expected the answer to be no.

"Party?"

"Shot and Joanie Barnes are having a cookout tomorrow night. I'd like it if you'd go with me. Maybe we could press Jill and Tony into baby-sitting duty."

The invitation was unexpected and appealing. Laurie brightened a minute, then reconsidered. "Thanks, George, but... You see, Melissa Barnes is a pupil of mine, and a certain amount of decorum is called for on both sides. I've met Joan at several parent-teacher meetings, and I wouldn't want to make her feel uncomfortable or anything like that."

George tried to imagine Joanie at a parent-teacher meeting and found he could not. But Shot's wife seemed to have a dual personality. He had to assume that on those occasions she managed to keep a lid on her godawful temper. "Oh, I can't believe that Shot and Joan, of all people, would mind if their daughter's teacher drank a beer or danced a little. Please come. You never get away from this place."

"You noticed." School and home—that was her life. To spend an evening with George in totally different surroundings... The prospect shouldn't have been as irresistible as it was. "Well, I suppose I can ask Jill and Tony if they have plans for tomorrow night that can't be changed."

"Good. You know, it's been some time since I've had a date."

Laurie would have bet he'd had dozens since her last one, and she was far more excited about this one than she would have wanted anyone to know. Jill registered outright surprise when she was asked to baby-sit. "Sure, Laurie, but what's the occasion?"

"George asked me to go to a party with him, and I thought it might be fun," she said offhandedly.

"You and George?"

"Yes."

"Well, I'll be!"

And what, Laurie wondered, was that supposed to mean?

CHAPTER SEVEN

SATURDAY WAS A BRIGHT, warm day, and the evening promised to be soft and gentle, a perfect night for a cook-out. The Barnes home was buzzing with activity when Laurie and George arrived. Since the weather had cooperated so splendidly, most of the party-goers were in the backyard, clustered around long tables laden with food that had been covered with huge sheets of plastic. Two portable barbecue grills had been fired up and were in the process of burning down to coals. An enormous plastic tub filled with ice contained beer and soft drinks. Laurie hadn't imagined there would be so many guests, but she was grateful for the mob scene. One could get lost in a huge crowd, which at the moment seemed desirable. Glancing around, she saw that she was acquainted with maybe a third of the guests and those mainly because their children were or had been students of hers.

No one noticed their arrival until Joan spotted them and called out. Then every head turned in their direction. Unconsciously, George stepped closer to Laurie and placed his hand on the small of her back. He surprised himself with the possessive gesture, but she looked so wonderful it made his heart pound. She was wearing a bright pink sundress and low-heeled sandals. The dress had a short jacket, which she'd slung casually over one shoulder. And she had done something different with her hair. It was pulled away from her face in a braid that started up at the crown and hugged the contour of her head down to the nape. George knew next to nothing about women's hairdos, but he doubted that many women could wear that one and look absolutely beautiful. They'd have to have a face as alluring as hers, and he doubted many of those existed.

He would have liked to tell her she was possibly the prettiest sight he'd ever seen, but he wouldn't have known how to begin. He silently cursed his lack of eloquence. Having spent his adult life working almost exclusively in the company of men, he simply hadn't had any practice at uttering those smooth phrases that rolled off some men's tongues so easily. He couldn't come on to a woman; it was that simple. Oh, maybe with a certain kind of woman in a certain kind of place after he'd had a few beers, and he could talk to Joanie like one of the boys. But a woman like Laurie—no way.

Joan was bearing down on them. She had on skin-tight white jeans and a flame-red blouse, both of which emphasized her voluptuous figure. Her smile was radiant. It was obvious that Joan, the chameleon, had donned her party face and manners; she was all Little Mary Sunshine. One who didn't know better would think that nothing but kind words had ever passed through those lips.

"George!" she gushed. "How wonderful to see you!"

It was all he could do to keep from bursting out laughing. "Hi, Joanie. Did you kill Shot in his sleep last night?"

He was aware that Laurie's head turned in his direction, and for a fraction of an instant Joan's sunny smile was obscured behind a dark cloud of irritation, but their hostess recovered quickly. "You crazy thing."

"Guess you didn't or I would have heard about it. I know Shot would want me to be a pallbearer."

Joan's eyes glared daggers at him, but she turned to Laurie with a smile. "George is such a kidder."

"He is?" Laurie cocked her head and pretended to study him. "I guess that's a side of him I've never seen."

"You know Laurie, don't you, Joanie?"

"Of course. I'm so glad you could come."

"Thanks, Joan. So am I. How've you been?"

"Oh, splendid! Listen, I want you two to mix and mingle and introduce yourselves to anyone you don't know.

There's lots to eat and drink, so if you go hungry, it's your fault.''

George turned to Laurie. "How about a beer?"

"I'd love one."

"I'll get it."

Just as he walked away, a woman Laurie knew slightly accosted her, so Joan took advantage of that to catch up with George. "How in the world did you ever wrangle a date with Laurie Tyler?"

"I asked her."

"And she accepted, just like that?"

"Yep."

"Hmm. You just advanced several notches on my list, George."

"Thank God," he said with an exaggerated sigh. "I spend a lot of time worrying about my position on your list, Joanie."

Shot's wife shot him her sweetest smile. "Bastard."

"And you're a living doll." George winked at her, then strolled off to get two beers. He didn't want to leave Laurie on her own too long. He doubted she was acquainted with too many of these characters, and she'd seemed a little nervous about the party to begin with.

Laurie, however, discovered that it was impossible not to relax and have a good time with Shot and Joan and their hardy band of exuberant friends. She'd never been around people who were so unrestrained and had such a good time together. Admittedly some of the conversation was on the bawdy side, and it got bawdier as the evening progressed, but she heard nothing offensive, and she was anything but a prude. The one thing she had dreaded was feeling like an outsider, but everyone treated her like one of the gang. She had a wonderful time.

Oddly, it was George who was uncomfortable, even though most of the people there were friends of his. The longer he kept a watchful eye on Laurie, the more he thought that bringing her hadn't been such a good idea. She was a class act, and his friends definitely were not. To him,

Laurie looked like a hothouse orchid in the middle of a briar patch, and he was damned embarrassed that he'd thrown her in with this bunch. To top it off, he wasn't too wild about the way some of the guys were looking at her—Don Hobson, in particular. He was even less wild about the way Laurie was laughing delightedly over something Hobson had just said. Don worked at the DO and was one of the few cowboys George had ever known who considered himself a ladies' man.

Just then Don reached out and touched Laurie on the arm, and George felt something splinter inside. *Hobson ought to save that suggestive leer for honky-tonks,* he thought sourly. *He damned sure doesn't have any business touching Laurie.*

"Somethin' stuck in your craw, pal?"

A voice behind him snapped George out of his reverie. He turned to see Shot grinning at him. "Yeah. What the hell is Don Hobson doing?"

Shot glanced out over the crowd. "Looks to me like he's panting after the Duchess."

"Who?"

"Laurie Tyler. The Duchess."

George fumed. "Who calls her that?"

"All the guys."

"She's Miss Tyler to the likes of you and the rest of these bums."

Shot rolled his eyes. "Well, excu-u-use me for livin'. I thought I was the only one around here nursin' a hangover. Have another beer. Maybe it'll sweeten that rotten disposition."

At ten minutes to ten, George gave up. He took Laurie by the arm and pulled her away from the group of people surrounding her. "Are you about ready to go?"

"Go?" Her mouth fell and she glanced around at the festivities. "But no one else has left."

"Somebody's gotta be first. We need to go home and check on the girls."

"That's ridiculous. You know they're fine. Jill knows where we are. She'd phone if anything was wrong."

"Let's go, Laurie. Okay?"

I've done something wrong, she thought. She couldn't imagine what it was, but she must have. George had been acting funny all evening, almost from the time they'd arrived. Every time she'd looked in his direction he'd seemed to be glaring at her. She tried to think how she could have misbehaved. All she'd done was have a good time. She'd drunk nothing but two beers. She hadn't talked too loudly or too much. She didn't understand it.

Then a dispiriting thought occurred to her. Maybe George was just bored; he certainly looked it. At least he looked something, and it wasn't happy. Since the party was an unqualified success, and since almost everyone there was a friend of his, she had to assume she was the cause of his boredom. So much for their first date and, no doubt, their last one. Struggling with her composure, Laurie nodded curtly. "Of course. Just let me find Joan and Shot and thank them for the nice time. I'll only be a minute."

THEY WERE A solemn pair during the ride home. There was no conversation, but an almost tangible tension filled the cab of the truck. Once George chanced a glance in Laurie's direction, but she was slumped against the door on the other side, staring out the window, stiff and uncommunicative. He supposed he owed her an explanation. Frankly he'd been surprised that she was so reluctant to leave the party. Maybe she'd been enjoying the hell out of Don Hobson's attentions. The thought further darkened his mood.

Lights were on in the big house. George pulled around in back, where the only illumination came from the back porch light, and parked. Laurie made no move to get out of the truck, so he rolled down the window and stared out. He was trying to think of something to say when Laurie spared him the necessity. Good and miffed, she turned to him. "All right, suppose you tell me what I did to make you want to leave. Did I commit some terrible social gaffe?"

"You? You didn't do anything."

"Then why did you insist we leave?"

George sighed. "Aw, Laurie, you don't belong with that scruffy bunch of friends of mine."

She stared at him a minute, her mouth slightly open, her brows knitted. Finally she spoke. "May I ask why not?"

"I'd think it would have been obvious."

"I guess I'm dense. Nothing was obvious to me."

"You're . . . different."

Laurie didn't have the slightest idea what he was talking about. She had worked hard at blending in with the crowd, but apparently she hadn't been successful. Maybe she had been away from the social scene too long. "In what way?"

"You've just got...too much class for the likes of them."

It took a minute for that to sink in. When it did, she sat back, shaking her head and laughing lightly. Perhaps she should have been flattered, but she wasn't. She was horrified. Given her position in a close-knit community, she was scrupulous about her behavior, but the last thing she wanted to do was come across like a prim schoolteacher. "Oh, that's so ridiculous! George, look around and tell me what you see. No mansion for sure. This old hard-scrabble ranch is where I was born and raised. It's me! I loved the party tonight. I liked being with your friends. You can't imagine how good it felt to have fun for a change."

George rubbed his eyes. He guessed he had pulled a boner, but he genuinely had been embarrassed for her. Now he could see he should have let her decide when they would leave the party. "I'm sorry," he said contritely. "I wasn't too crazy about the way everybody was talking, and—"

"Oh, God! I didn't hear anything tonight I haven't heard before. I wasn't raised under glass. My dad was an earthy man, and I lived with two teenagers who went through a stage of trying their dead-level best to shock me."

"And I damned sure didn't like the way Don Hobson was looking at you."

So he'd noticed. Laurie didn't know when anything had pleased her so much. Don had come on to her pretty strong, but she'd found it more amusing than anything. As she glanced sideways at George, she began to understand one of the reasons she'd never been able to get close to him. He had some ridiculous idea that they weren't on the same level, and the last place she wanted to be was on a pedestal. Impulsively she reached for his hand, held it a minute, then placed it on the side of her neck. "Feel me. Just flesh and blood. I'm not a porcelain doll, and I don't want to be treated like one."

For George, the touch of her smooth, warm skin was like an electric shock. Never would he have imagined touching Laurie intimately; he wouldn't have allowed himself such a flight of fancy. A few times over the years he had wondered what it would feel like to kiss her, but he'd never dwelled on it long, feeling that such a thing lay way outside the realm of possibility. Now his fingers pressed her skin, and his thumb went under her chin to tilt her face up. There was little light, but enough for him to see her steady, unwavering gaze. His eyes dropped to her mouth. Looking at those incredible eyes and that appealing mouth, he found it hard to believe that no man had claimed her for his own by now. He searched for some sign of willingness on her part for... for whatever was coming next. He swallowed with difficulty. One little kiss in a parked truck... was that asking too much? He saw the pulse in her temple begin to beat faster, and slowly it occurred to him that she just might want it, too. The thought was so exciting that he felt himself begin to tremble.

Laurie's heart was lodged in the middle of her throat. They seemed to have been sitting there gaping at one another for a long time. She was afraid to move for fear she'd break the spell, and George was as still as death, staring at her with a kind of wonder in his eyes. Was he silently quizzing her? *Yes, kiss me,* she thought, *yes.* How many times had she dreamed about this? She had wondered about it so long that she thought she would explode if she didn't satisfy her curiosity. And instinctively she knew that if she really wanted his kiss, she'd have to make the first move. George, damn him, might sit there staring at her for an hour.

She leaned forward slightly, and his hand moved around to her nape, then below. Laurie heard him suck in his breath. Melting, she moved nearer. Her arms went up his chest and around his neck. She raised her face, and his lips closed over hers.

It wasn't a little kiss. George's first touch was gentle, hardly more than an inquisitive nip along the seam of her lips, but Laurie's pliant response and the pressure of her hands at his neck prompted him to part his lips and draw hers gently into them. His hands roamed her back, kneading, pulling her against him. Though more than a little in awe of her, George kissed her inviting mouth and tongue, with nibbling bites and sure strokes. He was sure he had never tasted anything sweeter in his life.

So this was how it felt, Laurie thought, as a small gurgle of pleasure rose up in her throat. But even with his mouth pressed insistently against hers, with his tongue making those sensitive forays between her teeth, her maddening, rational mind would not rest. Gathered in the warmth of his arms, it was easy to slip into a state of euphoria, but nothing had really changed. Sharing a few kisses in a parked truck wouldn't change his rambling ways. He was what he was. And it well could be that she'd never again be able to look at him without thinking about this. Perhaps wondering how George's kiss felt had been far safer, far less painful than knowing.

It was a little late to be thinking that, she conceded as they broke the kiss, breathless. Fearing that every powerful emotion she felt for him was registered on her face, she buried her head in the curve of his shoulder and clung to him tightly. George held her in a strong embrace, speechless himself, and pondered what his next move should be, if anything. This had happened awfully fast. He was trying to remember if he'd instigated it, but his mind was in

such a fog he would have been hard pressed to stammer out
his full name.

One thing he knew for sure, though: Laurie hadn't re-
sisted. Hell, she'd responded eagerly, even ardently. He'd
always thought himself out of her league, but apparently
she had not. He had to come to grips with that, too.

He heard Laurie sigh, and she stirred in his arms. Somehow George didn't think they could sit in the truck indefinitely, wound around one another, without saying
something. "Laurie, I—"

"Please, you're not going to say anything dumb, are
you?"

"Well, probably."

"Don't." Lifting her head, she planted a firm kiss on his
mouth, deeper and more lingering than the first one. Then
she trailed her lips down to the hollow at the base of his
throat, loving the texture of his skin and its heady, musky
scent. She brought her hands around to rub his chest
through the soft cotton of his shirt. One palm stilled over
the hard thumping of his heartbeat, and she sighed again.
She rested her cheek against the vee of skin where his shirt
was open. Somehow she imagined that his entire chest was
just as smooth, and she longed to flick his shirt buttons out
of the holes and slip her hand inside to satisfy her curiosity. He felt wonderful—hard and warm. She'd always
known he would be. *Lord,* she thought, *I really am in love
with him! This is no crush, no silly attraction. I haven't
been remotely interested in another man since I first saw
this one.*

George propped his chin on the top of her head. Her
body felt unbelievably light in his arms. He'd never held a
woman who felt so good or smelled so good. The scent that
clung to her wasn't heavy or perfumey; rather, it was sweet
and clean, the way he imagined a baby would smell. Laurie was the last word in human perfection to him, but she
wasn't too perfect to go all warm and pliant and womanly.
That she'd shown him this side of her made his pulses
pound. He could hardly let himself believe it, but it oc-

curred to him that there was a very real possibility that this could escalate into something much deeper. After all, more incredible things had happened in the history of civilization. They both were unattached adults. And sharing an intimate physical experience with someone he felt genuine affection for, someone he thought the world of, was something George would definitely welcome.

Except that with each passing minute the gentle affection he felt for her was turning into pure sexual desire. He was aware of an uncomfortable tightness in his jeans. He had lusted before, many times, but it had never felt quite like this. Lusting for Laurie was tempered by a certain sweetness.

She stirred again, shifting her position in his embrace. His hand roamed down her back to her waist, and rested there a minute before moving upward. His palm encountered the side of her breast and he stopped to feel the gentle swell. He thought his heart had stopped, too. In fact, his whole body seemed paralyzed. With a slight movement, he could fill his hand with that soft mound. The thought was unbelievably exciting. He wished he could stroke her into senselessness. He wanted to press her to him, rub against her and try to relieve the ache. Instead, with some difficulty, he forced his hand to move up to her face. His fingertips lightly grazed her cheek and jawline. "Laurie?"

"Hmm."

"You're . . . very nice." *God A'mighty, Whittaker, couldn't you come up with something a little more profound than that?*

But she raised her head and gave him the sweetest smile he'd ever seen. "So are you. And you know something—I wouldn't mind being kissed again." She would have kept him out there all night if she could. It was foolish and unwise, probably, but after dreaming and hoping for so long, she wasn't going to spoil this delightful interlude with a lot of sensible, pertinent doubts.

"Scoot over," he said huskily. "It's impossible to do any serious courting behind a steering wheel."

She moved until her back was resting against the passenger door. "Are we about to do some serious courting?"

George slid free of the restricting wheel. "Unless you tell me to stop."

"Well, you can bet your sweet life I'm not about to do that." Her hand went to his nape to pull his face closer; her lips parted invitingly. Above her, his white teeth gleamed, then disappeared from sight as his mouth closed over hers again.

At that moment there was a pounding on the driver's door. George bolted upright, and his head swiveled. There, framed in the window, was Stacy, and she was grinning from ear to ear.

"What'cha doing?"

George struggled with his ragged breathing. "What do you want, sweetheart?"

"I saw your truck through the window, Uncle George. Jill won't let us have popcorn this late unless you say it's okay."

George muttered something under his breath. He wondered if Stacy had seen that tight embrace. Not that he cared, but Laurie might. When he spoke, his voice sounded deceptively calm. "I, ah, guess it's okay. What time is it, anyway?"

"Ten-thirty," Stacy said, trying to peer around him at Laurie.

"Okay. Yeah, sure, you can have popcorn."

She scampered down and headed for the house. "I'll tell Jill to make enough for you and Laurie, too."

George and Laurie exchanged glances. "Damn!" he muttered under his breath.

"The joys of parenthood," Laurie said.

They sat side by side in silence for a minute, regretful but resigned. Whatever might have been wouldn't be, not that night. *Maybe never again,* Laurie thought, but it had been a lovely interlude, one she could tuck away into her memory bank to be recalled time after time.

Finally, George stirred beside her and reached for the door handle. "I guess we're going to have to go in since everyone knows we're home."

"Yes," Laurie said with a sigh. "Popcorn, anyone?"

STACY HURRIED into the house and ran straight for the living room, where Jill, Tony and DeeAnn were. "Popcorn's okay," she announced. "Uncle George and Laurie are home."

"Where are they?" Jill asked.

"Out back in the truck." Stacy covered her mouth with her hand to stifle a giggle. "They were kissing!"

"Oh, you were imagining things!" Jill exclaimed with a laugh.

"I was not. They were kissing!" Stacy looked at her sister. "Really, Dee. They were!" And both girls promptly dissolved into a fit of giggling.

Jill turned to Tony, lowering her voice. "Laurie and George?"

"For pete's sake, they had a date, and he kissed her good night. I don't think that qualifies as a news bulletin." He looked at Stacy and DeeAnn, who were still giggling. "What's the matter with you two? You've seen me kiss Jill a hundred times."

"That's different," Stacy said.

"It just seems so strange," Jill mused. "George has been around forever, and nothing's happened between them."

Tony chuckled. "How do you know?"

"I'd know, I'm sure of it. My sister wears her emotions on her sleeve."

"Don't be too sure of that, love. Besides, a good-night kiss doesn't mean anything's happening between them." He got to his feet. "Come on, kids, let's go make that popcorn."

When Laurie and George joined them in the kitchen a few minutes later, Jill watched her sister carefully. Laurie wore a sort of bemused, faraway expression and, Jill alertly noticed, she wouldn't make eye contact with George during the remainder of the evening. George looked different, too—sort of off-balance. If there was anything more obvious than two people looking at each other, it was two people trying hard not to look at each other.

Well, if this isn't something, Jill thought. *Laurie and George, of all people!*

DURING THE WEEKS that followed, Laurie was to think it incredible that she was never alone with George, not even for a few minutes, but that was the case. Of course, she reminded herself daily, there were good reasons for that. As the daylight hours lengthened, so did the workdays over at the DO. Even though Cassie, sympathetic to George's new circumstance, had told him he could quit at the regular time, he was much too conscientious about his work to take her up on her offer. And with the end of the school year at hand, Laurie was busier than usual. On top of that, every spare minute outside the classroom had to be spent on wedding preparations. Somehow, between George, Laurie and Jill, the twins were never left on their own for long, but some days Laurie felt as though she was meeting herself coming and going.

As the days wore on, the memory of the night of Shot and Joan's party dimmed. Laurie wondered if she'd only imagined the intensity of George's kisses. A woman with her non-existent love life could conjure up anything and read into simple gestures things that didn't exist. George and the girls often had supper in the big house, and on several occasions Laurie thought she'd caught him giving her some rather longing looks, but that, too, could have been her imagination. If he wanted to be alone with her, she thought pettishly, he could have found a way. Men could be very resourceful when they wanted something badly enough.

When she was being sensible, she asked herself what she had honestly expected to happen, and she couldn't come up with an answer. That night in the truck she had been content to let one thing lead to another, and she supposed if they found themselves in a similar situation again, she would do the same. She further supposed that having the kisses develop into something more passionate wasn't all that impossible or incredible. George was a man, and she was a woman. They were heterosexual, and neither of them was engaged in an affair of the heart with someone else. For sure she wasn't, and if George was, no matter how casually, he had stumbled onto the world's most patient and undemanding woman. To call a spade a shovel, Laurie supposed she could lure him into bed without too much difficulty.

But then what? She wasn't the kind of person who could drift into a casual affair; sometimes she wished she was. And to dwell on something permanent with George was to give new meaning to the word "imagination." Hers seemed to be working overtime these days.

What she wasn't imagining was the loving care he lavished on Stacy and DeeAnn. They, in turn, all but worshipped him. Laurie fancied that the girls had grown fond of her, too, and she certainly was crazy about them. Every Sunday night she suffered through George's call to Oklahoma. She couldn't bear to think of what life would be like when they went away.

For George, the longing to be with Laurie again was close to unbearable. He thought about her at the strangest times. He didn't know what was worse—seeing her or not seeing her. His memories of the night in the truck hadn't dimmed; he recalled every single detail with amazing clarity. The episode still filled him with a kind of awe when he thought about it. Not only had he kissed Laurie, she had kissed him back, eagerly. Remembering the way her soft, light body had felt in his arms made his blood course hotly through his veins, and if he didn't feel her again soon, he was sure he would lose his mind.

Of course, he had no reason to think she wanted that, too. If she did, it seemed to him she would have given him some sign or made some overture. Maybe the episode in the truck hadn't had the impact on Laurie that it had on him.

He hadn't exactly been Mr. Suave that night. Thinking back, he seemed to have behaved more like a kid out on his first date. The sad truth was, the woods were full of guys who were smoother with the ladies than he was.

Life was strange. Until a few months ago his idea of heaven had been to pack some gear, mount a horse and ride to a remote place where he could spend the night under the stars. Now all he could think about was the welfare of two young girls and the warm kisses and sweet smiles of a beautiful woman. Shot and the others had given up asking him to join them on their nights out. "Hell, man," Shot had said, "You're more tied down than any married man I know." George's excuses usually involved the twins, but Stacy and DeeAnn were sensible girls who could look after themselves. The truth was, he'd lost interest in the old life.

Maybe it was age. Responsibility had a way of making one grow up. A lot of what he'd thought of as fun before now seemed like macho kid stuff. He didn't suppose he'd ever lose his love for horses, cows and the ranching way of life—that seemed to be in his blood—but lately he'd been giving some thought to doing it in one place. A few months ago that mere idea would have been enough to send him packing his bags and looking for the nearest bus station.

George paced the rooms of the little cottage like a caged tiger. The twins were blissfully engrossed in some bit of inanity on television. He wondered if he allowed them to watch the tube too much, but now that school was out for the summer and there was no homework....

He didn't know. Maybe he ought to ask Laurie what the guidelines should be. There was so much he still didn't know, but he'd sure learned a lot in three months. Mostly he followed his own instincts where the girls were concerned and consoled himself with the fact that he loved them. He would have fought lions with his bare hands for them, so he doubted he could go too wrong. Still, he was always aware that having them would have been so much more difficult without Laurie.

Laurie! He couldn't think the name, much less say it, without something peculiar happening to his insides. He walked to the front window and looked out. The big house seemed quiet now. Earlier it had been a beehive of activity with cars arriving and leaving every five minutes or so. Now that the wedding was only days away, something always seemed to be going on over there, and the tempo would only increase in the next few days. George didn't think he and Laurie had exchanged more than a few sentences in weeks.

Behind him he heard the television being turned off, and the girls stirred. "We're going to do our hair now, Uncle George," Stacy announced. "Jill taught us to make French braids, so we're going to practice on each other."

"Lord, you two spend more time on your hair," George said, turning to them. Maybe they weren't turning into TV addicts after all. They seemed to watch only their favorites and then go on to something else. "I guess this means you'll be tied up for a while."

DeeAnn rolled her eyes. "Forever!"

"Then I think I'll, uh, take a walk around, just get some night air."

"Okay," they chorused as they headed for the bathroom.

George stepped out onto the porch, shoved his hands in his pockets and took a deep breath. Then, without consciously intending to, he walked toward the house. Through the kitchen window he could see Laurie at the sink, head down, concentrating on something. Cocking his head, he listened for sounds but heard nothing except a cricket's chirp. He wandered around the side of the house to the front. Laurie's car and Jill's were parked there, but Jill could be with Tony in his. Or she might be inside the house.

Hell, what difference did it make? What was wrong with just going inside to say hello, see how things were going? Since when did he need an invitation?

Maybe since the ache to see Laurie alone had consumed him. Nothing was exactly as it had been. Without giving himself more time to think about it, George turned and hurried around to the back porch. He rapped on the door, then pushed it open. "May I come in?"

Laurie turned with a start, and the knife she held fell and clattered in the sink. Her heart gave a leap. She'd been thinking about him all day. Four dozen things to think about, at least, and she hadn't been able to get her mind off him. "Oh . . . George. Of course."

He pushed the door shut and stood looking at her for a second before moving toward her. "Busy?"

"Very. I'm making finger sandwiches to put in the freezer. For the reception, you know."

George noticed that she looked tired. "You work too hard."

"Well, there's a lot of work that needs doing."

"I'd help if I knew what to do."

"I know, but there's really nothing." Somehow Laurie couldn't see herself asking George to make finger sandwiches.

He moved closer and propped one hip against the kitchen counter. "I guess you're glad it's about over."

"I know it had better be over soon, or Jill's going to be in the hospital. Her nerves are about at the snapping point. These things get out of hand before you know it."

He listened for other noises in the house, but all was quiet. "Is the, er, bride-to-be around?"

Laurie methodically stacked the last of the sandwiches on a baking sheet and covered them with plastic wrap. "No, she and Tony drove into town to meet his parents. They're hosting the rehearsal dinner tomorrow night. They—I mean, not they, but Jill—should be back . . . pretty soon."

George felt his breath catch in his throat. "There was quite a crowd here earlier," he said.

"I know. Friends bringing gifts by. But . . . everyone's gone now."

Laurie thought she at last knew the full meaning of the term "pregnant silence." Gathering up the tray of sandwiches, she turned, but George stepped forward to relieve her of it. "Freezer?" he asked.

She nodded. "On the middle shelf. There are three others just like it. They should be solidly frozen by now, so just put that one on top."

While he was in the utility room, Laurie gave the sink a much more thorough scrubbing than it needed. Lord, she felt awkward...and rattled and grossly unsophisticated. What she wanted more than anything was to put her arms around him and just hold on tight. She kept scrubbing until he returned and stood behind her. Rinsing the sink, she grabbed a towel and began drying her hands with slow deliberation. Finally there was nothing she could do but turn to face him. He was watching her with a speculative expression.

"Coffee?" she asked.

"No, thanks."

"What are the girls doing?"

The semblance of a smile touched his lips. "Their hair. That keeps them busy at least an hour." Instinctively his eyes flew to the wall clock.

Laurie rubbed her palms on her jeans. "By the way, George, Jill asked me today if I thought you and the twins might like to attend the rehearsal dinner. Would you?"

"I...don't think so. We're not family...or in the bridal party, or anything like that."

"No, you're not, are you? Funny, I sometimes think of you as—"

"As family?" he asked.

"Well, maybe not you so much as...the girls...you know."

"Yeah, I know."

Laurie glanced down, then back up. "Is there any news from home about Ellen?"

"I talked to her at the hospital last week."

"Oh? That's something new, isn't it?"

"Dr. Ames thought it was time. She says Ellen's making progress."

"How...nice." Laurie swallowed hard and turned away. "How did she sound—Ellen, I mean?"

"Pretty good. But the doctor says she still cries too much." Suddenly George made an impatient sound and raked his fingers through his mop of dark hair. Last time they'd been alone she'd been wound around him like a coiled rattlesnake. Now they were behaving as though they'd just bumped into each other in the supermarket. "Laurie, I—"

At that moment the front door opened, closed with a loud slam, and Jill's voice rang through the house. "Damn, damn, *damn!*"

Laurie looked at George in alarm, then turned and ran for the front of the house, with him quick on her heels. They found Jill standing in the foyer, her face flushed with rage.

"Jill, honey, what on earth—"

"There's not going to be a wedding!" Jill yelled. "It's off!" And she turned to race up the stairs.

"What?"

"You heard me!"

Laurie went to the bottom of the stairs. Her insides churned like a boiling cauldron. "Young lady, you can't do this to me! The wedding is two days away! Invitations have been sent, dresses bought, tuxedos rented, and the freezer's full of food."

"I don't care!"

"Your brother's on his way here from San Antonio!" Laurie realized she wasn't making much sense, but who could make sense at a time like this?

Jill had paused at the top of the stairs. "Send everything back. I won't spend the rest of my life with a selfish, inconsiderate lout."

"Tony?" Laurie cried in disbelief.

"Yes." Jill began to cry. She hurried to her room and slammed the door.

Laurie turned to George, so stunned she didn't know what to say. "Well, I—I can't believe—"

The doorbell rang. Laurie didn't appear to have heard it, so George answered it. He found a distraught Tony standing on the porch. "I gotta talk to Jill," the young man said, brushing past George to confront Laurie. "There's been a little misunderstanding."

Laurie put a hand to her pounding temple. "Tony, what happened?"

"I just made an offhand remark. I told Jill that the hotel in Colorado organizes hunting expeditions for the guests and I thought that might be fun. Hell, she went berserk. She said if I could even think about going hunting on our honeymoon, I wasn't the man she thought I was. She hates hunting, and it isn't romantic. It was just a thought. If she doesn't want to go, we won't go, it's as simple as that. My God, she doesn't have to turn it into a global crisis."

Laurie simply stared at him a minute. "Do you mean *that's* what caused all this?"

"Yeah. I don't understand what's wrong with her these days. I can't say good morning without her picking a fight."

"Oh, Tony, be patient for two more days," Laurie begged.

"I... Oh, hell, I'm going to talk to her." With that he bounded up the stairs.

Laurie felt herself go limp. She threw up her hands, then let them fall to her sides. "George," she all but whispered, "this wedding is going to kill me."

He smiled at her sympathetically. "Maybe not."

"No, I really don't expect to live through it."

"You're tired. Why don't you try to get a good night's sleep. Everything will look rosier in the morning. And I really need to get back and check on the girls."

Laurie looked at him, smiling ruefully. "Isn't responsibility fun?"

He crossed the space between them and laid a hand on her cheek. "Yeah, a laugh a minute. Good night."

"Good night, George."

CHAPTER EIGHT

"HAPPY THE BRIDE the sun shines on!" Laurie called as she sailed into the room. At last the big day had arrived. At last the wedding would actually take place. At last it was almost over. She stopped dead in her tracks. She had seen her sister in the gown the day of the fitting at the bridal shop, but that hadn't made much of an impact on her. Now the bride was a vision. "Oh, Jill! Lord, honey, you look beautiful!" For at least the tenth time that day, her eyes began to fill with tears.

Jill slowly pirouetted in front of the cheval mirror. "Isn't it a glorious dress, Laurie? I can't thank you enough for letting me have it."

At that moment the exorbitant cost of the gown seemed insignificant. The dress had an off-the-shoulder neckline, puffed sleeves, a fitted bodice embroidered with seed pearls, and the skirt went on and on. Her sensible self was appalled at having spent so much money on a dress that would be worn once, but Laurie had discovered she had a romantic side, too, and it questioned putting a price tag on memories. "Tony may pass out when he sees you coming down that aisle. I must have a picture." She reached for her camera lying on the dresser. "And one of you and Andy."

"But you're paying Gordon Woods to take pictures."

"I want my own for the family album. Where's Andy?"

Her brother entered the room as if on cue, looking stiff and formal and utterly marvelous in his tuxedo. Seeing him again after so many months had almost done Laurie in. To her eyes he looked so much older, but she supposed "mature" was the word. He was a businessman now, a salesman for a large company. Somehow he had acquired self-assuredness and a kind of poise that surprised her. She still thought of him as the scamp who had given her three heart attacks a week while he was growing up. "Hmm, nice," Laurie commented, her eyes raking him from head to foot.

"Damn, I'm glad I don't have to wear one of these very often," Andy complained, tugging at the shirt's collar. "When I get married, we're just going down to the courthouse and getting it over with."

"Uh-huh," Laurie said with a smile. "Your bride may have other ideas. Hush and stand over there by Jill."

After she'd gotten a couple of shots, Andy stepped forward and took the camera. "We need one of you, too, Laurie. You look beautiful. Doesn't she look great, Jill? The old girl's holding up pretty well, don't you think?"

"What we really need is a picture of the three of us together," Jill said.

"But who'll take it?" Laurie wanted to know.

Andy headed for the door. "George and the girls are downstairs. Let me see if he'll do it."

"And send Stacy and DeeAnn up, too," Jill called after him. "I want to see their dresses."

A minute passed, then Andy returned with the twins in tow and George pulling up the rear. When the girls saw the bride, they let out squeals and rushed toward her, oohing and ahhing. Both Andy and Jill made a great show of admiring their dresses, leaving Laurie and George a scant minute to look at each other with unabashed admiration.

Laurie had never seen him in anything but cowboy garb. His idea of dressing up was trading jeans for gabardine Western-cut trousers, work boots for designer ones, and a straw Stetson for a felt one. This afternoon, however, he wore a dark blue business suit, a light shirt and striped tie. She was quite certain she had never seen a more handsome man in all her life—not in a magazine, not in a movie, and not on television.

For his part, George was all but speechless at the sight of Laurie, and he certainly didn't notice anyone else in the room once he laid eyes on her. He'd always thought she possessed the most unstudied elegance of any woman he'd ever seen, but now her beauty took his breath away. She wore a floaty peach-colored dress and a big flower-bedecked picture hat in the same shade. The color seemed to make her face glow, and her eyes shone radiantly as she looked at him.

"Oh, George," she breathed, coming closer to him. "You look marvelous."

"Do I? I feel like an undertaker." He stopped and took a breath. "I'm not sure it's fair of you to go to the wedding, Laurie. Who's going to notice the bride?" The words didn't exactly trip off his tongue, and he felt foolish saying them, but, surprisingly, he didn't care. She was...exquisite.

Then the chatter of other voices in the room interrupted their absorption in each other. They moved apart, and George took the camera Andy was holding toward him.

THE WEDDING was the biggest that had been held in those parts in some time. Though her bank account had taken a severe battering, when Laurie saw Jill walking down the aisle on Andy's arm she decided it had been worth every penny she had spent. She was more than a little embarrassed afterward by the number of people who took the time to tell her what a wonderful job she'd done with "those two kids." She'd never felt that raising Andy and Jill was in any way remarkable or noble. She had only done what needed doing.

The church was packed to overflowing. Laurie tried to catch sight of George and the girls in the crowd that mobbed the vestibule after the ceremony, but it was useless. And she couldn't dally long. She had to get home to make sure everything was ready for the reception.

She was hurrying toward her car when Ted Weeks from the bank halted her. "Beautiful wedding, Laurie. Now we have to talk...very soon. No later than next week."

Oh, Lord, she'd all but forgotten the offer, and she was no nearer a decision than she'd been a month ago. But this

was no time to be thinking about that. "All right...sure,
Ted. Next week."

Ted had no more than said good-bye when Laurie turned
to find Cassie at her elbow. "Everything was just lovely,
Laurie."

"Thanks, Cassie. I'm glad you could come."

"I wouldn't have missed it. By the way, I saw you talking to Ted Weeks. Please don't do anything. Some of us
ranchers are considering forming a co-op so we can buy
land like yours and hold onto it until the right kind of buyer
can be found. I'll be in touch with you soon."

Wonderful, Laurie thought grimly. It was amazing how
much interest that miserable patch of land had generated.

GEORGE HATED WEDDINGS. Not as much as he hated fu-
nerals, but almost. He had felt like a fifth wheel all afternoon. He saw perhaps half a dozen people he really knew.
He spoke to Cassie and Scott Maitland and to J.B. Ferenbach, Cassie's father. There were a few area ranchers he
knew because of his association with the DO, but mostly
the guests consisted of longtime family friends, the faculty
of the school where Laurie taught, and college friends of
Jill's and Tony's.

Not knowing anyone didn't seem to faze Stacy and
DeeAnn a bit. Their faces flushed with excitement, they
preened around in their beautiful new dresses. It occurred
to George that he didn't even know where the dresses had
come from. Laurie and Jill had arranged for them, he
guessed, and he made a mental note to insist on paying for
them. Looking at his nieces and noticing the ladylike airs
they were putting on, he felt a twinge of guilt. He'd thought
that keeping them in plenty of jeans and shirts was enough,
but he was beginning to realize that girls needed nice
dresses, too. That only reminded him for the umpteenth
time of how much he still had to learn about them.

He had promised Stacy and DeeAnn they could sample
the goodies at the reception, and he would keep that
promise. But at the earliest possible minute he was going to

take them to the cottage, make them eat a bowl of soup—
they wouldn't want much—and then get them to bed. They
were wound up like five-dollar watches, and he didn't suppose anyone would miss his presence. No doubt Laurie
would be busy until she dropped, so that meant he wouldn't
get to see her tonight. That was all he really wanted. She
and the girls were the only reason he'd even attended the
wedding. Usually he avoided these affairs like the plague.

He caught sight of Laurie on the church steps, talking to
a group of people. She had to be dead on her feet, yet to
look at her one would think she'd done nothing more
strenuous than thumb through magazines all day. The
whole affair had been great, if you went for that sort of
thing, and it definitely had been a one-woman show.
George could barely imagine the logistics associated with a
wedding like that one. If he remembered correctly, the last
wedding he'd attended was Ellen's, and it had been modest indeed. Laurie was probably in for a hell of a letdown
when the whole thing was finally over.

THE WHOLE THING finally did get itself over and done with.
One minute the house was filled with people, noise and excitement; the next, everyone was gone. Jill and Tony had
driven away. Tony's parents were on their way back home,
and Andy had left for a night on the town with some old
school friends. Laurie had no idea where George was—
getting the girls settled down for the night, she supposed.
They had had a busy, exciting day and weren't going to be
easy to calm down.

The house was, to put it mildly, a mess, but everything
had gone so beautifully that a mess seemed a small price to
pay for a perfect wedding. If she hadn't been so tired she
might have tried to give herself a pat on the back. She
wandered through the rooms, simply staring at the party
debris and thinking how much time, effort and money had
gone into something that seemed to have ended in a flash.

Suddenly, without warning, Laurie was overcome by an
overwhelming feeling of despondence. She had felt alone

before—many times when problems had been heaped upon problems—but that had been nothing compared to what she was now experiencing. What was she going to do tomorrow and the day after that? Suddenly there was no one to look after.

There are Stacy and DeeAnn, her inner voice reminded her. *With school out and Jill gone, you can look after them all you want.*

But Laurie quickly shook off the thought. She wasn't going to fall into that trap, learning to love them just so she could say good-bye to them.

She couldn't muster any enthusiasm for cleaning up the horrendous mess or for doing much of anything. She went into the kitchen and—forgetting she hadn't had a bite to eat since breakfast—took what was left of the champagne punch out of the refrigerator and poured a glass. Then she simply sat at the table, sipping the punch and feeling sorry for herself.

She didn't know how long she had been sitting there or how many glasses of punch she had drunk when there was a tap on the back door. It opened, and George came in. He had shed his jacket and tie, but he still wore the suit trousers. His shirt had been unbuttoned three buttons down, and its sleeves were rolled to the elbow. Even with her senses slightly numbed by the champagne, they leapt to life at the sight of him.

"Hi," he said, studying her. "I've been debating whether or not to look in on you. Do you want to be left alone or can you use some company?"

She wouldn't have wanted just anyone there, but George wasn't just anyone. "Please stay. Are the girls in bed?"

"Yeah. No easy task tonight. They had a great time. I guess it was the experience of their lives." His eyes made a quick survey of the kitchen. "It looks like there's been a terrible accident in here."

"The rest of the house is worse."

He returned his attention to her. "What are you doing?"

"Feeling sorry for myself."

"Miserable pastime."

"Tell me about it. Help yourself to a beer or whatever you want."

He went to the refrigerator, then came to the table, popped the top on the can and eyed her glass. "Is that the pink crap from the reception?"

She giggled. "Yes."

"I don't know how people drink that junk. I'd rather have moonshine than that stuff."

"Have you ever drunk moonshine?"

He grinned. "Yeah. There was a time when I'd go out in the country, leave a dollar bill on a certain tree stump, then come back in half an hour and there'd be a Mason jar full of it. Better'n a martini beside the pool at the Beverly Hilton."

"Have you been to the Beverly Hilton?"

"Of course not. What would I be doing there?"

"I'll bet you've done a lot, though."

"I don't consider drinking moonshine in the woods doing a lot."

"But I'll bet you've been to a lot of places."

George shrugged. "Oh, not so many, I guess, when you consider how many places there are in this old world."

"Have you ever been to Boston or New York or San Francisco or New Orleans?"

"No, but I've been to Guymon, Oklahoma and Craig, Colorado and Douglas, Wyoming," he said with a grin.

Laurie's response to that was to take another sip of punch, then run the tip of her finger around the rim of the glass. "It was a nice wedding, wasn't it?" she asked pensively.

"Sure was. You ought to be proud of yourself."

"I am. At least I think I am. Jill looked so pretty."

"So did the bride's sister."

"Thanks. Nice of you to say so."

"Where's Andy?"

"Oh, he's gone off with some of his old friends. I won't see him until the wee hours." She poured some more punch into her glass. George frowned but said nothing. If she wanted to get a buzz on, who had a better right?

"Did I ever tell you how much money I've been offered for this place?" she asked suddenly.

"No."

"Seventy-five thousand dollars."

George let out a whistle.

"Nice, huh? I could finally go to Hawaii and Tahiti and Sydney and all those places I've been reading about for years. I could do a lot with that much money, maybe move away and . . . I don't know, just do things. I've never done anything or gone anywhere."

"Is that important?"

"It is when nothing's ever happened to you."

She'd said she was feeling sorry for herself, and she sounded it. An odd feeling hit the pit of George's stomach. People did some weird things while feeling sorry for themselves. "Are you going to sell?"

A second of silence passed, then she sighed. "I don't know. Cassie doesn't want me to."

"Cassie? Why not?"

"Because the people who want to buy it are planning to develop it into homesites with swimming pools, and the ranchers association doesn't want that. I don't know if I want to go against my neighbors' wishes. Maybe it's time to file all that literature about the South Pacific into the wastebasket and just forget it. It was nothing but a pipe-dream, anyway."

The wistful quality in her voice touched George. And he couldn't understand why the thought of her selling her property should alarm him. "You might get another buyer," he suggested.

"That's Cassie's game plan, but what rancher around here is going to pay me seventy-five thousand?"

George guessed the main difference between them was that he'd spent most of his life doing exactly what he wanted to do, while she'd spent most of hers doing what others wanted her to. "What would you do if you didn't sell? Keep on keepin' on?"

"I don't know. That doesn't sound very promising—just growing old here all alone. I might get a dog. Maybe two. Maybe a horse, too. I always had a horse when I was a little girl." Her eyes grew dreamy. "My dad had such dreams for this place. He worked so hard. And Mom had a vegetable garden, not far from where the cottage is, and there were always flowers around, and..."

George watched her carefully as she continued talking. He didn't know how much of the punch she had drunk, but it was obviously more than just a little bit. If she stayed only charmingly tipsy, that was fine, but he didn't want her to get sick, and he sure didn't want her getting all sad and weepy. That would only embarrass her later.

But she was in such a mood. He'd never seen Laurie in anything but good spirits. He knew she couldn't always feel up—no one could—but she always managed to behave as though she did.

Propping an elbow on the table, he rested his chin in his palm and listened to her reminisce. She talked and talked and talked, going through junior high, high school and college. She told him about long-deceased relatives, Jill's appendectomy and Andy's youthful escapades. George heard maybe half the words since he was far more intent on watching her. She was still wearing the stunning dress she'd had on at the wedding. The hat had been discarded, of course, and her honey-colored hair fell just below her chin. Occasionally she reached up and tucked a strand behind her ear. Her eyes were bright, partly due to the alcohol, and her face was more animated than he'd ever seen it. He was glad he'd come over. She needed this thorough shedding of her inhibitions.

Suddenly she stopped talking and looked at him sheepishly. "Good heavens, I've been chattering away, haven't I?"

"I'm enjoying it," he said, but when she again reached for the pitcher of punch he laid a gently restraining hand on hers. "Watch that stuff. I've heard that a champagne hangover is the worst kind. Did you have supper?"

She shook her head.

"Then I'm going to get you something to eat."

"I don't want anything to eat."

George grinned and got to his feet. "When you reach the I-don't-want-to-eat stage it's time to eat something." He opened the refrigerator and peered at its contents.

"George?"

"Umm."

"What are you going to do when Ellen gets well and the girls go back home?"

The question knotted his stomach. "I don't know, Laurie."

"Montana?"

"Lord, I haven't thought of Montana in…I don't know how long." He found some sandwich-makings. He didn't suppose it mattered what she ate, as long as she ate something. Pushing the refrigerator door shut with his hip, he carried the food to the counter and opened the bread box.

"Would you take me with you?"

He looked over his shoulder. "What?"

"To Montana, if you go. Would you take me with you?"

He chuckled. "I'll remind you in the morning that you asked me that."

"I mean it. I could go along for company, and you can just do whatever it is you like to do."

"A lady like you would hate the life I've always led."

"Maybe I could stop being such a lady. It really isn't much fun, you know."

Oh, God, he'd waited too long to feed her. She really was gone. He cut the sandwich in half, laid it on a napkin and carried it to the table. "Maybe. And maybe it won't rain anywhere in the whole world tomorrow." He bent and placed a kiss on the tip of her nose. "Eat!"

But Laurie reached up, captured his face between her hands, and forced it down to hers. She planted a deep, clinging kiss on his mouth. George held the kiss for a minute, returning it, loving it. Then, through sheer force of will, he broke it. "Eat, Laurie!"

"You aren't much fun, either," she said, but she did manage to make short work of the sandwich. When she'd finished, she wadded up the napkin, put it in the center of the table and said, "Okay. Now what do you want me to do?"

"Go to bed."

She smiled seductively. "Are you coming with me?"

George laughed. "Boy, you're swacked! No, I'm not coming with you."

"Then I'm not going."

"Yes, you are." He got up, walked around the table and, with very little trouble, pulled her to her feet. She leaned against him for support and slipped her arm around his waist. "Come on," he said softly. "It's been a long day. You must be dead."

She buried her head on his shoulder, wound her other arm around him and began nibbling at his neck. "I feel wonderful."

"Oh, Lord!" he muttered. "Okay, I guess we're going to have to do this the hard way." Bending, he slipped an arm behind her knees and swept her up into his arms. Then he carried her out of the kitchen and wound his way through the shambles in the dining room.

Laurie laughed. "I've always dreamed of being swept up into a man's arms and being carried away from all this."

"I'm not carrying you anywhere but upstairs."

"Still, it's so romantic."

"It isn't romantic," George muttered as he began climbing the stairs. "You feel as though you weigh a ton."

"Thanks a lot! You have no poetry in your soul." But she laughed again and began kissing the underside of his chin.

He reached the second floor. "Which one is your room?"

She flung out an arm. "That one."

The room looked like her, all neat and feminine, with a big four-poster covered with a flowered comforter. When he set her on her feet, she continued to cling to him. Her appealing body was all over him, as were her hands, rubbing and petting. He felt as though he was being strangled. "Laurie, honey, please get undressed."

Her eyes brightened. "You called me honey."

"Just a slip of the tongue. Now, please, get undressed."

"Okay. Unzip me."

"I'm not going to undress you."

"Oh, okay! But I need help with the zipper." She released her hold on him and turned. He saw that a long zipper ran from the neckline to below the waist. He gave it a pull, and it fell open, giving him an enticing view of her smooth back, its expanse broken only by the band of her beige bra. His fingertips itched to touch her warm skin, and she was so willing. It would have been so easy. . . .

Too easy. There was no way he was going to take advantage of her now. He stepped back to preclude the possibility that desire would overcome reason. "There you go," he said huskily.

She turned to him, her lips slightly parted. "Thanks. I'll be right back." With that, she disappeared into her private bathroom.

While she was gone, George pulled down the comforter on the four-poster and flung back the sheets. They were pale blue, as smooth as silk, and they smelled as sweet as Laurie did. He could hear water splashing in the bathroom; then it stopped, and a drawer opened and closed. As long as he could hear some noise from in there, he supposed she was all right.

He was smoothing the spread at the foot of the bed when the door opened and Laurie stepped into the room. George straightened, his eyes widened and his mouth grew slack. She was wearing some kind of robe that stopped at the knee and fastened directly under her breasts. There was nothing indecent about the garment—if anything, it was on the demure side—but he thought he'd never seen anything so sexy in his life. Perhaps because it suggested bed.

"Here I am, Daddy. All dressed for beddy-bye like a good girl."

"And it's all ready for you. I'll even tuck you in."

"But first you have to kiss me good night."

"Laurie, for pete's sake . . ."

She walked straight to him and slipped her arms around his middle, locking her hands at the small of his back. His own arms instinctively went around her, and a storm of sensations deluged George at that moment. The sweet scent of her, the knowledge that two very thin layers of cotton were all that separated his hand from her bare flesh, her pliant eagerness—it all nearly undid him. And he knew she needed to be held and caressed and pleasured. Hell, so did he.

But not tonight. If they ever made love—God, he couldn't believe he was actually thinking they might some day—they were going to go into it cold sober, with their eyes wide open. He dropped his arms and reached around his back to take her hands. "Come on, it's way past your bedtime."

Laurie uttered some obscure sound. "Chicken," she said, but nevertheless she allowed him to lead her to the bed. She undid the robe and let it float to the floor, treating his avid eyes to a brief glimpse of her delectable body in a skimpy nightgown. Then she crawled under the covers and scrunched up the pillow. Her eyes drifted shut. "Feel better?" she asked sleepily. "Your virtue's intact for another day."

Standing there, watching her huddled in bed like a child, George's heart seemed to swell to twice its normal size. "Aw, Laurie," he said with a sigh. "I deserve to be canonized."

He waited there until he was sure she was asleep. Then he went downstairs and out the back door to the cottage to check on the girls. Neither of them seemed to have moved.

He scooped up the orange ball of fur at the foot of Stacy's bed, and the cat went as limp as cooked spaghetti.

"Come on, Princess. Nice try, but you know you're not supposed to sleep in here."

Once the cat had been deposited outside, George put on water to boil, then made himself a cup of strong instant coffee, which he carried back to the big house—he wanted to check on Laurie again. And he kept running back and forth until Andy got home at one o'clock. To say that Laurie's brother was surprised to find George holding down the fort would have been an understatement.

"I was keeping an eye on Laurie," George explained.

"Oh? Why?"

"She had a bit of the bubbly."

"Laurie?" Andy couldn't have been more surprised.

"I think the past few weeks have been a bit much for her."

"Yeah, I guess so. Well, sure do appreciate your keeping an eye on her."

"Don't mention it. I wouldn't have left her alone for the world. Good night."

George went back to the cottage and got undressed for bed, thinking all the while of Laurie's reckless abandon earlier and wondering if he'd ever again be witness to such behavior from her...without the help of champagne.

Tomorrow could be a bad day for her, he thought soberly. Andy had to get back to San Antonio, so that big old house was going to seem like a cavern. Maybe he could get her away from it for a few hours. The four of them—he, Laurie, Stacy and DeeAnn—could go somewhere... maybe drive up into the mountains and have a picnic. He'd think of something.

For a man who had lived thirty-three years without forming attachments, he seemed to have become awfully attached to three human beings in an awfully short span of time. Oddly, that didn't make him feel in the least fenced in or fettered. In some curious way, caring seemed to have set him free.

CHAPTER NINE

LAURIE WOKE the following morning with a pounding headache and no real recollection of having gone to bed. Bolting upright, she tried to clear her fogged mind. She did remember sitting in the kitchen, drinking punch and talking to George. She seemed to recall talking too much; otherwise, everything was sort of a blur. The feeling was so alien to her it was frightening.

But once she'd washed her face and brushed her teeth, she didn't feel much the worse for wear, just a little rocky. And when she came out of the bathroom she definitely smelled bacon and coffee. *How nice,* she thought. A bachelor's life had done wonders for Andy. He'd certainly never bothered cooking breakfast when he'd lived at home.

Slipping on jeans and a T-shirt, Laurie hurried downstairs. But Andy wasn't in the kitchen; George and the girls were. Had she known that, she might have done a little more to herself. "Good morning, everyone."

George was standing at the stove. Turning, he gave her a lopsided grin. "Good morning. How do you feel?"

"Oh . . . okay."

"Liar. I hope you don't mind our making ourselves at home."

"Of course not. That coffee smells divine."

"Sit down and I'll get you a cup."

Laurie sat next to DeeAnn and rumpled the girl's hair. "This is a real treat. To what do I owe the pleasure?"

George set the cup in front of her. "I thought you might appreciate some, er, assistance this morning." He grinned again.

As much as she would have liked to quiz him about the night before, Laurie decided it might be best to leave the subject alone. "Has Andy been down yet?"

"Not yet."

"Guess what, Laurie?" Stacy said. "Uncle George says we're all going to go on a picnic today."

"A picnic?" Laurie looked at George for confirmation. "A real picnic?"

"Why not?"

The plate of ham and eggs he set before her looked irresistible, and she began to eat hungrily.

"How long has it been since you were on a picnic?"

"I don't remember. A long, long time."

"And we're going to hunt for rocks," Stacy added enthusiastically. "Special ones. Uncle George knows how."

George as a rockhound didn't ring true, but Laurie was beginning to realize there were facets to his personality that she'd never dreamed existed. She'd once considered him a man of utter simplicity, just a footloose cowpuncher without a care in the world, as restless as west Texas wind. There was so much more to him than that.

"Well, it sounds as though the day's been all planned, so I'd better get busy. This house is a disaster."

"We'll help," Stacy said. "Right Dee?" Her sister nodded uncertainly.

At that moment Andy ambled into the room. "Gotta hit the road, Laurie," he said.

"Oh, Andy, so soon?"

"I want to make Uvalde tonight."

"Have some breakfast first."

"I'd rather stop down the road. I'm never hungry when I first wake up."

Laurie forgot her own breakfast. "It seems like you just got here."

"Yeah, it went pretty fast. But if I don't get back sooner, I promise to come for Christmas. Maybe Jill and Tony will, too."

Lord, where will I be Christmas? she wondered. "Drive carefully."

"I will."

"And call me when you get home."

"Sure."

She was saying the same things she'd been saying to him since he was sixteen, and she doubted he was paying any more attention to them now than he had then. Funny how hard it was to untie the apron strings.

George couldn't take his eyes off Laurie's sad face. Yes, the picnic was a good idea. The last thing she needed today was to be alone.

IT WAS A BEAUTIFUL Sunday. The floor of the valley was sprinkled with wildflowers, and the verdant hills undulated in all directions. The four of them squeezed into the pickup and drove as far up into the top country as George's truck could safely go, to a special area he knew where agate-laden rocks were plentiful. If they found any good ones, he promised, they would take them to a lapidary shop for polishing. Laurie thought it odd that as long as she'd lived in an area that drew rockhounds from all over the country, she'd never taken up the hobby. She was as fascinated by George's instructions on what to look for as Stacy and DeeAnn were.

While Laurie spread a blanket under a tree, George and the twins climbed up and down the hills in search of the semiprecious stones embedded in volcanic rock. Then she sat cross-legged on the blanket and watched them. She wished there was some way to draw the three of them close to her, so close that nothing would ever separate them. But, of course, that wasn't possible. None of them belonged to her, and soon she was going to have to make a decision about her property. If she sold the ranch, her last tie to her old life would be severed.

And why was she thinking such gloomy thoughts on such a glorious day? She'd worry about those things when the time came. For now she wanted this idyll to last as long as it possibly could.

Eventually, George left the girls to pursue the rock hunting on their own, and he joined Laurie on the blanket. Removing the ever-present Stetson, he laid it beside him, raised one knee to provide an armrest, then smiled at her...wickedly, she thought.

"Feeling all right?" he asked.

"Yes, I feel fine."

"No headache or anything?"

"No. I had one earlier, but—"

"I'll bet. Champagne's famous for that."

"I...guess I drank too much of the punch, huh? I don't know why I did that. I'm really not used to much liquor."

"I gathered as much."

Laurie hesitated. "Did I...do or say anything I shouldn't have?" she asked warily.

"No. You talked about buying a dog or a horse and about being a kid. Simple stuff. Well, come to think of it, you did ask me to take you to Montana." He couldn't resist adding that.

She gasped. "I didn't."

"And you did say that being a lady's no fun."

"Oh, God!"

"You also told me I'm no fun."

Laurie closed her eyes. "What on earth would make me say something like that?"

"I wanted you to stop kissing me and start eating your supper."

"Are you making this up?"

"Not a word."

"I'm sorry I asked. I don't think I want to hear any more of the sordid details, thanks."

George chuckled and watched as she brought her knees up and hugged them to her chest. Then she turned her head as if embarrassed, and sunlight danced off her hair. He thought about touching it—just touching, that was all. It looked so silky that he wondered how it felt. Finally he gave in to the impulse. The moment his fingertips grazed the strands, her head came around with a jerk. Their eyes locked, and his heartbeat rumbled like mountain thunder. How he wished that somewhere along the line he had learned all those smooth, courtly words that women liked to hear. He wanted to tell her not to be embarrassed. He wanted to tell her that seeing her last night—and right now in sun-drenched, unadorned beauty—made her seem so much more...approachable. He wanted to tell her that knowing her had changed him in ways he didn't understand so he couldn't begin to explain. There was a lot he wanted to say to her. He guessed what he wanted more than anything was to put his arm around her, draw her close and simply share a companionable minute with her—let her know that she wasn't nearly as alone as she thought she was.

But maybe that wouldn't be fair. Who knew what next week or next month would bring? One phone call from Oklahoma could change everything.

"They're having a wonderful time," Laurie suddenly said, wondering at the heavy silence between them.

"What?"

She inclined her head toward the two figures scampering up a hill. "Stacy and DeeAnn."

"Oh. Yeah, they always seem to have a pretty good time. It doesn't take much to keep them amused. Maybe that's because they have each other."

"They're sweet, unspoiled kids. You wouldn't be surprised if they had some problems as a result of what's happened to their parents, but they don't seem to. I'm prepared to say that the sharp points on DeeAnn's heart aren't there anymore. I guess they have you to thank for that."

George's eyes dropped. He thoughtfully raked a forefinger across his mouth, then uttered some obscure sound. "Funny, isn't it, that they should end up with me of all people? And, as you said, not suffer because of it."

"Not so funny. You've been wonderful with them."

"There are a whole bunch of people who would find that hard to believe."

"Maybe your life just needed a . . . focus."

"Maybe. It sure never had one before."

Another minute of silence passed before Laurie asked, "What was the woman in Wyoming like?"

George frowned. "Who?"

"The woman in Wyoming. Your only 'meaningful relationship.'"

Lord, that she'd remembered that! "Oh, I don't know..." He had to dip way back in his memory bank to come up with the first detail.

"What was her name?" Laurie prodded.

"Wanda." At least he remembered that. "She was nice, a country girl who'd grown up around horses. I guess we thought that gave us a lot in common, but it didn't. She wanted a heckuva lot more out of life than she would have gotten with me. I was only twenty-four, full of sass and vinegar and as restless as they come."

"Do you ever wonder what happened to her?"

"I know. A fellow I worked with up there hired on during the DO's roundup a couple of years ago. Told me she has three kids, stair steps. And her husband enlarged his store. Guess they're doing all right."

"That's good." Laurie didn't have the first idea of why she'd said that. She really didn't care anything about Wanda from Wyoming. Maybe she just liked the thought of people getting married and having babies and prospering. She lifted her eyes and said, "Here come the girls."

Stacy and DeeAnn raced toward them, their arms laden with rocks. While Laurie knelt on the blanket and spread out the food, she listened to George explain which rocks should be kept and which left. "You just might have a red plume agate here," he said excitedly at one point.

"Is that good?" Stacy asked.

"Wait'll you see it all polished up. They're beautiful."

"Are the rocks worth money, Uncle George?" practical DeeAnn wanted to know.

"I imagine so, especially if you have a bunch of them. But you won't want to sell 'em. They're too nice to look at."

The four of them sat cross-legged in a circle on the blanket, pow-wow style, and ate fried chicken, beans, bread-and-butter sandwiches and drank lemonade. After that came grapes and plums. "Where'd you get the chicken?" Laurie asked George.

"It's the frozen kind. You just stick it in the oven."

"It's good."

"Yeah, I'm great with things that just have to be stuck in the oven."

"You're not doing badly. Neither one of these two look like they've been deprived of food." Grinning, she poked at DeeAnn's belly.

"I'm stuffed," the girl complained.

"Me, too," Stacy said.

"Well, clean up your mess and take a nap," George suggested. "As a matter of fact—" he reached for his hat and settled his back against the tree trunk "—that sounds like a good idea."

Once the picnic debris had been put away, Laurie glanced around her at the picture of pure bliss. George had covered his face with his hat, folded his hands on his midsection, and stretched his legs in front of him, crossing them at the ankles. DeeAnn was slumped against Laurie's hip, with Stacy fit against her. They looked like two interlocking pieces of a puzzle. The only place available for her own head seemed to be George's lap.

When George felt the weight of her head on his lap, his stomach muscles tensed, then relaxed. He tipped his hat back with his thumb and looked down to see her hair fanned across the whiteness of his shirt. Just then her head moved. She looked up and smiled gently. He laid his hand on her cheek. She raised her arm and rubbed his throat with the back of her hand; her touch was as light as the brush of a butterfly's wings. The simple gesture filled him with wonderment and sent his spirits soaring off on some wild, uncharted course.

The first time he'd kissed her, that night in the truck, it had happened quickly; the impulse had been unrooted in conscious thought. Perhaps it had been nothing more than the inevitable conclusion to an evening with a lovely woman.

The second time—no, last night didn't count. She didn't even remember those kisses.

But next time... Ah, next time it would be premeditated, anticipated, welcomed with open arms. Next time the kisses would precede something more—he could feel it. He thought he could read longing in her eyes, and he knew he was eaten alive with it. He tipped his head back again, against the tree trunk, and sighed. Had there ever been such a day? Six months ago who would have thought he could sit in a field strewn with wildflowers, share a picnic with a beautiful woman and two little girls, and feel so utterly, blissfully content? Where was the urge to mount a horse and ride, ride, ride? What amazing metamorphosis had taken place inside him? When had it happened? How had it happened? And now that he thought about it, hadn't Laurie warned him months ago that it might? And he'd been so sure it wouldn't.

How differently all this might have turned out if it hadn't been for her, he mused. Thanks to Laurie, he was far freer of responsibility with Stacy and DeeAnn than she'd ever been with Andy and Jill. On top of that, he never got tired of being around her. He could take her in enormous doses and always be ready for more.

For the first time a thought took form inside his head, a thought that was to occupy his mind for far longer than he could have imagined at that moment: *I don't ever want to say good-bye to these three people. The four of us are closer than most families.* It was so unexpected, so definite, that it shook him.

What is he thinking? Laurie wondered while he was dealing with his newfound realization. He had the strangest look on his face. Instinctively she knew his thoughts were somehow connected with the twins, and she hoped she was in there somewhere, but that might have been hoping for too much. In all the times she had fantasized about him, not once had she been able to envision the two of them sailing happily through life together. A few lovely interludes like the night in the pickup or this golden afternoon was the best her limited imagination could come up with.

The halcyon day inevitably ended. The sun was sinking low in the western sky when they at last packed up and went home. The phone began ringing the minute they stepped into the kitchen. Laurie rushed to answer it.

"Hello."

"Laurie? Well, at last! This is Joan Barnes. I've been calling all afternoon. I decided to try one more time and then forget it."

"We went on a picnic. It's nice to hear from you, Joan."

"I'm calling to ask if the girls can come over. Melissa's coerced us into a wiener roast and slumber party. Would Stacy and DeeAnn like to come?"

Laurie felt her heart trip, then race out of control. It would be the first time since they'd arrived that the girls would be away from the ranch. She looked at George, who was busy unpacking the picnic basket. All afternoon the sexual tension between them had been thick enough to cut with a knife. Now they had a chance to be absolutely alone.

But it wasn't her decision to make. "You'll have to ask George, Joan. Just a minute." She handed the phone to him. "It's Joan Barnes."

"Hi, Joanie, what's up?" There was a pause while he listened. As Joan's message was conveyed, his eyes widened slightly, then flew to Laurie, who was trying to look anywhere but at him. "I see.... Well, just a minute." His voice sounded tangled up in his throat. "Stacy, DeeAnn...Melissa's having a slumber party, and she wants you guys to come. Want to?"

"Yeah!" they cried in unison.

George lifted the receiver again. Though he spoke to
Joan, his eyes were riveted on Laurie. She knew what he
was thinking because she was thinking the same thing.

Alone at last, he thought. *No kids, no Jill, no Andy, no
one. Just the two of us.* "You bet, Joanie. I'll have them
there in half an hour." Hanging up, he motioned the girls
out the back door, still looking at Laurie. Not one word
had passed between them. In fact, except for that night in
the truck, and last night, nothing much of anything had
passed between them. And if he were in the mood to analyze, which he wasn't, he would have admitted to knowing
next to nothing about women like Laurie. Yet he was consumed with the feeling that tonight was going to be the
night of his life. "Don't go anywhere," he said to her in a
husky voice that didn't sound much like his own. "I'll be
back in less than an hour."

FOR LAURIE it was the longest hour of her life. She paced
the rooms of the house, alternately excited and appalled by
the prospect of what the night might have in store: excited
because her deprived body longed to savor romance again;
appalled because of the lack of permanence associated with
George. She had honestly believed that if love happened to
her again, it would come fully equipped with promises and
plans for the future. How could she possibly be palpitat-
ing for a man who thought of the future as no further away
than tomorrow afternoon?

She had to do something to keep from thinking about his
return. Racing upstairs, she took a quick shower, then
pondered what to wear. Had she been staying home alone,
she would have slipped on a robe, but there was no way she
was going to greet George wearing a robe. Almost any
drastic change of clothing seemed obvious. She settled for
clean jeans and a fresh shirt, then went back downstairs to
pace some more.

Her nervousness made no sense. While she would never
qualify as an experienced woman where men were concerned, she wasn't a total novice. But George was different

from other men she had known. There was an innocent quality about him. The thought caused a smile to touch her lips; she imagined George would have laughed out loud. Still, it was true. He did hard, physical work around rough-talking men, but somehow he'd retained a gentle kindness. She couldn't imagine George doing anything crude or coarse, certainly not in front of a woman. And he certainly didn't come across as being self-absorbed, nor did he flaunt his superb masculinity. Unlike so many men, he didn't appear to believe he had been put on earth to please and delight women. His only real fault was his maddening wanderlust.

Only fault, Laurie? It's the worst one he could have! Don't start rationalizing it away.

The Thermos and the plastic tumblers they'd taken on the picnic were in the kitchen sink, so she washed them. When she heard the truck rumble past the window, her stomach knotted into a tight fist. But when George tapped lightly on the back door, then pushed it open and stepped into the room, she turned from the sink and smiled easily at him. With George, she'd had so much practice at pretending one thing while feeling another that she donned her casual role effortlessly, like an actress doing the two hundredth performance of a play.

She studied him for what seemed like minutes but could only have been seconds. Some men looked younger with a hat on, especially if the hat covered a less than flattering hairline, but George looked younger without one—almost boyish—and very appealing. "Got them to the party safe and sound, I guess," was all she could think of saying.

"Yes. I have to hand it to Joanie—I wouldn't want that bunch of giggling girls on my hands all night."

"Slumber parties were the bane of my existence when Jill was in high school. Would you like something to eat?"

"I . . . no, not really."

"A beer, coffee?"

"No, thanks . . . unless you want something." George felt far more awkward than he'd thought he would.

"Well, I sure don't want a beer, not after last night," Laurie said with a smile.

At the mention of the previous night, George could feel some of the tension leave him. Last night he'd been the sensible one, the one in control, and she had been vulnerable. He grinned his lopsided grin. "That wasn't beer you were drinking last night. Not only was it champagne, it was laced with sugary glop." He crossed the room to stand by her. "It sure made you sugary."

Laurie expelled her breath. "Please, George, I don't think I want to know any more about last night. I must have done some dreadful things..."

"Dreadful? Naw." His grin broadened. "Unless you call this dreadful." Bending, he captured her mouth with his, turning his head this way and that, sipping and savoring, but otherwise not touching her. When he broke away from her, she saw sparks flashing from his eyes. They were like blue diamonds.

"There. Was that so dreadful?" he said quietly.

Laurie's cheeks flushed. She would have liked to tell him she thought it was just about the most wonderful thing in the world. "I guess it is if you don't remember doing it."

"Believe me, you didn't do a thing that would embarrass you," he assured her quickly, seeing the grim look coming into her eyes.

"I guess I'm going to have to take your word for that."

Not knowing what else to do, he put his arms around her and gathered her into a gentle embrace. For the time being it was enough just to hold her. He bent his head to rub his cheek against her hair, loving its smell, like springtime itself. Never had he held a woman who felt as good as Laurie did. It took all of his control to keep the embrace light until she gave him some sign that she was ready to progress to the next natural step.

Laurie felt his touch, light and soothing, and she melted against him, laying her head on his chest, putting her hand over his heartbeat. It had a strong rhythm. For the moment she could forget that he represented the kind of freedom she could barely imagine, freedom he wouldn't want to give up for anyone. It simply was good to hold him and to have him hold her. Her arm circled his taut waist, and her body seemed to lose all its bones. She uttered an involuntary sigh.

Her pliancy was all George needed. His arms tightened around her. With the barest nudge of his chin he tilted her face up and kissed her closed eyes, the tip of her nose, her cheeks and the corners of her mouth. Impatiently, Laurie turned her face slightly, and they kissed fully, their tongues exploring.

George broke the kiss. Anticipation tightened his stomach and made him feel weak. He looked down at her upturned face. He could hardly let himself believe that the promise of fulfillment was at hand. "Laurie, right now you could tell me to go and I would. But if I stay—" his voice shook "—if I stay, I'm going to make love to you."

It seemed an eternity before she spoke. "Turn out the lights and lock the doors."

"You want me?"

"Yes."

"Now?"

"Yes."

His throat was so dry it hurt. He couldn't say anything, but there really wasn't anything that needed saying. He simply nodded, released her and locked the back door while she turned off the light over the sink. Then he held her hand and followed her through the house, pausing only while she locked the front door and flipped the wall switch that darkened the foyer.

At the foot of the stairs George momentarily thought about carrying her up them again, but tonight that seemed unbearably corny. He followed her, watching the movement of her hips, and the ache inside him was so strong it was like fire.

In her room Laurie went to close the blinds and turn on the bedside lamp. George reached for the door, then realized there was no need to close it. They were blissfully alone, far from anyone. It was heaven.

Laurie bent to fling back the bedcovers. He watched her movements in a daze. When she straightened and walked toward him, he had never felt more awkward in his life. Did he remove her clothes layer by layer and murmur all the nonsensical words normally employed at a time like this? Most of his sexual encounters had been delightful romps with no consideration given to such matters, but the emotions in the room he was in now were so intense that the walls seemed to reverberate with them. Then she touched him, running her fingers across his tight stomach muscles and up his chest, and what little rational thought he still possessed evaporated. He reached for his shirt buttons.

Laurie stayed his hand with hers. "Please, let me."

Though her fingers shook, she quickly dispensed with the buttons and jerked his shirttail free from his jeans. Then her hands roamed the broad expanse of his chest. It was as smooth, tanned and hairless as she had imagined. She pushed the shirt off his shoulders; he shrugged out of it and let it fall to the floor. Laurie fumbled with his belt buckle and thought, *My God, it's really going to happen!* The realization was so overwhelming that she faltered; it was George who removed the belt. It joined the shirt on the floor, and Laurie reached for the snap of his jeans.

"Boots," he muttered. "The boots have to come off first."

Laurie swallowed hard. "Of course."

George sat on the edge of the bed and removed his boots; one thudded to the floor, then the other. *Now comes the awkward part,* Laurie thought. But it wasn't. She stepped back and kicked off her shoes, then unzipped her jeans and shoved them down her hips, taking her panties with them. That seemed to galvanize them both into action. Two pairs of jeans were hastily discarded, then Laurie removed her shirt, leaving him to unhook her bra. Then he turned her around to face him, and there was nothing at all between them: they stood flesh to flesh and had all the time in the world to explore each other, which they did languorously.

He's so beautiful, Laurie thought.

She must be the most perfect woman alive, George thought. He fondled her breasts, drank from her mouth, and stroked the core of her femininity until he felt her tremble. Her knees seemed to buckle, so he tightened his hold on her. "Tell me what you like, Laurie. I want to make this perfect for you."

It's already perfect, she thought. Simply being held against him was perfection. "Just . . . love me."

He nodded humbly and guided her between the sheets. Then he turned his back to her and sat on the edge of the bed a minute. She heard some kind of movement, and when he turned back to her, she realized what he'd done.

"Are you always so, er, prepared?" she asked in surprise.

George smiled as he joined her beneath the covers. "No. I stopped at a drugstore on the way home. I didn't figure you used anything. You don't, do you?"

"No, there's not been a need." His consideration touched her. She stroked his face, staring at him in wonder. Desire made him even more handsome, and she wouldn't have thought that possible. Those blue, blue eyes had darkened, like a summer sky as a thunderstorm approached.

Mindlessly they embraced, touching and kissing in harmony. Laurie's breath escaped in a garbled sound. George's lips were on her neck, her breasts, her stomach, her thighs. He damned sure didn't need the foreplay, but he imagined she would. Then his fingers encountered her warm moistness, and he knew she would never be more ready for him.

Laurie squeezed her eyes tightly shut, then felt him crush her to him as he moved over her. He made his first tentative entrance. She was unbelievably tight but accepted him eagerly. Sinking deeply into her, he stilled, as if afraid to move. She wound her legs around him and held him, waiting.

Gradually the natural rhythms took over. Laurie thought it was the perfect union, a beautiful thing of twining arms and legs and hungry mouths. She had dreamed of it more times than she could count, but none of her fantasies had done justice to the reality. She wished it could go on forever. George was a powerful and sensitive lover, not shy in that respect. She was obsessed with him; it was as simple as that. She'd never get enough of him.

The rhythms grew strong and hungry. Laurie felt an awakening of passion that she feared had wasted away from neglect. George was whispering something against her neck, but she couldn't make out his words. It didn't matter. There were no words for this, just feelings. And she wanted him to remember it always. Maybe that wasn't possible, but that was what she wanted.

He stilled in her arms and hovered above her slightly, matching her undulations in perfect tempo. With his hands he cupped her face. Laurie opened her eyes to reassure herself that it really was him. "George," she crooned. "Ge-orge." It was as though the sound of his name triggered his release. He thrust, lunged, and, shuddering violently, collapsed on top of her again. Simultaneously the golden fireworks began in Laurie, bathing her limbs in liquid heat. The ecstasy was indescribable.

MUCH LATER, Laurie lay sleeping peacefully beside him, curled into an embryonic position, her lips against his shoulder. George didn't know how long he had lain there, watching her, but it had been some time. When he had finally released his bruising hold on her and rolled away, he had drawn her into the cradle of his arms where she had fallen asleep almost immediately. But he couldn't sleep. To sleep would be to lose the wonder.

What they had shared had been pure magic. What now? Perhaps a less conscionable man wouldn't have cared, but he did. Laurie needed more than a man's comfort on one night. She needed someone to hold her at night and share coffee with in the morning. She needed and deserved someone she could depend on morning, noon and night, someone to talk to, to laugh with, to commiserate with when necessary. She needed the kind of man he had worked hard to avoid becoming.

Could he change that much? Did he want to? He didn't know, and that frightened him. He wasn't in charge of himself or of the events swirling around him.

Laurie stirred beside him just then, and she stretched, purring softly. Struggling up on one elbow, she looked down at him. Her eyes were soft with the residue of sleep. "Mmm, you're very masterful," she cooed.

"I thought I'd died for a minute. Maybe I have and this is heaven. If so, I'm glad I always led such an exemplary life. You were a bundle of dynamite."

"Was I? That's nice to know. I wondered how I would measure up on your personal scale."

"Lord, Laurie, I'm not a man who's had a lot of experience with women, but if it got any better than that, I wouldn't be able to stand it."

"And to think I always considered you shy."

"Maybe I was with you. Every time I was with you my tongue seemed to get twisted in knots. You were such a patrician lady. I thought I was beneath you."

She smiled seductively, then bent to nibble his earlobe. One silken leg moved sleekly across his hard stomach. Her fingertips teased his flat nipples, then forged a trail downward. George could feel himself rising and hardening again. Her fingers closed around his arousal, effectively reducing him to a conquered male animal, hers to do with as she wished. She moved over him to straddle his hips, and her pink-tipped breasts hovered enticingly above him. He captured one with his lips.

"Get underneath me now," she whispered, "and I'll show you what a patrician lady I am."

CHAPTER TEN

FOR THE FIRST TIME in memory George was late for work the next morning, although no one else was aware of that. If anyone had given his absence a minute's thought, he or she would have assumed that George was in the house talking to Cassie. It was the nature of their business that none of them needed the foreman to tell them what to do. The work always was there for anyone to see.

George felt great; he was fairly bursting with energy, and full of goodwill and kindness toward his fellow man. Shot was the first to notice his unusually good spirits. During a lull in the morning's work, he sidled up to his friend and spoke in a low voice. "What's got you in such a good mood, pal? You just get laid or something?"

"Nicely put, Shot, as always. I want to talk to you."

"Talk away."

"Not now. I'll tell you when."

At mid-morning, George decided he wanted to check on some colts in one of the top pastures. At least that was the excuse he used. Motioning for Shot to come with him, he drove his truck along a rutty trail that climbed high above the vast valley. Near a windmill, they spotted six colts, and when George whistled, the animals came straight to them. Looking them over, he noticed that one of the colts had a nasty gash on his foreleg.

Shot examined it. "Reckon we got us a lion up here?"

George shook his head. "I don't think so. He probably got that playing with these other fellows. Doesn't look serious. I'll come back later and put something on it." He straightened. "Shot, tell me something about... women and...marriage." He felt a little foolish. He didn't know how Shot would respond to this kind of questioning.

"What?" His friend guffawed. "Well, wha'da'ya know! Don't tell me you finally got the hots for some little filly."

George ignored that. "I really don't know a whole lot about women."

"Show me a man who says he does, and I'll show you a liar."

"I guess what I mainly want to know is, if you had it to do over, would you get married again? Would you marry the same woman?"

"Hell, yes!"

"Really? Seems like all you and Joanie do is fight."

"Naw, that's not all we do, pal. That's just what we do to keep life from gettin' too dull. Like I told you once, it's kind of a game. But, shoot, I couldn't do without Joanie. Kinda scares me to think about ever havin' to."

George thought of all the times he had driven away from Shot's house thinking that a man could dream of being married to a woman like Joanie and wake up in a cold sweat. Yet he'd suspected there was some deep affection there, something that bound them together. Otherwise, how could they have stayed married so long? That was why he had chosen Shot to talk to. He wanted someone who'd been over the long haul. "What is there about her you like so much?"

"I dunno. What is there about my right arm I like so much?"

George shook his head in bewilderment. "I guess I don't understand."

"Guess you don't. Look, I admit it ain't hearts and flowers all the time, but given my fondness for alcohol, women and cards, I figure if I wasn't married I'd probably have cirrhosis of the liver, a social disease and be dead broke. I reckon little Joanie kept this ol' boy from an early grave."

"You've been married fifteen years. Do you and Joanie ever run out of anything to talk about?"

Shot laughed. "Can't say I recall too many lulls in the conversation. There's always something to talk about."

George kicked at the ground with the toe of his boot, then looked up at the sky. "Don't you ever miss being single?"

"Guess I did a time or two in the beginning. Can't recollect just why, though. If you wanna know the truth, I can't really remember just what there was about that life that I thought was so all-fired red-hot."

George digested that for a minute. "Tell me something else. When you're married and have kids all over the place, when do you and your wife find time for...well, you know, just being together, alone? You know what I mean."

"Yeah, I know what you mean."

"Do you always have to wait for bedtime?"

Shot shrugged. "You just lock the bedroom door. Once kids get to be a certain age, they're not all that interested in what their parents are doin', especially if they're bein' left alone. Just lock the bedroom door. Sometimes a quickie in the middle of the afternoon is the best there is."

"I've heard that after a while, wives don't like it much, that it gets to be a chore, like ironing their husbands' shirts. Is that true?"

"God, I hope not! If that's true, Joanie's some kinda actress. She ought'a get in the movies. As a matter of fact, I think once women get some years tucked under their belts, say 35 or 40, they like it better'n their husbands do."

"You're kidding."

"What am I, a sex therapist? Why don't you get yourself a book?" He looked at George with as much seriousness as he was ever able to muster. "This has kinda thrown you for a loop, right, pal?"

George tugged on his chin. "I—I guess I didn't expect it to happen to me, not when my back was turned, anyway."

Shot smiled sympathetically. "There's a test, you know."

"A test?"

"Sure." Shot pointed in the distance. "Wha'd'ya see over yonder?"

George squinted. "Well, I see mountains and the valley and a canyon and the sky."

"And you don't feel nuthin' tuggin' at you, beggin' you to come on and see what's on the other side of the mountain?"

"I know what's on the other side," George said with a shrug. "More of the same."

"Then you just might be ready to settle down." Shot gave him a hearty slap on the back. "Cheer up, pal. Just remember that you fought it longer'n most of us did."

George had hoped that talking to Shot would miraculously make up his mind for him, but nothing in life seemed that simple. He was stunned by the realization that Laurie had worked her way into his heart so thoroughly, and succumbing didn't come easily for him. He'd always thought of himself as a happy man, content to live his own life and let others live theirs. He didn't bother anyone or let anyone bother him. "Love" came in the form of brief flings with lusty, earthy women who didn't consider a night in bed an earth-shaking event. That way no one got hurt.

But not getting hurt probably just meant no one cared that much about you, he reflected, and that was a pretty sorry way to live when you got right down to it. He knew Stacy and DeeAnn cared about him, and he liked that. He fancied that Laurie cared, too, and that made his heart thump crazily. Last night had been earth-shaking.

In retrospect...well, maybe the ramblin' life hadn't been all that great. Maybe he'd actually just been searching for constancy and a purpose in life. Now he could feel them within his grasp. Why didn't he just reach out and take them?

It wasn't an easy question to answer. For one thing, he didn't think Laurie would be getting such a bargain. He was better about thinking of others and looking after them now than he had been four months ago, but sometimes he had to work at it. Old habits were hard to break, and he'd had only himself to answer to for a long time.

He'd never want to hurt her, but he was sure he would occasionally and not even know he was doing it. Then he'd feel rotten for days and try to make it up to her, but he probably wouldn't do such a good job of that, either. Moreover, though he had a little money saved, it wasn't much, so he couldn't rescue her from her financial woes, only ease them a little.

Also, he was not her intellectual equal, although she would have pooh-poohed that notion and told him he was being ridiculous. But he had neither class nor means, and she deserved a man with both.

He guessed about all he could do was love her, and never having loved a woman, he wasn't sure he'd be any great shakes at that. He wasn't even sure that this was love, but it definitely was something he'd never felt before.

Ah, hell! he thought. Attachments were the damnedest things to live with.

SHORTLY AFTER LAURIE and the twins had finished lunch, the telephone rang. It was Jill calling from the plush hotel in Colorado. She'd barely said two words before Laurie knew something was wrong.

"Honey, are you crying?" she asked incredulously.

"Oh, Laurie, I'm sc-scared."

"What in the world are you afraid of?"

"I'm . . . homesick. And I'm m-m-married."

You're not kidding you're married, Laurie thought. *I have the sad bank account to prove it.* "Of course you're married."

"I'm going to have to live with Tony every day for the rest of my life!"

"Where's Tony now?"

"Downstairs getting a haircut."

"You two haven't had a fight, have you?"

"N-no, but . . . it's so scary."

Laurie sank wearily to a chair in the kitchen, and for the next twenty minutes she employed her most soothing and reassuring voice, explaining that probably ninety percent of newlyweds had these moments of doubt, but everything was going to be just fine. She and Tony were going to have a wonderful life together. She was just experiencing a letdown from all the hoopla surrounding the wedding, and things would look much rosier when she was rested. Laurie talked until she couldn't think of anything else to say, and by the time they'd hung up, she thought Jill had a more upbeat attitude. But Laurie herself was a little teary for a while after the call.

She'd barely recovered from that when the doorbell rang. Visitors in the middle of the afternoon were a rarity. Even more surprising was the contingent of community leaders she found standing on her front porch. There was Ted Weeks from the bank. And Rebecca Spenser, who owned the area's largest real estate company. Rebecca and Laurie's mother had been friends, but Laurie hadn't seen the woman in ages. Laurie knew the two men with Ted and Rebecca only slightly—Chester Dobbs, who owned an automobile dealership, and Hoyt Bennett, the president of the Chamber of Commerce. They were, along with four or five others, the community's movers and shakers, the ones who formed committees and organized drives and got their pictures in the Sunday paper. It was, to say the least, an unusual group to be calling at the Tyler Ranch.

Hoyt Bennett took the initiative. He was a tall, nicelooking, affable man, the kind who was born to be president of a Chamber of Commerce or to run for public office. "Good afternoon, Laurie," he said jovially. "I think you know everyone here. Forgive us for just stopping by unannounced, but we have a little business to discuss with you if you can give us a few minutes."

What kind of "business" could these people possibly have with me? she wondered, even as she stood back and held the door open. She shooed Stacy and DeeAnn out of the living room and invited her callers to sit down, offering them refreshments. Everyone assured her they wanted nothing.

Since Ted was closely acquainted with Laurie, he did most of the talking. "We've come to discuss the offer on your property, Laurie," he said, getting right to the point.

"Oh?"

"We understand that some of the local ranchers have been giving you a little trouble about it."

"Well, I'm not sure 'trouble' is the proper word, but there's no question that they're unhappy about the way the property would be used."

Ted chuckled and shook his head. "I won't pretend to understand those people. They're constantly talking about tradition and loss of old values, but what they really mean is that they want to keep the High Country the way it was a hundred years ago. But we must move forward. Progress is the key word here."

It occurred to Laurie that so much of what was termed "progress" often wasn't very progressive. She guessed she had a lot of her parents in her. They had been people who lived close to the earth, so her sympathies tended to lean toward the ranchers.

Rebecca leaned forward and spoke earnestly. "Laurie, think what a shot in the arm for the local economy a development of such magnitude would be—the jobs it would create. The construction business alone would be booming."

As would the real estate business, Laurie thought wryly. Rebecca was an aggressive go-getter. Laurie was willing to bet that it was she who had been in touch with the development company and sewed up the sale of the proposed homes for her agency. That was the way Rebecca operated, and it had made her a very wealthy woman.

"Well, I... really haven't made a definite decision to sell." Laurie's plans were even less definite after her night with George. She knew she couldn't allow her hopes to soar out of sight simply because of one night of lovemaking, but there was a very real possibility that she and George were on the verge of... something. Whatever it was, for however long it lasted, she'd take it. So she didn't want to rock the boat or disturb the status quo.

She studied her group of callers, suddenly aware of their vested interest in the development. Rebecca's was obvious. A six percent commission on a sale of several million dollars was a tidy sum. And people who could afford homes like the ones that would be built opened hefty bank accounts and bought expensive cars, so that took care of Ted and Chester. And as president of the Chamber, Hoyt was driven by the desire for growth. The ranchers had their own interests; now all Laurie had to do was decide where hers lay.

The four visitors continued talking, more among themselves than to Laurie, reaffirming their belief that the development would be of enormous benefit to the area. Finally all eyes turned expectantly to Laurie.

"All I can tell you right now is that I haven't made up my mind," she repeated.

Ted played his last ace. "Laurie, dear, I told the man I've been dealing with over the phone that the ranchers had approached you. He said I'm authorized to offer you whatever is necessary. Perhaps as much as eighty-five thousand."

Laurie tensed. So that was what this was going to turn into; they were going to make her an offer she couldn't refuse—more importantly, an offer the ranchers couldn't match.

"That's very generous," she said, "but I have some people renting the cottage out back—a man and two little girls. They aren't in a position to be displaced at the moment."

Ted hesitated. "I can't keep these easterners dangling forever, Laurie."

"I understand that."

"They're very anxious to raze this house and get started."

"Raze?"

"Well, of course."

Of course. Why hadn't she thought of that? The house would hardly look right smack in the middle of fifty expensive homes. Odd that the thought should be so alarming. If she sold, what did she care what happened to the house? "I...just can't give you a definite answer yet," she said, glancing down at her hands.

"I see." Ted cleared his throat. "I don't want to pressure you, dear, but I'll have to have an answer soon...say within three weeks at the latest."

"All right. I'll tell you something in three weeks."

Since there was nothing left to say, her visitors stood, exchanged the usual amenities, then left. Laurie went in search of Stacy and DeeAnn and found them happily skipping rope in the backyard. Then she headed back to the house to begin supper preparations. She just assumed that George and the girls would share the meal with her, just as she assumed she and George would find time for themselves before the night was over. She'd kept the girls busy all day, not only because she didn't want them to be bored but because she wanted them to sleep soundly. Now, as five o'clock approached, she could feel the anticipation building within her.

And she didn't want to think beyond that, even though she was aware of how foolish that was. Eighty-five thousand, for heaven's sakes! Talk about a change in destiny. If she had an ounce of good sense she'd grab it and begin planning her future.

Then the truck rumbled past the kitchen window, and anything smacking of good sense quit her. The only future she cared about was at hand. There was something almost coldly calculating about her resolve. She knew exactly what she wanted at the moment.

Walking to the back door, Laurie watched the girls run toward the truck. George got out and gave both of them a big hug. Then he reached into the truck and withdrew a small sack, which he handed to one of the girls. They went to sit under a tree and inspect its contents while George made straight for the back door. Seeing Laurie standing there, he grinned disarmingly. He opened the door, closed it and reached for her, seemingly all in the same movement.

"Hi."

"Hi."

"What did you bring the girls?"

"Something called mind-benders. Puzzles. Guaranteed to keep inquisitive minds busy for hours." He tapped his forehead. "Always thinking."

Laughing, she slipped her arms around his firm middle and gave him a resounding kiss, the tip of her tongue making quick darting movements that taunted him beyond belief.

George groaned. "Damned if I haven't thought about this all day."

"So have I," Laurie admitted.

"Feels as good as it did last night?"

"Yes. How can a man who works with cows and horses all day smell as divine as you do?"

"I took a shower in the bunkhouse before I left. Didn't figure I'd want to take the time when I got here." He took off his hat, placed it on the nearest surface, then grabbed her hand and began pulling her through the kitchen.

"George?"

"Upstairs."

Laurie's glance darted toward the back door. "But...the girls..."

"What do you think the puzzles are for?"

Laurie couldn't believe she was so eager. She was almost skipping in order to keep up with him. Halfway up the stairs George began removing his belt. When they reached her room, he pulled her inside, then closed and locked the door. Suddenly she was being held in his arms so tightly she thought he was trying to squeeze all the breath out of her. Finally he released his viselike grip and began covering her face with hot, avid kisses, while his hands made a voyage of rediscovery up and down her body, cupping her buttocks and bringing her up to meet the thrust of his hips.

A minute of that was all it took. He backed her toward the bed, unsnapped and unzipped her jeans, then hooked his fingers in the waistband and tugged downward, taking her panties at the same time. Then she lay back on the bed, her eyes closed, her heart pounding. She heard the rasp of his zipper; a second or two passed, and he was over her.

There was no time for play. Both of them were filled with urgency. Laurie whispered her desire, and then George was hard and thrusting inside her. She wound her legs around his hips, almost dizzy with enchantment. They were perfect together. She wished the magic never had to end.

It was, of course, over much too soon, but the frantic nature of their coupling hadn't diminished the ecstasy. They lay very still; one of George's legs was thrown possessively across her, and his breath was tickling her ear.

"Is that what is affectionately known as a 'quickie'?" she asked.

"Sorry."

"Don't be. It was wonderful and...exciting."

"Good."

"Are you going to sleep with me tonight?"

"I was sure planning on it."

"We'll let the girls stay up until they drop. Then they can sleep in one of the other rooms."

George grunted his approval. "But don't let me be late for work again."

"Speaking of the girls, get up and look out the window. Are they still in the backyard?"

George pushed himself off the bed and, after rearranging his clothes, he complied. "Yep. Doesn't look as though they've moved."

Laurie stepped into her jeans and stuffed in her shirt. "Good. It does bother me to think they might...oh, I don't know. Think we're...improper."

"Twelve-year-olds?" he asked in astonishment.

"George, I teach that age group, remember? Some of them know things that would blow your mind. It depends on their upbringing, of course. But generally, twelve is about the age when sex starts creeping into their humor.''

"Twelve? You're kidding!"

"No, I'm not. Our girls are still innocents, but you never know what they'll hear from someone else."

Our girls, he thought as he followed her downstairs. *Ours.* Stacy and DeeAnn did seem like theirs in so many ways. *We could be so wonderful together, the four of us.* He honestly had planned to have a long talk with Laurie later in the evening, to discuss the feasibility of their making this a permanent arrangement. Marriage. He even could think the word without blanching, something that would have been impossible only a few short months ago. All afternoon, working in the sun and dust, he had listed the reasons in favor of living with Laurie the rest of his life. She was beautiful, and she made his heart pound. He never got tired of being around her. She was the only woman he'd ever made love to that he wanted to return to again and again and again. She wasn't moody or flighty or extravagant. She had brains. She was born to be somebody's mother. The list seemed endless, and way down at the bottom, just in case the cake needed some frosting, she was the best cook in the whole damned world.

It could be perfect, he knew. So why was he hesitating? Was he afraid he'd wake up some morning and find that the wanderlust had returned? Was he afraid she'd say no? She liked their lovemaking as much as he did—no one was that good an actress—but that didn't mean she wanted to spend the rest of her life with him. But suppose she said yes, a small voice asked. Was he afraid she would wake up some morning and wonder how in hell she'd ended up married to a cowpoke?

George couldn't take his eyes off her while she bustled around the kitchen getting supper ready. He set the table for her and filled the water glasses, but still he watched. And he watched when she went to the back door and called the girls, then made sure they washed their hands before sitting down at the table. They ate like starving field hands, but they were the picture of health and happiness, George thought. Throughout the meal, Stacy chattered like a magpie, with DeeAnn putting in a word now and then. A stranger happening on the scene would have immediately surmised that here was an average middle-class family having their evening meal together. There was such a feeling of rightness to it, a feeling that was underscored when no one jumped up immediately after eating, anxious to be off doing something else. Laurie's influence on the girls had been thorough and wonderful. Ellen could never accuse him of not taking good care of them.

Thinking of Ellen was somewhat sobering. He glanced at Stacy and DeeAnn, and something squeezed at his heart. He had let them get to him. He'd become so fond of them. Then he looked at Laurie. So fond of all of them, he quickly amended. But he and Laurie could have a couple of their own. Then the girls would have cousins.

It could be so perfect, George thought again. *Ah, Laurie, I wish you'd give me some sign, something that would tell me how you feel about this abrupt change in our relationship, something that would encourage me... or discourage me completely. I need to know if I'm way off base or moving along on the right track.*

"You haven't said much tonight, Laurie," he said. "How was your day?"

"Some of our illustrious community leaders called on me. They're as anxious for me to sell this place as Cassie and her cohorts are for me not to. They upped the offer to eighty-five thousand." She looked at him to see his reaction.

"That's . . . a lot of money," was all he said.

"Yes. And it's just for the land. They...want to raze the house."

George tensed. "This house?"

"Yes."

He looked around as if seeing the house for the first time. He'd known a lot of happiness in it, more than in any place he'd ever been before. The house meant Laurie to him. And someone wanted to tear it down. "What did you tell them?"

"That I didn't know if I wanted to sell or not."

"Is that true?"

"Yes. I . . . that is, certain recent events have . . ." She let the words trail off, mainly because she had no idea how to finish the statement.

George stared at her. Certain recent events could mean only one thing: them. Was this the sign he'd been waiting for?

"And Jill called from Colorado, all teary and confused and homesick." She chuckled lightly. "She isn't sure she wants to be married. Fine time to be thinking of that, right? I told her I was sure all newlyweds felt that way occasionally."

Oh, geez, Laurie, George thought. *Why did you have to say that?*

The telephone's shrill ring interrupted his thoughts. Laurie got up from the table to answer it. When she turned around again, she was holding the receiver in her hand and had a peculiar look on her face. "It's your dad," she said.

George slapped his forehead with his palm. "I forgot to call him yesterday." Getting to his feet, he walked to her and took the phone, smiling at her wickedly. "I can't imagine why."

Laurie went back to the table and began clearing it. "You girls can have ice cream bars if you'll take them outside."

They nodded enthusiastically and hurried to the freezer to get their treats. The back door opened and closed, and then Laurie listened to George's end of the phone conversation fearfully. He was always the one who called; his father never did. Of course, Jonas's call could have been prompted by his son's failure to check in Sunday, but Laurie didn't think so. Some sixth sense told her there had been a change. Her throat tightened with trepidation.

"Yeah, Dad . . . sorry I forgot to call yesterday, but . . ." There was a long pause, then George shouted, "What?"

The outburst was so untypical that Laurie turned to watch him. He was gripping the receiver so tightly his knuckles were white, and as he listened, his eyes widened, then narrowed, and his mouth set in a tight line. "That son of a bitch! You're dammed right I'm protesting!" he exploded. "I'll take it to the Supreme Court!"

Laurie couldn't have been more startled. Thank goodness the girls had gone outside. George wasn't a particularly profane man, nor was he given to bursts of temper, but the veins were standing out at his temples. One did not have to be too smart to know that something dreadful had happened.

Finally George sighed a struggling sigh and rubbed his eyes. "Okay, Dad. Sure, I understand. I'll ... take care of it." He slammed the receiver into the cradle with such force that Laurie wondered how the telephone remained on the wall.

Her hand went to her chest. "George, what on earth is wrong?"

"Plenty. Steve's back from South America and raising all kinds of hell because that saddle bum—that's me—has his daughters."

"Oh, no." Laurie placed a sympathetic hand on his arm.

"He's gone to the juvenile authorities, and the sheriff paid Dad a call about an hour ago." His eyes came to meet hers. Laurie had never seen such a look on anyone's face. He was absolutely furious, but frightened, too. "Laurie, I have four days to get Stacy and DeeAnn back to Oklahoma or ... Steve's charging me with kidnapping."

CHAPTER ELEVEN

IT'S OVER, Laurie thought and wanted to cry, *and that's so unfair. It's barely begun, and now it's over.* They'd never even had a chance to find out where they might be heading. Once George took the girls back to Oklahoma, he'd keep on wandering. He'd only come back in the first place because of the girls; he'd admitted that. "I'm so...sorry," she said weakly.

He made a fist with one hand and slammed it into the palm of the other. "Dammit, I can't let that sorry-ass Steve have them!"

"What...are you going to do?"

"I don't know, but I'm going to do something. How can the authorities, whoever the devil they are, give those two girls to a man who ran out on them and their mother?"

"George, goodness knows I'm no expert on this, but working with children as I do, I've known of a few custody cases. The courts always lean heavily in favor of the natural parent, no matter how unsuitable the parent seems to be. As long as the children in question aren't being abused, a parent who wants them gets them."

"Where in the hell is the justice in that?" he roared. "Steve doesn't want those girls. He just doesn't want me to have them. Well, we'll see about this. I'm going to do something."

"What?"

"I don't know. Talk to Ellen. If she was okay, the girls would go to her without question. Steve ran out on them."

"You can't talk to Ellen without consulting her therapist first. You might do all sorts of damage."

"Okay, I'll . . . Hell, I don't know what I'm going to do, just something. But first I've got to get Stacy and DeeAnn back to Oklahoma. I can't do anything if I'm in jail."

Laurie turned toward the sink and began rinsing dishes. She felt as though her heart was being ripped out a tiny piece at a time. Behind her, George paced restlessly and muttered under his breath. He seemed to have already forgotten about her, about later tonight, about everything but the threat to Stacy and DeeAnn. Laurie knew that should be uppermost on her mind, too, and it was—to a point. However, her own disappointment and the prospect of her impending loss were there, choking her.

A heavy weariness settled over her like a shroud. How would she ever say good-bye to the three of them? Perhaps when they actually drove off, she could be away from the house, away running errands or something—anything. But then, how could she ever come back to an empty, empty nest? The loneliness would chew her up and spit her out. Before George and the twins she had learned to accept her life of minimal peaks and valleys, the days so alike that they virtually were indistinguishable. Then they had come, filling the house with noise and laughter, filling her heart with emotions she hadn't known existed. How would she ever do without them? She'd never be able to walk through these rooms again without the memories crushing down on her.

And that was why she couldn't stay. She'd sell this place to the highest bidder—to hell with the ranchers with their enormous spreads and centuries of traditions and credit at the bank. She wouldn't spend one week in the house with everyone gone.

"There's a hearing Monday," George said suddenly.

"What?" Laurie spun around.

"Monday," he repeated. "A preliminary hearing for all 'interested' parties. And since I have to have the girls back at the farm by Thursday, I guess that means we'll need to be on the road pretty early Wednesday. Lord, there's a lot to think about. I have to tell Cassie. I'm sure she'll understand, but I hope I don't put her in a bind."

"She'll understand," Laurie mumbled. Hot tears welled in her eyes, but she didn't want to call attention to them by wiping them away. She simply tried to stem them by gulping hard, and she kept her back to George.

But just then he took her by the shoulders and spun her around. "Laurie, I... Hey, what's this? Tears?" Gently he drew her to him and held her. Her tears made a damp spot on the front of his shirt. "Don't cry. I'm not going to let anything happen to Stacy and DeeAnn. I'll raise a ruckus everyone will still be talking about twenty years from now. Steve is not going to get those girls."

It's not that, you big galoot, she wanted to scream. *I'm going to lose you. I can feel it.* Of course, it was stretching things a bit to say she had ever had him, but she'd had something, more than she'd had in her life. Once before she had watched him walk away, and she'd missed him terribly. But back then they'd shared so little. Now.... She decided she would be a fool if she let him leave without a word or an effort. All her life she would wonder if theirs would have been a fleeting affair or the stuff dreams were made of.

The plan took hold in her mind in a flash. Well, it wasn't a plan exactly, more of a need born of desperation. Stepping back, she squared her shoulders and looked George straight in the eye. "I'm going with you."

"What?"

"You heard me. I'm going to Oklahoma with you and the girls. Look, George, I'm the only person on the face of the earth who knows first-hand what kind of guardian you've been. I'm not going to let you go into that hearing without someone in your corner. Don't try to talk me out of it."

A slow smile spread across his face. Why hadn't he thought of that immediately? He knew she was doing it for the girls, but he'd have her there with him. It would make the whole business more tolerable. "Why would I try to talk you out of it?"

"We'll take my car. That'll give the girls more room to spread out." It would also mean that, regardless of the outcome of the custody fight, he would have to come back for his truck. She was amazed at her deviousness. "And you're right. We have a lot to do. What are you going to tell the girls?"

George scratched his head. "I'm not sure, but I'll think of something. And I guess I'd better do it now."

He was gone maybe ten minutes. When he walked through the door Laurie quizzed him with her eyes. "I told them their grandfather just called," he explained, "and that I need to go to the farm to take care of some family business. I said you'd decided to go along for the ride, so we were going to make a family trip out of it."

"They're pretty sharp. Did they believe you?"

"I don't know." He lifted his shoulders. "It was the best I could do."

Laurie was thinking out loud. "I need to let Andy know where I'll be. Jill, too, if I can reach her. But I guess they're the only ones."

"I'll tell Cassie at work tomorrow. Shot, too. But I don't think anyone but Cassie needs to know the seriousness of the situation, right?"

"Right."

"And I'd just as soon Stacy and DeeAnn didn't have any idea that this might be—" he swallowed as if the word was stuck in his throat "—permanent."

Laurie's chin trembled. "I agree."

George felt himself relax a little. He was beginning to be confident of his ability to take care of the situation once they got to Oklahoma. He could even allow himself to smile and glance at Laurie speculatively. "Tonight... later? Is it still on?"

"Yes," she said softly. "I've discovered that I like waking up beside you."

His face sobered slightly. "Once we get to the farm there won't be much privacy."

She nodded. "All the more reason to make tonight special." Within the short span of twenty-four hours she'd been transformed from wanting to just plain wanton.

That night George didn't make his usual announcement about bedtime when nine o'clock rolled around, and the girls didn't remind him. It was almost ten when they began yawning and nodding sleepily.

"You know, I think your uncle wants to watch the late movie tonight," Laurie lied. "Why don't you run and get your pajamas and sleep upstairs?"

She would never know why a change of bedrooms appealed to them so much, but that was the case. Once they were bedded down, she and George sat on the sofa, kissing and hugging like a couple of teenagers. At ten-thirty Laurie stood, turned off the light, held out her hand to him, and arm in arm they went upstairs.

"I'll check on the girls," she whispered.

George nodded and went into her room. When Laurie joined him a minute later, he was unbuttoning his shirt. She closed and locked the door, then wordlessly went into his arms. Laurie refused to allow herself to think, because thinking would bring pain with the pleasure. Even so, their lovemaking had a bittersweet quality to it. All she could see ahead was uncertainty. Who could predict how much time would pass before she again could lie in his arms...if ever.

TUESDAY WAS a busy day. There were dozens of details to be taken care of, but by nightfall Laurie's car was packed and ready to go, the refrigerator had been emptied of everything except what was needed for breakfast, and everyone who needed to be notified had been. There was nothing to do but get up on Wednesday, eat something and go.

It had been a long time since Laurie had taken a prolonged motor trip, and the one to Oklahoma was not a particularly good one with which to become reinitiated. It was a grueling journey of over five-hundred miles, much of it on two-lane highways through farm and ranch communities, which necessitated a lot of stopping. And once they left the mountains the day turned murderously hot. There obviously had been no rain in that part of the state in some time. The further north they drove the more the fields flanking the highway took on the color of a corn tortilla.

Moreover, though George felt sure that with him and Laurie sharing the driving they could make it straight through with no trouble, the girls were another matter. After six hours in the car they were growing fidgety and what passed for cross with them. They needed a respite, and he realized that he could use a meal and a good night's sleep himself. He wanted all his wits about him when he got to Oklahoma. They found a nice-looking, mom-and-pop motel with a café and swimming pool in a farming town that was built around a Victorian courthouse. The owners, who manned the front desk, naturally assumed they were a family.

"We're pretty full up," the wife said pleasantly. "Peanut growers are meeting at the library tomorrow. You folks with them?"

George blanched at the thought of being mistaken for a peanut farmer. "No, we're from down in the Davis Mountains."

"Oh. Must be ranchers, right? Well, I can put you and the wife up in 117. A roll-away for the kids will be two dollars extra. The room has twin beds. Is that all right?"

George glanced uncertainly at Laurie. He naturally had expected to get her a room by herself. "That's fine," she said. "All we need is a place to lay our heads."

"We want to swim," Stacy said.

"Did you bring suits?" Laurie asked. She had no idea what personal things they had brought.

The girls nodded. "There's a pond on Grandpa's farm. He lets us swim in it when there's enough water."

The motel room was cramped once the rollaway was brought in, but it was clean, and, as Laurie reminded herself, they weren't setting up housekeeping, only spending the night. Stacy and DeeAnn, now that they were free of the confining car, seemed imbued with renewed energy. They were in their swimsuits within minutes and outside at the little pool. George went along to keep an eye on them, leaving Laurie with a few peaceful minutes alone. She stretched out on one of the beds and fell sound asleep.

The next thing she knew she felt a hand brush at her hair. Opening her eyes, she saw George standing by the bed looking down at her. "Sorry," he said softly. "You had hair in your eyes. I didn't think I'd wake you."

Laurie's arms went over her head, and she stretched. "I shouldn't be sleeping this late. I won't be able to sleep tonight." Raising herself up on her elbows, she glanced around the little room. "Where are the girls?"

"Still at the pool. There's a whole family out there, and they're having a ball. They really don't need watching. They could teach the fish a thing or two. Scoot over."

Laurie did, and George settled full length beside her. For several long wordless minutes they simply contemplated the ceiling. Then he sighed. "Look at this. Here we are—in a motel room in an obscure town where not a soul knows us. We could close the blinds, lock the door and just let the rest of the world go by for a few days."

She smiled and patted him on the arm. "Instead, we've got two girls on our hands, and tomorrow we'll be in Oklahoma for... God knows what."

More silence. "I don't know what I'd have done without you these past months," George said.

"I didn't do anything."

"You did more than you know. More than once I might have just packed up and taken the twins back to the farm. You always managed to do or say something to make me think I could make a go of it."

Laurie hated his tone of voice. There was so much finality in it. No doubt he was thinking that it was likely the girls wouldn't be making the return trip with them.

She was sure of it when, in a flat, lifeless voice, he said, "Laurie, I'm worried."

"I know." She sighed. "So am I." Silently she added, *And I have more to be worried about than you do.* If they returned to the High Country without the girls, what would keep him there? It would have been nice to be able to hon-

estly say, *There's me,* but Laurie was a realist. She knew
George thought a lot of her, knew he liked her as a person,
and certainly knew he liked their lovemaking, but to seriously hope he was falling in love with her was to stretch the
bounds of hope and imagination. She felt sick at the
thought of having him leave again. Possessiveness was one
of her great faults, she decided. Once she cared for someone, letting go became devastating.

George turned on his side so that his face was only inches
away from hers. He nibbled at the tip of her nose. Laurie
took his hand and held it warmly in hers. All was so peaceful and companionable that neither of them moved, not
even when the door opened. The twins burst into the room,
each swathed in one of the motel's towels. When they saw
Laurie and their uncle lying on the bed, they stopped, but
if they found the scene unusual they gave no sign. In fact,
they joined the adults. Stacy scooted in beside George and
laid her face against his back. Laurie raised an arm to allow DeeAnn to snuggle up under it. They were damp from
head to toe, but who cared? The four of them lay entwined
and still on the small bed meant for one.

A lump formed in George's throat the size of a cork. It
wasn't right for the four of them ever to be separated.
Laurie was so good with the girls, teaching them constantly in little ways that would never occur to him. *Teaching me, too,* he added. He used to think he had everything,
the freedom to go and come as he pleased and to keep his
life uncluttered. Hell, he'd had nothing. But for a short
time now he'd had everything, thanks to the three female
persons lying on the bed with him. And it all could come to
an abrupt end by the rap of a gavel or the solemn pro-
nouncement of some obscure social worker.

He tried to envision a life that didn't include them, and
discovered that what he came up with wasn't very appealing. His old way of life suddenly seemed narrow and self-
centered. He knew now that self came to mean something
only when it was shared with others.

DeeAnn was squirming. To accommodate her, Laurie moved even closer to George. Her breasts brushed against his chest. Her breath fluttered against his chin. Her eyes, wide and luminous, met his. One slight movement in her direction, and his mouth captured hers in a slow, drugging, drinking kind of kiss. The cork in his throat refused to budge. "Laurie," he whispered. "I can't stand this."

"I know. I know. Neither can I."

George closed his eyes, breathing deeply, feeling Laurie against him. Placing a possessive hand on her stomach, he felt himself slipping into a hazy state, somewhere between sleep and daydreams. He didn't want to move, even though he was aware that they needed to get up. The girls needed to get dressed, and they all needed to have supper and get to bed early. Tomorrow promised to be a difficult day. But for now...

Someone moved eventually; George thought it was Stacy. Then DeeAnn yawned and shook herself out of her stupor. "This bed is too little for all of us," she complained.

"I'm hungry," Stacy announced. "When are we going to eat, Uncle George?"

"Soon, hon. You and DeeAnn get out of those wet suits."

The peaceful interlude ended.

SINCE THEY HAD PUT so many miles behind them the first day, they were able to reach the farm by noon Thursday. George had called Jonas before leaving the motel that morning, so they were expected, and lunch was waiting.

Jonas met them on the front porch. "So you're Laurie. Don't recollect ever hearin' so much about anybody as I have you. Sure do want to thank you for all you've done for those twins. For my boy, too. Reckon you made things lots easier for him."

George's father was something of a surprise to Laurie. He was a small, spare man with a wizened face, permanently bronzed by years of working in the outdoors. He looked far too old to have a son in his early thirties, but then Laurie remembered that he would have to be seventy-three or -four. She could understand why two twelve-year-olds had been too much for him.

Stacy and DeeAnn had hurried on into the house, and Jonas took advantage of their absence to ask, "How much do the girls know?"

"Nothing," George said.

Jonas nodded. "Then I guess we oughta leave it that way, huh? We'll talk after lunch. Come on in. Anna's waitin' with a spread that looks like the preacher's comin' to eat. You can bring in your gear later."

The farm house reminded Laurie of home. It had probably been built about the same time as hers, and the floor plans were similar. Lunch, which they called dinner, was the biggest meal of the day, and two farm hands shared it with them. Laurie was dying to know where things stood with Steve, and she was sure George was about to burst, but because of the girls' presence, conversation around the table was small talk. Mostly she answered polite questions about her background. She was quick to notice how quiet Stacy and DeeAnn were. Back home, conversation during dinner usually was pretty animated, but here, apparently, children were meant to be seen but not heard. *They're happier in the mountains,* she decided, and her heart ached for them . . . and for George . . . and for herself.

After lunch, the farm hands scattered, and the girls went upstairs to their room. George closed the door between the kitchen and dining room to preclude the possibility that their voices might carry. Then he and his father got down to business. Laurie and Anna mostly just listened.

"Have you seen Steve?" George asked.

Jonas shook his head. "Nope. But I've talked to him over the phone. He wanted to know what the devil I was thinkin' of when I let you take the girls."

"What did you tell him?"

"The truth. Told him you wanted them and were young enough to ride herd on them. He's convinced you're roamin' all over the place with them, driftin' from job to job, and nothin' I said made a bit of difference.''

George's mouth was set in a tight line. "So, where do we stand from a legal aspect?''

''Well, for the time being, those child welfare people are sayin' that the girls can stay here until some kind of ruling can be handed down. At first they were sayin' that Steve got the kids, period, but I told 'em how he ran off and left the family and put their mama in the hospital because of it. I also told 'em that the girls love you to death and are happy with you. Sure hope I was tellin' the straight story.''

Jonas looked to Laurie for confirmation, and she nodded. ''They adore him, and he's been wonderful with them. The girls are happy, Mr. Whittaker. I can tell.''

''You got any kids of your own, Laurie?''

''No, I've never been married, but I'm a schoolteacher. I teach twelve-year-olds, and I know them. George has been a better father to them than a lot of natural ones I could tell you about.''

Jonas shifted his attention to his son. George? A good father? This was the kid he'd given up on a dozen years ago. Interesting. And he wondered just how much the pretty young woman had had to do with that. But he'd lived too long to be much surprised at human behavior, no matter how unusual.

''Anyway,'' he said, ''that social worker, Mrs. Prescott, finally said they would listen to both sides, and that's what Monday's hearing's all about. She said they would be fair and impartial, but the judge will be the one who has the final say. She also warned me that the courts almost always lean in a natural parent's favor. Lettin' you have the girls would be like puttin' them in a foster home, as far as they're concerned.''

George rapped his fist on the table. ''Dammit, that's not fair!''

''Well, if you ask me, you can thank your sister for this. If Ellen was okay, none of this would be happenin'. Her husband walked out on her, so she'd get custody of the kids, simple as that. You need to get your butt over to that hospital and talk some sense into her."

"I can't do that, Dad, not without talking to her doctor."

Jonas scoffed. "She might listen to you. She's started asking about the girls and seemed to be relieved that you have them. I talked to her on the phone yesterday and told her you'd all be here this weekend. She says she wants to see you."

"Does she ever ask about Steve?"

"No."

"She doesn't know he's back?"

"No. One of those fancy shrinks says she's accepted the fact that he's gone, so best leave well enough alone. Her problem now is coping. Hell, last time I went to see her everybody was dancin' a jig 'cause she'd been to the store with one of the aides and actually bought some shampoo. Silliest damned thing I ever heard of. They have her on some kind of drug with a name a foot long, and I have to admit it's made a difference. The doctor says she's all right until she starts thinkin' about comin' home, then she panics. If you ask me, she's been in that hospital too long. She needs to get out and just start doin' things. She'll be all right."

George sighed. "I wish it were that simple, Dad. Surely do."

Silence fell over the table for a minute. Then Jonas got to his feet. "Well, I gotta get back to work. When push comes to shove, I don't know a thing about how to handle any of this." With that, he walked out the back door.

"This has been awful hard on him," Anna said. It was the first time she'd spoken since being introduced to Laurie. "He's not a young man."

"I know, Anna, but Ellen needs lots of encouragement, not criticism."

Anna looked down at her hands, frowning. "I'm going to tell you something, George. When Ellen gets out of that hospital, she's going to have to stay here for a spell. The doctor says she's going to be afraid and shouldn't try living alone right away. I . . . worry about how that's going to work out."

Laurie was thinking about Stacy and DeeAnn. That meant they were going to have to live here, too, and she knew only too well how they felt about that. It was a no-win situation for them, no matter how one looked at it.

"Well," George said miserably, "I guess we're all going to have to take it one day at a time."

Anna nodded and got to her feet to begin clearing the table. "Guess so," she said.

Laurie jumped up. "Let me help you, Anna. That meal was delicious."

"Thanks, dear, but you go on with George. I got me some thinking to do."

Laurie understood. Sometimes well-meaning helpers only got in the way and required unwanted conversation, so she didn't protest. She followed George through the dining room, across the foyer and into the living room. It was a bright, hot day, and the house wasn't air-conditioned, but the room, with its ceiling fan and shuttered windows, felt pleasantly cool. Laurie thought about going up to check on the girls—it was awfully quiet up there—but George looked so patently miserable that she wanted to be with him. He sat on the sofa, shoulders slumped, the picture of worry. Laurie took a seat beside him.

"If you'll turn just a tad, I'll massage your shoulders," she said softly. "I'm awfully good at it."

He turned. "I'll bet. You're awfully good at a lot of things."

Her deft fingers began kneading the tense, hard muscles; her thumbs rotated at the nape of his neck. Gradually she felt him relax.

"Laurie, did it sound to you as though Ellen might be ready to come home if she wasn't so scared?"

"Yes."

"Well, if a mother got scared for her kids, wouldn't she stop thinking about herself?"

"Seems like it."

There was a minute of silence before George said, "I'm going to see Ellen tomorrow. I can't sit around here doing nothing."

"You have to be awfully careful about what you say to her."

"I know. I'll just talk to her about the girls, about what they've been doing and how cute they are. That kind of stuff. I won't mention Steve unless she brings him up." His head fell forward slightly. "Mmm, that feels great. You really are good at this."

Laurie continued her soothing ministrations until she felt him go almost limp. Then she slipped her arms around his middle and pressed her cheek against his back. She knew the inner turmoil he was going through. If Ellen came home, the problem of Steve would be solved, but it still meant the girls wouldn't be going back with them. She had been so proud of him, of the way he'd stepped in with Stacy and DeeAnn and made them his, but perhaps that hadn't been wise. Sometimes it seemed that nothing was wise where the heart was concerned.

George reluctantly stirred and shook himself out of his half stupor. "Ah, hell, I don't guess worrying ever accomplished a damned thing. I'll find out which room Anna wants you to take. We might as well unload the car and get settled in. Then let's gather up the girls and drive into town. The three of you can go shopping or get ice cream or something. There's an old friend I want to look up."

CHAPTER TWELVE

AFTER DROPPING LAURIE and the twins off at a shopping center, George drove to the police station. The man he wanted to see was Detective Tom Sargent, a friend from high school days. After the customary glad-handing and reminiscing, they walked down the street to a café for coffee, and George got right to the point. He told Tom the whole story, beginning with Steve's leaving his family last November and ending with Jonas's phone call on Monday night.

"Tom, I know you worked in Juvenile Division for a long time. Give it to me straight. What are my chances of keeping those girls?"

"Lousy."

"That's it?"

"I'm afraid so."

George's face flushed. "But why? Goddammit, Steve doesn't deserve them!"

"Maybe not, but he's their daddy." The policeman settled back in his chair and regarded George levelly. "Let me tell you a story. A few years ago a local fellow got himself killed in a hunting accident. He and his wife had a little boy who was about five or six. Well, the mama went to pieces and ended up getting hooked on tranquilizers. She went to every doctor in town and a few over in Duncan. I guess she had a prescription in every pharmacy in the county. She was a basket case. I wouldn't have left my cat with her for an hour. The little kid might as well have gotten his own apartment for all the supervision he had. So the mama's sister came for him and took him home. A year passed.

Then mama claimed she'd cleaned up her act and wanted the boy back. The aunt said no way, and they went to court. Three guesses who got the boy."

George sighed. "Mama."

"Right the first time. And the last I heard, the mama was back on pills, and the aunt had come to the boy's rescue again. Auntie may have herself a case this time, but I wouldn't swear to it. The thing is, the courts figure that any kid is better off with a natural parent, no matter how mediocre, than with a foster parent. I've seen it over and over again."

"I'm not a foster parent!" George exploded. "I'm their uncle, and I love them."

"Okay, pal, okay. And I know you, so I figure you're sincere. But that judge won't know you. He's gonna want to know what you do for a living, whether you're married or not, stuff like that. And when you tell him you're a single cowpoke... Well, it won't play good."

"What about Steve? He left his wife and kids and has been down in South America playing house with another woman for six months. How does that play?"

Tom smiled ruefully. "Sorry, friend, but the way I see it is, the only way Daddy doesn't get the kids is if their mama gets out of that hospital and takes over."

"You're telling me there's no chance I'll get to keep them until Ellen's okay?"

"Oh, I'd never say there's no chance... but that's sure the way I'd bet."

"Jesus, that's not right."

"Maybe not. But that's the way it is."

GEORGE WAS SULLEN and preoccupied during the drive back to the farm, and Laurie couldn't ask any questions because the girls were in the car. But when they parked at the side of the farmhouse, she opened the door and held her seat forward so Stacy and DeeAnn could get out. "You two run along. I want to talk to George a minute."

She waited until they were inside the house, then turned to George. "Whatever happened in town wasn't good."

He curved an arm around the steering wheel and shook his head, feeling older than he'd ever felt in his life. "I'm not going to get them, Laurie. I'm just not."

Laurie felt as though her heart was in a vise. "But you have to try!" she cried, alarmed over his defeatist attitude. "You have to go to that hearing and try."

"Oh, I will, I will. But the fellow I saw in town is a policeman who's done a lot of juvenile work. He didn't give me the slightest encouragement. Quite the opposite."

Laurie placed a sympathetic hand on his arm. "I'm going to that hearing, too, you know."

"Good."

"If they'll let me, I'll have my say."

George looked away and snorted. "They! They don't know any of us, but they are going to decide our fate."

"I guess . . . they do their best."

A long minute of silence passed before George said, "I don't know how I'm going to let go of those girls."

Laurie studied a fingernail. "I'm hurting, too. I love them, too." She badly wanted to add, *And I love you, too. If you would accept that and let me into your life, heart and soul, then this wouldn't be the end of the world. We'd have each other. We could have our own babies. Then I'd be the girls' aunt, and they could spend summers with us, and . . .*

But, of course, she'd never say that, not without some sign from him. She'd just put him on the spot, force him to say something noble or, worse, let her down as gently as possible. Regardless of what happened here, they were going to have to go back to the mountains together, although how long he stayed remained to be seen. She didn't want him feeling embarrassed or uncomfortable with her. She didn't want him running away.

George reached out and took her hand. It was a companionable gesture between two human beings who shared a problem. "I know," he said. "And the girls love you. I wish the judge and the social workers and the psychiatrists could see you with them, see the way they respond to you. Who makes up these rules, anyway? Who decides how something like this should be handled?"

Laurie smiled ruefully. "They."

"Yeah," he said, and his voice was bitter. "They."

Frustration permeated the cramped confines of the car. It was almost a tangible thing. Finally, as if on signal, they opened the doors and got out. But when they stepped up onto the porch, George stopped and turned to Laurie. "Something just occurred to me," he said with a thoughtful frown.

"What's that?"

"You've been with the girls every day for months. Have you ever heard them talk about their dad?"

Laurie thought about it. "No, I don't think so. They talk about Ellen sometimes, but their father...no, not that I can remember."

"I can't, either. Strange, isn't it? It's almost as though he doesn't exist for them."

"Maybe talking about him is too painful," Laurie suggested.

"Or maybe they don't care all that much that he's gone."

"You're reaching, George."

"You're probably right, but I've got to do something." His hand dropped to the small of her back, and he gently propelled her into the house. "Before I go to see Ellen in the morning I'm going to try to talk to Dr. Ames. Maybe she has some clout with that judge."

"MR. WHITTAKER, it's so nice to see you again," Frances Ames said. "Please have a seat."

Once again George took a seat in one of the wing chairs in front of the fireplace. He found it hard to believe it had been only a few months since he'd last been in the psychiatrist's office. In some ways it seemed like years. A lot had happened. For one thing, he wasn't even the same person he'd been on that first occasion. All that remained unchanged was his fear. He'd been afraid then, and he was afraid now, albeit for different reasons.

"I want to thank you for seeing me on such short notice, Doctor."

"I was delighted to hear from you. I'm anxious to find out how you and the girls are getting along."

"Pretty good. No, make that real good. I've gotten very attached to them. To be honest, that's the reason I'm here."

"Oh?"

"Their father's back from South America and wants them. Or rather, he doesn't want me to have them."

"Ah, yes, I seem to recall your telling me that you and your brother-in-law are not...er, close."

George had vowed he would be calm, cool and collected during the visit with Dr. Ames, but already he could feel the anxiety building within himself. He couldn't disguise the quiet desperation in his voice. "Stacy and DeeAnn are happy with me, Dr. Ames. We've become a family. Steve doesn't have any right to them."

"He's their father, Mr. Whittaker," the doctor said quietly.

God, if he heard that one more time he was going to smash something! "What kind of a father would run off and leave his family?"

"Making financial arrangements for the girls precluded his being charged with desertion. He's never physically abused the children or his wife. I'm afraid adultery isn't grounds for taking children away from parents." Dr. Ames settled back in her chair. "Tell me something about these past months, Mr. Whittaker. Have they been difficult for you?"

"If they were in the beginning, I've forgotten. Mostly they've been the best months of my life." As succinctly as possible he recounted the events of the past months. He hadn't planned to mention Laurie, but when Dr. Ames questioned him about the girls' care while he was at work, he was forced to. "Miss Tyler, our landlady, is great with them. She's a schoolteacher and has a knack for kids. Stacy and DeeAnn adore her."

Frances Ames had a soft spot in her heart for George Whittaker. Back in March she had been struck by his concern, and now she thought it remarkable that a free spirit like him could step in and take charge of two young girls. On top of it all, he obviously had grown attached to them. But the doctor didn't want him to get his hopes up. "Mr. Whittaker, do you understand how this will appear to the court? The girls' natural father versus a single uncle who is forced to leave them in the landlady's care much of the time."

"It's not like that!" he exclaimed, his face reddening. "We're all...very close—almost like a family. And the girls are happy. Doesn't that count?"

"I suppose I could suggest that the judge who hears the case—no doubt it will be Fred Benson—talk to the girls. But that sometimes is difficult for children. Let's not do that just yet." The doctor smiled at him. "We seem to have forgotten that the girls have a mother. Aren't you curious about Ellen's condition?"

George rubbed his eyes wearily. "Of course. I'm sorry. This business with the girls has me so upset I'm not thinking straight. I'm going to see Ellen when I leave here."

"She's responding wonderfully. I'm very pleased with her progress."

"But when can she come home?" George asked impatiently.

"She could go home now...if she would. She has to conquer her fear."

"I don't understand. What's she afraid of?"

"Life. Ellen married right after school. She's never held a job outside the home. She's a professional wife and mother, and she depended on her husband for everything, including her emotional stability. When she's ready to rejoin society, she's going to have to get a job. She's going to have to make the kind of decisions she's never had to make before. It's not easy to take on responsibility when you've never been given any. Ellen's aware of all these things. She's not just afraid; she's petrified. And that's compounded by what she considers her father's indifference to her problems."

Ah, me, George thought. *It's all too much for me. My mind can't handle all this heavy stuff. I just wish Laurie and the girls and I could pack up and go home.* He did not remember just when he had begun thinking of the four of them and home in the same breath, but the thought was now a natural one. It had grown gradually and taken hold.

But it wasn't going to be. The girls didn't belong to him, as everyone told him over and over. Hell, Laurie didn't belong to him, either. For all he knew, she was going to take that eighty-five grand and run. Maybe she was thinking about Hawaii and Australia and all those places. Certainly she deserved the time and money just to do what she wanted to do for a change.

Unconsciously he was trying to adjust to a life that didn't include her or the girls. It should have been easy, he kept reminding himself. He'd always been able to adjust, to say good-bye to the old and hello to the new. This time, however, not only was it not easy, it bordered on the impossible.

"Tell me, Doctor, what can I talk to Ellen about?"

"Why, anything you like."

"Is it all right to tell her about Steve?"

Dr. Ames frowned. "Let's not hit her over the head with that right off. I'd like for you to stress how much you and the girls want her to come home. Make her feel wanted and needed. Encouragement and support are what she needs now. Let her know she's loved. The wonders that can work would stagger you."

Thanking Dr. Ames for her time, George left and drove to the hospital where Ellen was staying. The modern brick complex reminded him more of an exclusive motel than anything, bright and cheerful, completely unclinical, and Ellen's room resembled a pleasant bedroom-sitting room combination.

His reunion with his sister was an emotional one. Ellen was pitifully glad to see him, hugging and kissing him and clinging to him as though she never wanted to let go. Her greeting was so touching that George felt his own eyes sting. He didn't know what he had expected, but she looked fairly healthy and happy... if he didn't look into her eyes long. They were eyes that had done too much crying. She was four years older than he was, but when they were growing up there were many who'd thought he was older since Ellen had always looked young for her age. She no longer did. And she was too thin. Holding her, he could feel her bones.

But, all in all, she was a pleasant surprise. Even now her beauty was startling in its vividness. All their lives people had told the brother and sister how much they favored each other, but George had never been able to see it. When he looked in the mirror, he saw an ordinary face, but Ellen's was captivating.

"Oh, George, it's so good to see you." Her grip on him was all but smothering, and her eyes misted over. "Please, come over here and just let me look at you."

"It's good to see you, too, hon. Real good."

Sitting beside him on the love seat in front of the window, Ellen took his face in her hands. "I love you. You always hated for me to say that to you."

"Well, I don't hate it now. I love you, too."

"I thought you might bring the girls."

"Not today. I had some other business to take care of."

"How are they?"

"Great. Wonderful."

"Do they ask about me?"

"Yes," George lied. "All the time." Stacy and DeeAnn seldom mentioned their mother anymore, but that didn't make him think they didn't miss her. It was more that he and Laurie had kept them busy enough to take their minds off their family problems. "We all want you to come home."

Ellen bit her lip and smiled a small smile. "Every morning when I wake up I tell myself that today is the day, but..."

"Let it be. Today or tomorrow. I'll come and get you, and I'll be there to lean on."

"Will you? For how long?"

That was a stickler. How long could he reasonably ask Laurie to stay? There wasn't a thing for her to do at the farm since Anna was possessive of her bailiwick and didn't kindly tolerate help in the kitchen. Laurie was going to get restless soon, and, frankly, so was he. "For as long as you need me," he said gently. "Please come home."

"Where's home? I'm not going back to that house."

"No, I don't think you need to be there. I was thinking of the farm."

Ellen grimaced. "And watch Dad disapprove of my every move?"

"He doesn't disapprove, hon. He doesn't understand. Dad thinks the entire world should be as uncomplicated as he is, and you and I know that isn't possible or even very desirable."

"Oh, George, I don't know. When I get out of here, I'm going to have to make a new life for myself and the girls, and I don't have the slightest idea where to begin. For sure I can't do it at the farm. I've got to get a job, but doing what I can't imagine. When I think about it, I feel ... I feel like a load of stones is pressing down on my chest. I've never done anything."

"How a woman who's raised two kids can say she's never done anything is beyond me. It's the hardest job in the world."

"You know what I mean. I've never done anything marketable."

"Just take it a step at a time," he said. "There's no requirement that you go out and conquer the world tomorrow. Focus on the girls. They're the greatest kids I can imagine. You can absolutely lose yourself in them. I've learned that first-hand."

Ellen cocked her head and studied him. "You've changed."

"In what way?"

"I don't know, but you've changed."

"Well, I guess you can thank parenthood for that."

Ellen's smile was warmer. "Oh, I'll bet the girls have had a grand time. You always were their hero. I suppose they've been spoiled rotten."

"No, rest your mind about that. I've had a good advisor." Then George told her about Laurie, taking care to make it sound as though they were nothing more than friends. He didn't think Ellen would want to hear anything about a romance—if indeed he and Laurie were engaged in a romance. He tended to think of it as one, but how she felt might be something else entirely.

Ellen, however, was finely tuned to her brother, and she sensed more to his story than he was telling her. "Do you realize that this is positively the first time you've ever told me so much about a woman—any woman? She must mean a lot to you."

"I don't know what I would have done without Laurie, especially in the beginning." George hoped she would let it go at that.

She didn't. "What's she like?"

Lord, how to describe Laurie? If he told Ellen his true thoughts about her, it would sound unbelievably corny. "Nice," he said inadequately. "You'll like her."

"I hope I get to meet her sometime."

"You will. All you have to do is come home."

Taking his hand, Ellen got to her feet. "Let's go to the dining room and get coffee. I want to hear everything about you and the girls and Texas and . . . just everything. I'm so glad to see you I could cry."

George stood, and to his astonishment, Ellen slipped her arms around his waist and rested her cheek against his chest. At that moment he felt sorrier for his sister than he'd ever felt for anyone in his life. She reminded him of Stacy or DeeAnn—small and vulnerable.

"Could you stay the afternoon, then have dinner with me? The food's not bad."

"Aw, hon, I'd like to, but it's not right to leave Laurie out at the farm to fend for herself."

Ellen sighed. "No, I suppose not."

"But we'll have coffee and a nice long visit."

He was anxious to get back to the farm and "rescue" Laurie from what surely was a heavy case of boredom by now, but Ellen needed him, and so he would stay until he absolutely had to go. His days of backing away from attachments were long gone.

CHAPTER THIRTEEN

LAURIE GLANCED at the clock for the dozenth time in two hours, wishing George would hurry and get back. The afternoon had seemed interminable, and the weekend promised to be a long one. The girls already were restless and asking when Uncle George would finish his business so they could go home. The question had torn at Laurie's heart. That they thought of the ranch in the mountains as home seemed the final unbearable straw. Over and over in her mind she'd tried to rehearse her goodbye to them, but nothing would form, and the exercise only depressed her. She supposed when the time came she would handle it the way she handled everything difficult that life had pitched at her—with stoic determination.

It was too hot to do anything outside, and there was nothing much to do inside. Anna was a nice woman but totally uncommunicative, not that Laurie thought they would have much to talk about even if she weren't. She went into the girls' bedroom and found them stretched out on their beds with a fan blowing on them. DeeAnn was reading, and Stacy had fallen asleep. DeeAnn looked up, smiled and returned to her book. For want of anything else to do, Laurie took a shower and shampooed her hair, then changed into a gauzy cotton sundress, the coolest thing she owned. That done, she went downstairs and rifled through a pile of magazines in the living room, looking for something to read.

Overcome by lethargy, she was half dozing when the doorbell rang. Rousing, she waited for Anna to answer it. But when it rang a second time she decided the woman must have gone outside, so she went to the front door. A tall, nice-looking, sandy-haired man dressed in tailored slacks and a polo shirt stood on the porch. He gave her a quizzical look, then said, "I'd like to see Stacy and DeeAnn, please."

Laurie tensed. She couldn't have explained why, but she suddenly felt threatened. "They...taking a nap."

"Well, wake them up. I'm their father."

"Oh. You're Steve."

"Yes. Who are you?"

"My name is Laurie Tyler. I'm a friend of George's."

His gaze became downright speculative. Too late Laurie decided it would have been better to tell him she was a friend of the family's. "I see. Well, Miss Tyler, I want to see my daughters."

"They...were very tired. I...hate to wake them."

The man fastened her with an icy stare that made her cringe inside. "Let me rephrase what I said. I'm here, and I intend to see my daughters. Where are Jonas and Anna?"

"I'm not sure. Around somewhere."

"And George?"

"Also around...somewhere," she lied.

"But none of them are in the house?"

"N-no."

"Good. I'm not the least interested in seeing the rest of the family, just my daughters."

Laurie didn't know what to do. The man's manner was brusque and insufferable. Perhaps he had expected to get an argument from whoever answered the door and had decided to go on the offense. He would have to know he wouldn't be welcome here. Every instinct Laurie possessed told her that letting Steve talk to the girls was not a wise thing, but how could she refuse to let a man see his children?

As it turned out, it was out of her hands. Steve rather rudely brushed past her and entered the house. "Well, I'll...go get them," she said.

"No need. I know where their room is." He headed straight for the stairway, leaving Laurie to wish with all her heart that George would walk through the door that instant. He was the one who should be handling this.

She didn't know how long Steve was upstairs, not more than twenty minutes, she guessed. During that time she went outside to look for either Jonas or Anna, thinking some member of the family should know Steve was there, but she found no one. So she returned to the house and waited.

Soon the girls' father stalked down the stairs and out of the house, tight-lipped, without a word. Laurie's heart was tripping like mad. She raced upstairs into the twins' room. The minute she walked through the door, two pairs of agitated eyes turned on her.

"Laurie, what's going on?" Stacy asked in a tremulous voice.

"Wh-what do you mean, honey?"

"Daddy was just here. He says... he says we're going to live with him... in South America." She began to cry, and the minute she did, DeeAnn did, too.

Laurie rushed across the room to sit between them on the bed and gather them close to her. "No, no, don't cry. Now you know that no one's going to let the two of you go to South America. Don't cry."

"Where's Uncle George?" Stacy asked.

"He went into town to see your mom, remember?"

"When he comes back, couldn't we all just get in the car and go back to the mountains?" This from DeeAnn.

Lord, don't I wish, Laurie thought but said nothing.

"Laurie, we're scared," Stacy said. "Uncle George has been acting funny ever since we got here. Something's going on, but you're probably not going to tell us what it is. Let's just go, okay? Please!"

"Honey, don't get upset. You and DeeAnn don't have a thing to worry about. George will take care of this, I'm sure of it." Laurie hoped her voice carried far more conviction than she felt.

"D-daddy asked questions about you, too, Laurie," DeeAnn said.

"M-me? What kind of questions, sweetheart?"

"Oh, who you are—stuff like that."

"What did you tell him?" Laurie was fighting to keep her voice low and casual.

Stacy took over at this point. "We said you own the house where we live. Then he wanted to know where you live, and we said you live there, too...only in a bigger house next to ours. Then he asked about you and Uncle George, if you were really good friends or what."

Oh, God, Laurie thought, *why did I feel compelled to tell him I was a friend of George's?* "I see. Anything else?"

Stacy thought about it. "Oh, I can't remember all of it. He asked if we'd ever seen Uncle George kiss you or anything like that. We said sure, but it was okay because you're such good friends." The girl noticed the look on Laurie's face and began to whimper. "Did we do something wrong?"

"No, darling, no. You can't do wrong when you tell the truth—you know that." Laurie felt sick inside. While it was true she had insisted on coming along on this mission to give George moral support, her motives hadn't been entirely altruistic. She'd been thinking of herself, too, of keeping him close, making sure he would have to return to the mountains. Maybe she should have stayed out of it altogether. If her presence here caused him any trouble, she'd never forgive herself.

She could have cheerfully killed their father. For months she and George had worked hard to keep things on an even keel during this difficult time in the girls' lives. Now their father had been with them less than half an hour, and they were truly upset for the first time since Laurie had known them. And how dare he question these girls about George's behavior!

Oh, where was that man? Depending on someone else to take care of something was new to her, but she really didn't feel she had the right to do...well, to do anything about

this. In her heart she might feel that the girls were partly
hers, but in her mind she knew better. "Come on, you two.
Anna baked some cookies earlier. Let's go snitch a few and
have some of that lemonade."

By the time George showed up sometime later, Laurie
had managed to get the girls settled down and their minds
on other things. She herself was a nervous wreck, though
no one would have known that by looking at her. When she
heard the front door open and close, she told the girls to
finish their cookies and lemonade, then she hurried to the
foyer to intercept him.

"I've got to talk to you," she said.

"What's wrong?"

She pulled him into the living room and spoke in a low
voice. "The girls' dad came to see them."

"Steve? Here?" He set his mouth in a tight line. "Did he
see them?"

"Yes."

"Dammit, why did you even let him in?"

Laurie was taken aback by his sharp tone. "Be reasonable. What could I do?"

"I'm sorry. I feel like a time bomb about to go off. What
did he want?"

"He told them they were coming to live with him... in
South America."

George's eyes widened. "The hell they are!"

"He got them so upset they both were crying. They're
scared. I don't blame them. I'm scared, too. He couldn't do
that, could he, George? Take them to South America?"

"No! At least...I don't think so." He heard voices in his
head, and they all were saying the same thing: *But he's their
father, he's their father....*

"Unfortunately there's more bad news. Steve questioned them about us."

"You and me?"

She nodded. "My fault. I made the mistake of telling him
I was a friend of yours. I guess he's clutching, too. I'm

sorry. Also unfortunately, the girls told him they'd seen us kissing...."

George gave her a quick hug. "Don't be sorry. Don't give it another thought. Is either one of us cheating on a spouse, huh? Has either one of us run out on a family?" He pulled on his chin. "So Steve's going back to South America. He must have come back here to get a divorce."

"That won't do Ellen any good if she's still crazy about the guy."

"Listen, Laurie, Ellen seems fine to me. We had a great visit. I even had her laughing before I left. If only I can convince her to come home. If I can break through that wall of fear and confusion. That's all I need to do. Get her home and the problem with the girls is solved."

Laurie fell silent and stared down at her hands. When she looked up, her eyes were teary, and her chin trembled. "Will it? They'll still be here ... not there. They must have asked me a half a dozen times when you were going to finish your business so they could go home."

George expelled his breath. "At least they'll be with Ellen, and Steve won't have a leg to stand on."

Laurie nodded. "And if they're with Ellen you'll be able to see them all you want ... for the rest of your life. And you're so good for them. Girls need heroes—dashing masculine figures. They love you so much."

"Not any more than they love you."

"But you're their uncle. I'm only—"

"The best friend they've ever had. I don't wonder why Jill and Andy turned out so well, not with you steering the ship."

Laurie managed a small smile. "This sounds like a meeting of the Mutual Admiration Society."

"Doesn't it, though?" He slipped his arm around her shoulders and began walking toward the kitchen. "We're not going to be able to do a damned thing until that hearing Monday, so why don't we put our heads together and come up with some ways to keep the girls entertained this weekend. We all need to get our minds off this mess for a couple of days.''

''Sounds great. Got any ideas?''

''We don't have to do anything elaborate. Make home-made ice cream, cook hot dogs over a campfire, maybe take them into town to a movie or to play miniature golf—any-thing. I just don't want them thinking about this stuff. God knows, we'll all have to think about it soon enough.''

AFTER SUPPER, which was always served early, the four of them drove into town for ice cream. When they returned to the farm, they sat on the front porch steps and watched the sun go down. Darkness fell very quickly in the mountains, but here on the level plains, sunset was a spectacular show that seemed to go on and on. The house faced west, so the view was fantastic, with a practically unbroken 180-degree horizon. Mesmerized, Laurie watched the last golden glow fade from sight, then said, ''Lord, I feel like applauding.''

''So do I,'' George agreed. ''Now it'll start to cool off.''

Stacy's head was in his lap; he stroked her hair. DeeAnn was fastened to Laurie's left hip, a place the girl seemed to stay more and more. Laurie's gentle nature appealed to the quiet twin. George shifted slightly, and his thigh settled against Laurie's. Her hand went to his knee. He just wished he had a picture of the four of them like this to show to whoever the ''authorities'' turned out to be. Then he'd ask the ''powers that be'' if they honestly thought the girls would be better off in South America with a father they hadn't seen in eight months and an unknown woman.

''Hey, you two,'' Laurie finally said, ''don't you want to take a bath and call it a day?''

''Guess so,'' DeeAnn said sleepily. ''I feel all sweaty and yukky.''

''You go first, Dee,'' Stacy said, stifling a yawn. ''I'll be up in a minute.''

DeeAnn nodded and stood up, then bent to give both Laurie and George a hug. Once she was inside the house, Stacy rolled her head over so she could look up at her uncle. "Uncle George, if Daddy tries to take us to South America, Dee and I've decided we're going to run away."

Laurie sucked in her breath, and she and George exchanged a startled glance. He frowned, looking down at his niece. It bothered him enormously that they were worried enough to discuss that in private. "Is that a fact? Where're you planning on running to?"

"Back to the mountains."

"I see. Have you given any thought to how you'll get there?"

Stacy nodded seriously. "On a bus."

"Oh? A bus, huh? You can't ride those things for free. Did you come into some money I don't know about?"

"Grandpa would have to give us some, I guess."

George smiled at her fondly. "Well, I reckon we can save your grandpa some money, because there's no way I'm going to let you go to South America."

Stacy grew thoughtful. "Suppose someone says we have to go?"

"Someone? Like who?"

"I don't know. Whoever does that kind of thing. The police or somebody like that."

"Hmm. Well, in that case...I guess Laurie and I would have to go to South America, too."

Laurie's heart missed a beat. "Laurie and I," he'd said. "Laurie and I would have to go." Of course, it was only a story designed to make the girls feel better. Still, it pleased her enormously to hear him say "Laurie and I."

Stacy's eyes widened, and she bolted to a sitting position. "Really? Would you?"

"I don't see how we could let you and DeeAnn go and us stay behind."

"Oh, boy! I gotta tell Dee." Giving George a hug, then Laurie, she raced into the house.

Laurie expelled her breath. "I hope you didn't paint yourself into a corner," she said.

"So do I. I just don't want them thinking about this garbage all weekend."

"You were pretty convincing. You almost had me be-
lieving that story for a minute." She rubbed at her nape,
which was very damp. "I didn't ask about Ellen earlier, and
I meant to. You say she seems all right?"

"To me, yes. But she's afraid. She said she feels like a
load of stones is weighing on her chest."

"How awful."

"To tell you the truth, when I think about the girls I feel
something like that myself."

"I know," Laurie said with a sigh.

George moved his hand behind her to rest his weight on
his palm, and Laurie settled her head in the comfortable
curve of his shoulder. They both sat in silence and stared
into the twilight. An evening breeze came up, bringing a
moment of blessed coolness. A nearby honeysuckle vine
perfumed the air, and the night air was alive with the
sounds of insects. Laurie certainly wasn't anxious to go inside and try to sleep in the airless little bedroom. It was too
nice here, and she was drawing comfort from George's so-
lidity and watching the night come. It was the first time
they'd had a few minutes alone. She closed her eyes, rel-
ishing the moment. At a time like this, with a little effort,
she could believe that their troubles were far away.

George nuzzled her hair. It had a freshly shampooed
smell that filled his nostrils. It wasn't easy to smell fresh
and clean in this godawful heat, but Laurie did. He hadn't
been able to take his eyes off her during supper. She had
looked sweet and pretty and thoroughly embraceable. He'd
never wanted to make love to her so badly. Thinking about
that now brought the feeling back.

Laurie stirred just then. "I'm going to check on the
girls."

"I'll wait here."

She was back in a few minutes. "They're about to settle
down for the night. I guess that fish story you concocted
helped. They seemed convinced that you're going to rescue them from a fate worse than death. They'll be asleep in
a few minutes."

There was no need to ask if Jonas and Anna were down for the night. Except in winter, their days were ordered by the sun. When it came up, they got up; when it went down, their heads hit the pillow.

Before Laurie could sit down, George stood up. For a minute she was afraid he was going to call it a day, too. Instead he said, "Let's go for a drive."

"A drive?"

He grinned. "It's taken some doing, but I finally thought of a way for us to be alone."

"I do appreciate a resourceful man."

"Wait here. I'll be right back."

The keys to Jonas's ancient pickup always hung from a peg on the kitchen wall. George grabbed them, then went out onto the screened-in porch that was used more as a storeroom than anything else. Rummaging through the incredible mishmash of things piled there, he found what he was looking for—two bedrolls. Gathering them up, one under each arm, he went out back and tossed them in the bed of the truck. Then he went to get Laurie.

"We'll go down to the pond," he told her. "When I was a kid it always seemed ten degrees cooler down there. The road, if you can call it that, is miserable, but Dad's old pickup makes it just fine."

The truck was nothing short of a relic, and it had not led a pampered life, but it was kept in good running order. The engine roared to life the second George turned the key in the ignition, and the vehicle rumbled off down a rutty road that sliced through the cotton fields.

The pond was like a mini-oasis in the middle of the flat landscape. It nourished the few really grand trees that grew on the farm. With a constant supply of moisture, a stand of giant cottonwoods flourished. George stopped the truck near one and switched off the engine. The open windows drew the prevailing south wind.

Laurie realized he had been right; it did seem much cooler here. And the world was so quiet it was almost eerie. The house stood in the far, far distance, its few burning lights looking like tiny fireflies twinkling in the black night. She settled back, folded her arms and looked at George, who was smiling at her. She smiled, and a tiny laugh escaped her lips.

He cocked his head. "What's so funny?"

"I was thinking about the last time we sat together in a parked vehicle."

"Ah. I was so damned excited that night I thought I was going to choke." He moved closer to her. "But I didn't know the half of it, did I? Not then. A lot has happened since then."

"Yes. Some of it very nice."

He quickly closed the small space between them and gathered her to him for a lingering kiss. "I hope that's the nice part."

"You know it is." She sighed, burying her head on his shoulder. "It's so peaceful out here. We could be the only two people on the face of the earth."

"There have been plenty of times when I've wished to heaven we were."

Her arms went around his waist and she clung to him. Resting her head on the back of the seat, she accepted the kisses he lavished upon her, kissing him back hungrily. His petting, restless hands were all over her, eliciting wonderfully warm, entrancing sensations. Finally one came to rest at the row of buttons on the bodice of her sundress. He undid the top four and slipped his hand inside. She wasn't wearing a bra, and her response was instantaneous. Moaning against his mouth, she took his head in her hands and urged it downward. The moment his lips closed over the puckered nipple she shuddered.

The knowledge that he could make Laurie tremble with desire filled George with a kind of excitement he wouldn't have imagined existed. He had been amazed to discover what a sensitive, sexy woman lurked under that poised exterior. She didn't just make love with her body but with her soul and mind, as well. Now, with his hand covering one breast and his mouth avidly drinking from the other, he could hear her kittenish whispers, feel her straining against him. His free hand moved to the bottom of her dress, and slipped under and up it. Her legs were smooth and bare. She wore only flimsy panties, not surprising in this heat. He stroked her, and her responding moan was soft and yearning. He lifted his head and stared into those lovely eyes, now glazed and dark with desire.

"Please..." she whispered. She looked as though she wanted to cry.

"It won't be comfortable for you in here,"

"I don't care."

"I do." Reaching across her, he opened the door. "Get out."

Laurie wasn't sure she could walk, but somehow she managed to get out of the truck. George jumped down beside her, and together they walked around to the rear, kissing all the while. Reluctantly releasing her, he lowered the tailgate, then effortlessly lifted her up onto it. He joined her and with a quick motion he unrolled the two sleeping bags, laying them one on top of the other in the truck's bed, before guiding her down onto them.

Laurie smiled up at him. "You are resourceful."

"Desperate is the word. And very hungry. I need you, Laurie. I never dreamed I could need a woman so much."

"Oh, George, I need you, too. And it's a new sensation for me, too."

He sank to his knees and simply stared at her a minute. Then his eyes fell to the open bodice. His hand slipped inside to fondle a breast, and its nipple hardened immediately. "They're very sensitive."

"Apparently. I...never knew that before, either. There's so much I never knew."

Slowly he stretched out beside her. One arm slipped under her neck while the other continued to cup and fondle her. After kissing her mouth soundly, he let his lips replace his hand. Laurie moaned softly, straining her hips toward him. Again his hand found the hem of her dress. This time he pushed the garment to mid-thigh, then hooked his fin-

gers over the top of her panties. Laurie wriggled to facili-
tate their removal. She reached for his belt buckle. When
that had been dispensed with, she unsnapped and unzipped his jeans, and slipped her hands inside, closing her
fingers around him. He trembled violently.

"I wish," he whispered in her ear, "we had a bed. I wish
I could strip you. I wish I could make it last all night."

"When two people want to make love, a bed isn't necessary," she said. "Another revelation."

He moved over her. She pushed his jeans down low on
his hips, taking his undershorts with them. "Will that be
uncomfortable for you?" she asked.

"No, no," he said huskily.

She unbuttoned several buttons of his shirt and teased his
flat nipples with her fingertips. Then she lifted her head
slightly and touched each one with a darting movement of
her tongue. "You could feel more of me than I could of
you, and that wasn't fair."

George was on fire. Never had he experienced feelings
even remotely like the ones Laurie inspired in him, and he
figured her actions were instinctive. She was not a woman
with a lot of experience with men, yet she could melt his
insides. When he entered her, he was afraid his explosion
was too near.

She wrapped her legs around him, binding him with loving ropes. With his first thrust, passion shot through Laurie as though it had been injected. She pushed against him,
writhing and straining, unable to get close enough even
though their bodies seemed welded together. When she was
poised on the brink of climax, she gasped loudly, her face
contorted, and she bit her lip.

Above her, beads of perspiration had broken out on
George's forehead. "No, honey, no, don't hold back.
Please don't. You can scream if you feel like it. No one can
hear you."

She didn't scream, but his name escaped on a high,
arching cry. The moment he felt the walls of her body con-

tract, he gave himself up to his own release. It seemed to go on and on.

When Laurie's breathing became normal again, she opened her eyes and saw George's face looming over hers. "Oooh, that was wonderful," she breathed.

"You're going to start thinking I'm the most impatient man on earth."

"No, really... it was... wonderful."

He loved the way she looked now—tousled and disheveled, fresh from uninhibited sex, a sensuous aura surrounding her like a halo. He didn't know why he couldn't just open his mouth and say the words he felt. *I need you, Laurie. I need your taut, warm body, I need your soul and your sweetness, I need your class and your encouragement. I just need you.* In fact, he was beginning to think he couldn't exist without her.

So why didn't he tell her that? Most men his age had uttered those words, or similar ones, dozens of times to women they no longer remembered. Why couldn't he? What did he fear? Settling down? Laurie's possible rejection? The differences between them? When he got right down to it, the twins were the only thing they had in common, and he was dangerously close to losing them.

And, too, Laurie needed to make up for all those years that should have been carefree and weren't. How well he remembered the wistful quality in her voice that night of Jill's wedding when she'd said, "I've never done anything or gone anywhere." Hell, he'd probably never have the wherewithal for travel and excitement, and she'd realize that if she gave it two seconds' thought. He didn't have a thing to offer her except needs and desire and white-hot passion. What they had together was the most beautiful thing that had ever happened to him, but he didn't know if that was a good basis for marriage. He didn't have the faintest idea how to care for a woman the way Laurie deserved to be cared for, and it frightened him to think the day might come when she would regret casting her lot with him.

Then, for some unknown reason, he thought of Shot and Joanie. A casual observer of that domestic scene would immediately conclude that theirs was a marriage made anywhere but in heaven. Yet, not only had it survived, but Shot—coarse, crude Shot—had admitted that the thought of having to do without Joanie scared him to death. Once George had felt sorry for Shot, married to that shrew; now he envied him. How wonderful it must be, he reflected, to go through life with someone you didn't think you could live without.

All those thoughts churned inside George's head and had the effect of confusing him even further.

Laurie reached up to stroke his face. "What are you thinking?"

"How pretty you are." She had pushed her dress down, which was a shame. He loved looking at her legs. But the bodice was still open, and he loved looking at her breasts, too. He touched one, and she smiled through her lazy languor.

"Careful. You know how I am. A little more of that and I might go on the attack again."

"I promise not to scream or anything," George said.

He smiled and she smiled. Then her face sobered somewhat. "George?"

"Hmm."

"Hold me."

"Gladly."

He lay down beside her, gathering her into his arms as he did, and it never crossed either of their minds that there were dozens of more comfortable places to lie than the back of a pickup. Laurie wanted to expire from happiness. She lay in his arms, blissful and sated, watching the stars. Her gaze fixed on a distant one. "Venus," she murmured.

"And the moon must be in the seventh house or something," George said. "I feel like the whole world's changed."

"Maybe it has."

They kissed once, then twice, sweetly, tenderly. At some point the kissing grew more sensuous, and then they began petting and fondling one another again until they were ready for more lovemaking. This time it was less frantic, slower and sweeter. The foreplay was prolonged, and Laurie's anticipation was heightened.

"I'm not going to be impatient this time," George said thickly. "We've got hours if we want them."

To her delight and astonishment, he then began uttering unbelievably sexy, erotic phrases to her. He told her how he felt when he was inside her. He told her how he felt when she climaxed. She wouldn't have imagined he would ever say such things, and George himself had no idea where the words had come from. He had to believe they were inspired. The spell his words wove was intoxicating. He brought her to the zenith of passion, until she begged him to enter her.

It was their time. They were the only two people on earth, and not once would either allow the thought to form that everything could change drastically on Monday. There was no tomorrow, only now.

CHAPTER FOURTEEN

LAURIE AND GEORGE ran themselves ragged that weekend, trying to keep the girls busy, and themselves, too—anything to keep their minds off the upcoming hearing. They were trying hard not to speculate on what could happen, while constantly rehearsing what they planned to say. The twins, aware of certain undercurrents but blissfully confident that Uncle George would take care of everything, simply enjoyed the attention and activity.

The hearing was scheduled for ten o'clock Monday morning. Laurie couldn't remember ever being so nervous, even though she reminded herself over and over that it was only an informal preliminary hearing, that nothing would be determined that morning. Still, in her mind, nothing involving a judge and a courthouse could be considered completely "informal." The waiting was terrible, and she was almost relieved when she and George were in her car driving to town.

Several times during the trip she glanced at him surreptitiously. His agitated state was apparent, and he'd been totally uncommunicative all morning. He had picked at breakfast, which he normally ate with gusto, and had wandered through the house, looking for all the world like a man with the weight of the world on his shoulders. She was sure he hadn't slept, at least not much. Neither had she. This business had to be resolved soon, or they would both be mental wrecks and of no use to anyone.

Laurie was pleased to discover the hearing wouldn't be held in a courtroom, but in the judge's private chamber. They were seated in leather chairs arranged in a semicircle in front of the judge's desk. Steve and another woman, whom Laurie correctly guessed was his lover, were seated at the far end. The woman could not possibly have been over twenty-five, Laurie surmised, and her expression clearly revealed that she would have preferred being anywhere but in that chamber. Seated between the two brothers-in-law were a Mrs. Prescott from Child Welfare and a grandmotherly woman whom George introduced as Dr. Ames, Ellen's psychiatrist. To George's everlasting gratitude, the doctor had driven from Oklahoma City to be at the hearing.

Judge Fred Benson opened the proceedings by explaining that the hearing was designed to determine the best interests of the girls in question. He wanted to give all interested parties a chance to present his or her case, and he wanted everyone present to feel free to express an opinion. Then he asked Mrs. Prescott to briefly explain the case to him, which she did in a crisp, businesslike manner. It all boiled down to one sentence: Ellen Greene's brother was disputing her estranged husband's right to have custody of the couple's two daughters.

The judge digested that, thanked Mrs. Prescott, then turned to George and gave him the floor, telling him to take all the time he needed. Laurie's heart was in her throat, and her stomach was somewhere down around her knees, so she could imagine the turmoil churning inside him. He looked so tired and miserable and frightened, but when he spoke, his voice was amazingly strong and controlled.

"Your Honor, last November, when my brother-in-law left his family, my sister, understandably, was quite upset. No...I'm sorry...not upset. She went to pieces. I didn't think that was too unusual, given the circumstances, so maybe I wasn't as concerned as I should have been. I just thought she had a case of the blues, and so did my dad. We assumed she'd get over it in time, just as soon as she realized what a rat she'd married."

The judge raised a hand. "Please, Mr. Whittaker, no editorializing."

"Sorry. The temptation was too great. So...that was just before Christmas. We got through the holidays as best we could for the girls' sakes—" he paused to shoot Steve a scathing look "—and maybe we were too busy to give Ellen the attention she needed. But one day it occurred to me that not only wasn't she getting better, her blue mood had turned black. Now, my father and I aren't too sophisticated about things like that, but I insisted she go see our family doctor. He gave her some tranquilizers, which seemed to help until...until the day she polished off half a bottle of them. That's when she was diagnosed as being severely depressed."

He paused to take a breath. Laurie briefly placed an encouraging hand on his arm. She thought he was doing marvelously well. He started speaking again. "I met Dr. Ames about then, and she said that Ellen was being hospitalized. She also told me that the twins needed a stable environment. There was the farm, of course, but the girls don't much like it there, and my dad's in his seventies and just can't handle large doses of young children. That's when I decided they should be with me. I'd been working on a ranch down in southwestern Texas, so I decided to go back. It's worked out great. The girls are happy, and they live a good life. We're renting a house where they have people around and plenty of room to run and play. They've made friends. Their grades are above average. I love them very much, and they love me. We're like a family. Of course when Ellen's well...and according to Dr. Ames that could be any day now...they'll live with her, but in the meantime—" George's voice rose slightly "—why should I let them go off to South America with their father, a man who ran out on them, when they live such a happy life where they are? I promise you, Your Honor, if you were to ask Stacy and DeeAnn where they wanted to go, they'd tell you they want to stay with me. In fact, they've threatened to run away if they have to go to South America. I don't think they'd actually do it, but they've mentioned it, so that ought to tell somebody something."

The judge's face was completely impassive. He folded his hands in front of him and nodded to George. "Thank you, Mr. Whittaker. Now, Mr. Green, if you have something to say, this is the time to say it."

Steve cleared his throat. "Thank you, Your Honor. You bet I have something to say. My brother-in-law painted a very rosy picture of domestic bliss, but he seems to have forgotten that I've known him for fifteen years. During that time he's never held a job for more than a few years, never taken on responsibility for anything or anybody but himself. He's never been married, had a home, or owned a car. For all I know, he's never had a woman—"

"Mr. Greene," Judge Benson interrupted, "I'll repeat my warning about editorializing."

"Sorry. The point is, he's a cowboy, a drifter, a vagabond. He shows up every once in a while, mainly for life's major events, then just rides off into the sunset. Now, human nature doesn't change. I would like to remind everyone here that Mr. Whittaker has only been in charge of the girls for five months. What will happen when the urge to roam comes over him again? And it will. Oh, it will. Once a saddle bum, always a saddle bum. My wife always had some rather romantic notions about her brother, as though his way of life was admirable, but I don't see it that way. I absolutely refuse to allow my daughters to be in his care, and I have that right because I'm their father."

"Seems to me you waived your rights when you ran out on them last November," George said angrily.

"Mr. Whittaker, I don't want to have to remind you again," the judge said sternly. He returned his attention to Steve. "Yes, that is something that must be taken into consideration, Mr. Greene. You did leave your family and have made no attempt to contact them in almost nine months."

Steve shifted uncomfortably, and the woman beside him just looked embarrassed. "How did I know Ellen was going to go off her rocker? People divorce every day, and everything remains normal. But, no, my wife has to turn it into an emotional crisis. I didn't contact them because I wanted to give her time to settle down before trying to discuss divorce.''

It had been a long time since George had wanted to punch someone in the nose, but at that moment, if they had been anywhere but in a judge's chamber, he thought he would have done just that.

Judge Benson addressed Dr. Ames. ''How is Mrs. Greene, doctor?''

Dr. Ames told him essentially what she had told George. The judge listened thoughtfully, then asked, ''What are the chances of a recurrence of this mental illness? I confess to knowing very little about depression.''

''While it's true that some people fall victim to depression many times in their lives, others have only one bout with it,'' Dr. Ames said. ''This seems to be particularly true when the depression is triggered by a specific event, such as a death in the family or, in Mrs. Greene's case, a divorce. I'm certainly not going to sit here and tell you she'll never have another depression, but I don't anticipate one. And, Your Honor, I'd like to add a personal word, if I may.''

''Of course.''

''When I met Mr. Whittaker in March, I was impressed by his concern, not just for his sister but for the welfare of the girls, as well. I think his willingness to completely change his way of life for them is commendable. And, of course, he did what so many people fail to do—he made sure his sister got proper treatment.''

Laurie had been struck by one thing while the twins' father had been talking: not once had he mentioned fervently wanting his daughters. In fact, the girls' welfare seemed the last thing on his mind. George had been right; Steve didn't want Stacy and DeeAnn as much as he didn't want George to have them. The animosity between the two men was thick enough to cut. She thought of some of Steve's remarks, and it occurred to her that the man might just have been jealous of Ellen's love for her brother. Possibly he had envied George his freedom from responsibility. She supposed anything was possible. And she couldn't remain silent any longer. She made a motion with her hand that caught the judge's eye. "Your Honor, may I ask something?

"Of course."

Using her best schoolteacher's voice, which could be riveting when she put her heart into it, Laurie said, "I want you and everyone else here to know that the picture Mr. Greene painted of Mr. Whittaker simply isn't a true one. I've watched him with those girls. No one could have been better with them than he's been, and they adore him. I've had the chance to observe them every day for the last few months. If you could see him with them, you'd know he's not only a suitable guardian, he's a superb one. I'm a schoolteacher, and I can spot behavioral and emotional problems a mile away. The girls simply don't have any, and considering that their family life has been destroyed, it would be understandable if they did. That cannot be an accident. One of the twins, DeeAnn, likes to write stories, and the ones she wrote when she first came to the mountains were heartbreaking, all about a little girl who was devastated over the breakup of her family. I wish you could read the happy stories she writes now. I honestly think Mr. Whittaker is responsible for that. Furthermore, to characterize him as a drifter or 'saddle bum' is grossly unfair. He's worked for my best friend almost five years now, and she swears by him. I doubt that he's more mobile than, say, a military man or a junior executive or...a geologist. And I certainly can't imagine a man like George ever leaving his family." She shot Steve a contemptuous look before sitting down.

Steve spoke up again. "Your Honor, I think we should establish just who this woman is. From what I've been able to gather, she owns the house my brother-in-law rents, the house where my daughters have to live. It's on this woman's property. She and Mr. Whittaker are—again, this is from my daughters—'good friends.' They, er, kiss each other. Furthermore, when he's at work, my daughters have to stay with this woman. Now, I'd like to know who she is."

With all eyes turned on her, Laurie felt her face color. "I'm . . . Mr. Whittaker's fiancée," she said. She wouldn't look at George since she didn't particularly want to see his reaction to learning he was engaged. "We're going to be married . . . soon. We'll live on a ranch down in the Davis Mountains. It's a . . . beautiful place." *Oh, God, please don't let any of these people go down there and look at that pitiful patch of land.* "Stacy and DeeAnn just love it."

"Your Honor, this is ridiculous!" Steve exclaimed. "My daughters are in the hands of a saddle bum and a stranger who are 'good friends.'"

"Listen, I've never run out on a family!" George all but yelled. "Spare me your moral gymnastics."

"I respectfully request that my daughters be placed in my custody," Steve said.

"And I respectfully request they remain with me until their mother can take care of them," George retorted. "She's the one who should have them."

"I'm not too sure of that," Steve said. "My wife is obviously emotionally unstable."

George leaned forward and spoke earnestly. "Your Honor, if this hearing really is to determine the girls' best interests, then I submit to you that taking Stacy and DeeAnn away from me at this point would not be in their best interest. It would be a crime to allow those two girls to go to South America to live with a father who left them and a woman they don't even know. While we're at it, Steve felt free to question Miss Tyler, so I'd like to ask—" he glanced at the unknown woman seated next to Steve "—I'm sorry, ma'am, I didn't catch your name."

"Cynthia Black," she said in a small voice.

"Miss Black, I assume you're returning to South America with Steve," George said.

"Y-yes."

"You're a very young woman. How do you feel about taking on the responsibility of two twelve-year-old girls?"

The woman glanced uncertainly at Steve. "Well, yes . . . sure, if that's what Steve wants."

George wanted to yell or hit something. That woman no more wanted those girls than Steve did. His shoulders slumped, and when he spoke he sounded weary and defeated. "Stacy and DeeAnn don't want to go to South America."

"Kids hate change," Steve said. "But they adapt."

"A stay in a foreign country can be very broadening for twelve-year-olds, Mr. Whittaker," the judge said. "I don't think where Mr. Greene chooses to take them will have any bearing on the case. I believe I've heard all I need to hear. I'll take this matter under advisement and discuss the pros and cons with Mrs. Prescott. You'll both be hearing from me soon. As I understand it, the children are presently staying at their grandfather's farm. Is that correct?"

"Yes," Steve said, "and I'd like to protest that."

"Mr. Greene, I think we'll leave that arrangement as is for the time being. Good day."

And just like that it was over. George had never felt so powerless. There were scuffling sounds as everyone stood, then he realized that Laurie's hand was on his arm, and she was urging him out of the chair. Heaving a sigh, he stood and took her by the hand, and together they walked out into the hall. Dr. Ames was standing there, waiting for a word with George.

"Doctor, I can't tell you how much I appreciate your coming," he told her, taking her hand.

"I wish I could have been more help."

"Tell me something, and please be honest. What are my chances?"

Dr. Ames smiled sadly. "I wish I knew. I only know what I would do if it were up to me."

"What's that?"

"Why, I'd give them to you, of course. I don't think Mr. Greene shows enough compassion. As someone who works with mental illness every day, phrases like 'off her rocker' just—if you'll pardon the expression—irritate the hell out of me. Please stay in touch. Goodbye.''

"Goodbye, Dr. Ames."

The psychiatrist turned to go, but stopped. "Oh, by the way, congratulations." Her smile was for Laurie, too.

"What?"

"Congratulations on your upcoming marriage. I hope the two of you will be very happy."

"Oh, er, yes, thanks."

When the doctor was out of sight, Laurie looked at George sheepishly. "I'm sorry about that. I really didn't know I was going to say it until it was out. But your single status didn't seem to be helping anything, and it occurred to me that if the judge thought you were about to get married...."

"Well, I'll admit I was a little surprised to find out I was engaged, but... Oh, get that naughty girl look off your face. I knew why you did it, and I appreciate it."

"I wonder if I perjured myself."

"You weren't under oath."

He took her arm and they left the building. It was a blistering hot day, and the blast of heat that greeted them was a shock after the coolness of the courthouse. "Want to have lunch somewhere?" he asked.

"I guess so."

"The café near the police station has pretty good food. At least, it used to."

"That's fine. Anything."

"Isn't it odd?" Laurie said when they were seated and had ordered. "I feel guilty when we go somewhere and don't include Stacy and DeeAnn. I know how bored they get out there on the farm."

"Yeah. Poor things." George studied the glass of water in front of him. "I'm not going to get them, Laurie. I can feel it in my bones. We're going to have to leave them behind."

"I'm afraid you might be right," she said, feeling hot tears form in her eyes. She envisioned life back home without the girls. George wouldn't want to stay at the house. The sensible thing for him to do would be move into the DO's bunkhouse. That meant they wouldn't see very much of each other, not unless he made the effort. And without the girls as a link, who could predict what he would do? There had been no avowals of undying devotion on his part. As badly as she hated to admit it, Steve Greene might have been right. George had "settled down" for only five months. Could he honestly say that wanderlust wouldn't overtake him again? Maybe human nature didn't change after all, at least not that much.

So that left her with some decisions to make. Should she stay or sell? And who was she to sell to? Where would she go? She had conveniently avoided making all those decisions the last few months. She wouldn't be able to procrastinate much longer.

George was deep in thought. "I've got to concentrate on keeping them from Steve."

"George, it's out of your hands."

"I know. And it's in Ellen's hands. She's got to come home."

"I think that's out of your hands, too. The judge will decide the girls' fate, and the doctors will decide Ellen's, and there's nothing you and I can do about any of it."

"No, there's got to be." His voice shook. "Ellen's got to know about all this. When she does, I'm confident she'll come home."

Laurie looked at him warily. "You're not considering talking to her without Dr. Ames' permission? Tell me you're not."

"Oh, I'll call the good doctor this afternoon and tell her what I want to do. I don't think Dr. Ames is any crazier about Steve than I am. The man has the personality of a mongoose."

"What if she tells you to butt out?" Laurie wanted to know.

There was a pause while George stared at the food on his plate. "I'm going to do it, anyway."

Laurie set down her fork and put a hand to her forehead. "Then suppose you tell me just what you plan to do."

"Tomorrow, you and Stacy and DeeAnn and I are going to pay Ellen a nice long visit. I want her to see the girls. They'll touch her, I know they will. And once they've cozied up to her, I want you to take them down to the cafeteria for a drink or something. Then I'm going to tell Ellen that Steve wants to take them with him to South America. If that doesn't bring her to her senses, nothing will. I'm banking on that lioness-and-her-cubs instinct, with just a little help from a less admirable instinct. Dr. Ames said once that Ellen has accepted the fact that Steve is gone. Translation: he cheated on her. I'm hoping she's had enough time and enough therapy to just be good and mad."

"Oh, George," Laurie breathed, "I have the worst feeling we're playing with fire, tampering with something neither one of us knows a damned thing about."

"Maybe. But I have to do it, Laurie. I just have to."

Laurie toyed with her food, then looked at him and smiled. "'Then I'm behind you one-hundred percent. You just tell me what you want me to do."

All of a sudden he grew pensive. His eyes got a faraway look in them. "I can't do that, because what I want you to do is put them in the car and take them back to the place they call home. You warned me about this, that first day—warned me about getting too attached to them. I was so sure I wouldn't, but...here I am, feeling like a little boy lost at the county fair."

Laurie reached across the table to cover one of his hands with one of hers. "You look like one, too. No, more like a basset hound. It's crossed my mind that you, George Whittaker, have been living a lie all these years."

"Oh?"

"You're not the free spirit you make yourself out to be. You're actually a card-carrying member of that limited species known as natural hearth-huggers. You like to nurture people."

"Me? You're wrong, Laurie. Do natural nurturers have killer instincts?"

"The worst. Remember the lioness with her cubs?"

"Well, I know one thing—Steve is not taking those girls to South America. If he wants a fight, he's sure found someone who'll give him one."

Once that decision was made, George seemed to relax. Now he had a mission, a purpose. When they returned to the farm, Laurie headed straight for the twins, and he headed straight for the telephone. He and Dr. Ames talked for almost half an hour. After hanging up, he was actually smiling.

"She wants to be with me when I talk to Ellen. She says Ellen trusts her," he told Laurie, obviously overjoyed that the psychiatrist hadn't forbidden him to talk to his sister. "Dr. Ames is going to meet me at the hospital tomorrow afternoon at two. That'll give the rest of us a chance to visit first."

"Oh, George, that's wonderful. Maybe it won't turn out to be much, but it seems like the first break you've had."

"Yeah. The doctor only cautioned me about one thing. If she tells me to be quiet, I'm not to say another word, no questions asked. Hopefully, she won't have to do that." He paused and heaved a sigh. "Now comes the hard part."

Laurie looked at him quizzically.

"I've got to have a talk with Dad. I haven't been through all this just to have him ruin it. He's got to understand that Ellen's truly been sick and is going to need his help. Believe me, I'm not looking forward to it. I'd about as soon explain something to that wall."

GEORGE FOUND JONAS standing and looking out over the cotton fields, so absorbed that the younger man wondered what on earth could be so fascinating about rows of green plants. To George it was the most uninteresting sight on earth, yet his father could spend long minutes simply gazing at his fields. He supposed that mystique about the land was what made some men farmers.

"Got a minute, Dad?"

Jonas smiled. "I'm not doin' much but watchin' 'em grow. Guess I got all the minutes you need. How'd it go this morning?"

George hunkered down on his heels, a comfortable position learned around hundreds of campfires, but his father remained standing. "Not too good. At least it didn't seem so to me. That's what I want to talk to you about. We're taking the girls into the city to see Ellen tomorrow. The doctor's going to meet me there. If everything goes all right, I'm going to do my damnedest to get Ellen home. It's the only way to make sure Steve doesn't get Stacy and DeeAnn."

"Seems funny to me he's settin' up such a howl over this. I never figured him as a dotin' daddy. He was gone more often than not, especially just before he left for good."

"Well, he doesn't want me to have them, and he is their father. Everyone seems to have tunnel vision when it comes to that. Anyway, if Ellen comes home, she's going to need a lot of TLC."

George waited for Jonas to say something, but when nothing was forthcoming he continued. "She really has been sick, Dad. Just as sick as if she'd had a heart attack. Depression isn't an act or a lack of willpower—I've learned that. And she's going to need a recuperation period, just like anyone else who's been sick. She's going to need lots of encouragement to overcome her fear of getting a job and making it on her own. She's probably going to have to take a nothing job at first, and that'll be a blow to her pride. And she'll have to stay here on the farm for a while, just until she gets her confidence up. No adult likes having to run home to Daddy. I'm . . . just counting on you. I'm not asking you not to be yourself—Ellen would see through that right away. Guess what I'm asking for is . . . kindness."

It occurred to him that, for someone who'd never been any great shakes with words, he'd been doing an awful lot of talking lately.

Jonas fixed his glance on the distant horizon, and for a long time he didn't say a word. Finally he made some kind of sound in his throat. "Know somethin'? I'm glad I'm not young anymore. Life was simpler back when I was. Back then the only people who went to shrinks were movie stars and other such crazy people. When your mama died, I was just as sad as I could be, but I didn't let it knock me down. Where would you and Ellen have been if I had? If I'd told anybody I was depressed and needed to see a doctor, I'd'a been laughed out'a town. And when I was your age I didn't know a single person who'd been divorced. Not one. Guess no one ever told us we were supposed to be happy all the time. What's the word everybody uses these days? Fulfilled. Everybody wants to be fulfilled. I never even heard anyone use that word when I was a young man. Everybody was too busy tryin' to put food on the table. Yeah, life was just a whole lot better back then."

The last thing George was in the mood for was one of his father's back-when-I-was-a-kid speeches. Frankly, some of Jonas's "good old days" sounded downright awful to him. "Different, Dad. Not necessarily better. The sickness wasn't Ellen's fault. Neither was the breakup of her marriage. Can I count on you?"

"Reckon so. We got those two young'uns to think about."

George stood up and stuck out his hand. "Appreciate it."

Jonas looked at his son's hand, then took it and shook it firmly. "Don't mention it."

And that, George reflected as he strode back to the house, was the nearest they'd ever come to having a father-son discussion.

STACY AND DEEANN had been quick to notice George's unusual mood since they'd arrived at the farm, and they were just as quick to pick up on the relaxing of the tension. When their uncle informed them that they would be going to visit their mother the following day, the girls naturally assumed that was the reason for the change in Uncle George's spirits—their mother was getting better. That realization was greeted by excitement on their part, tempered by some regrets. Alone, they discussed it.

"Maybe Mom's coming home," Stacy suggested.

"Maybe. If she is, I guess we'll be staying with her from now on," DeeAnn said.

"I guess so." There was a minute of silence. "I wonder if that means living in our old house."

DeeAnn shrugged. "I dunno." Then she remembered Laurie's constant admonitions to her to enunciate more clearly. "I don't know," she said again. "I heard Grandpa say that the house needs to be sold. I don't care. I don't much want to live in it again anyway."

"I'm going to miss the mountains," Stacy mused.

"And I'm going to miss Melissa and having Laurie for a teacher."

"Silly," Stacy said. "We wouldn't have her next year, anyway. We're going into the seventh, and she teaches the sixth."

"Yeah, I forgot. We'll never see Princess again."

"We haven't seen much of her lately, anyway, not now that the Millers have their grandkids visiting. Listen, Dee, I don't think we ought to tell Uncle George and Laurie this stuff. We'll just make them feel bad. And if we make too big a fuss over leaving Laurie, we'll just make Mom feel bad."

"Okay. I won't say anything."

"Do you know what I wish?" Stacy asked.

"Yeah," DeeAnn said without hesitation.

"Well, if you're so smart, suppose you tell me what I wish."

"You wish that you and me and Mom and Uncle George and Laurie could all live together."

"Yeah. I feel sorriest for Laurie," Stacy said. "She won't have anybody."

"Maybe Uncle George will stay with her," DeeAnn suggested.

"No, he won't. You know how he is. He likes to go different places. He only stayed at Laurie's because of us."

"Maybe he will if we ask him to. Tell him that Laurie's going to be all by herself, so maybe he should stay with her a little while."

"We aren't going to talk to Uncle George about any of this, remember?" Stacy propped her chin on her palm. "I'll never get to add more rocks to my collection. Where're you going to find pretty rocks around here? Where're you going to find anything around here? Grandpa's grumpy half the time, and Anna's busy. This farm is—" she searched for the word "—dreary. Besides, I heard Uncle George and Grandpa talking the other day. They said Mom's going to have to go to work."

"I guess that means Daddy's not coming back."

"Do you care?"

DeeAnn shrugged. "Not really. Seems funny that I don't. I felt just awful when he left, but I don't really care anymore."

"Sure will seem weird having Mom go to work. Guess we'll see a lot of this farm."

"And Uncle George and Laurie won't be around." DeeAnn pursed her lips. "But at least this farm isn't South America." The future novelist had a gift for cutting through the nonsense and getting to the heart of the matter.

CHAPTER FIFTEEN

ELLEN CRIED when she caught her first glimpse of her daughters, but those tears didn't cause anyone distress or alarm. They were tears of joy. The girls looked a little embarrassed, but there was no doubt they were glad to see their mother. Laurie had fussed over them too much that morning, but she had to admit that they looked wonderful. They never dressed alike, but that morning they had instinctively eschewed the shorts they'd lived in all summer and put on the same cool cotton dresses. Stacy's was blue and DeeAnn's coral. Stacy's curlier hair formed ringlets around her elfin face. DeeAnn's had been braided, which was the way she liked it—neat and out of the way. Laurie had to forcibly restrain herself from hugging them to death. It was never far from her mind that she and George were, a tiny step at a time, giving the twins back to their mother. The emotional void in her life that their departure would leave was something to be dealt with later, in private.

"Oh, you're going to have to excuse me, all of you," Ellen sniffed. "I didn't think I'd be so emotional. This seems to have knocked the props right out from under me."

She had an arm around each twin and alternately hugged them and looked at them in awe. She began fingering DeeAnn's braid. "What an intricate hairdo."

"I did it," Stacy beamed. "Jill taught us how."

"Jill?" Ellen asked.

"My baby sister," Laurie interjected. "She took quite a shine to these girls."

"Jill got married," Stacy said, "and we got new dresses for the wedding. Wait till you see 'em, Mom. They're bee-utiful!"

"I'll bet." Ellen finally tore her eyes away from her daughters to look first at George, then at Laurie. "Both of you... I know I... owe you a million thanks."

"You don't owe us a thing, hon," George said. "I'm sure Laurie will agree with me when I say that every minute we've spent with these two scamps has been pure pleasure."

Stacy squirmed out of her mother's embrace. "I gotta show you my rocks, Mom. Where's your purse, Laurie?"

Laurie indicated her handbag with a nod of her head and watched while Stacy proudly showed her mother her prized agates, explaining very carefully what each one was. Studying Ellen, she thought there were no outward signs that the woman had been ill, except for a certain fatigue around the eyes. But then, she hadn't known George's sister before; therefore, she couldn't know if she'd changed.

One thing was certain: Ellen was absolutely delighted to see her daughters, and that was a definite plus. Looking at George, Laurie could tell he was filled with encouragement. Things seemed to be moving along very quickly, almost at breakneck speed, so perhaps it would all be over soon. Then they could go on to other problems, of which there were many.

The visit undoubtedly was an unqualified success, and promptly at two o'clock, as planned, Laurie stood and said, "Girls, why don't we go down to the cafeteria and get something to drink? I'm parched. That way your mother and Uncle George can have a few minutes alone." If a visit to the cafeteria didn't eat up enough time, she had noticed a plant-filled atrium on the way in, and also a gift shop. She'd find a way to give George the time he needed.

Stacy and DeeAnn had grown so accustomed to following Laurie's lead that they stood and followed her out of the room without hesitation. "What a lovely woman, George," Ellen said. "No wonder you're so taken with her. Not many people can just step in and ingratiate themselves with two strange children."

"Well, she's a schoolteacher, you know. And she had to raise her brother and sister when their folks died. Kids don't faze Laurie a bit." George got up and walked to the window. He was suddenly overcome by an attack of nervousness, and he wished Dr. Ames would show up so they could get this over with. Having the psychiatrist present would be a blessing, he decided. Recalling all of Laurie's warnings about tampering with something he knew very little about, he realized he was skating on thin ice, and the doctor might keep him from falling through.

"You seem nervous, George," Ellen said. "Is something wrong?"

"No, no. Tell me, what did you think of the girls?"

"Oh, they look wonderful."

"They do, don't they? Healthy and happy. We've had a pretty good time together."

Ellen folded her hands in her lap and gave him a small smile. "When Dad told me that you had taken the girls with you, once I could think at all I thought oh, my God, they'll drive him nuts! But apparently that didn't happen."

George grinned charmingly. "Well, I have to admit that a couple of times in the beginning . . ."

"I can imagine. You amaze me, bro."

"Aw, they're just so damned much fun."

Ellen laughed. "Sometimes it's the people you least expect . . ."

"What?"

"Nothing. Confess now. How much did Laurie have to do with this startling transformation?"

"Plenty," he said honestly.

"Maybe you'll have a family of your own one of these days. Funny, I never would have thought so, but I'll bet you'd make a great father. Have you been considering it?"

"Well, yes, occasionally."

"You know, I used to worry that in the unlikely event you ever showed up with a woman on your arm, she'd be a honky-tonk queen or some plain Jane rancher's daughter who looked like she'd just slid off a horse. And here you are with a beautiful, poised woman who looks like she'd be at home in a drawing room."

"That was my impression of Laurie, too, but once you get to know her, she's very down-to-earth."

"So, you're really considering marriage." Ellen shook her head in disbelief.

"Let's say it's crossed my mind, and it never did before. But I haven't mentioned it to Laurie."

"What's stopping you?"

"I don't have any idea how she would feel about it, for one thing. She missed out on some carefree years, and I wouldn't blame her if she wanted to make up for them now. And, too, I worry about what kind of husband I'd be. What the devil do I have to offer a woman like Laurie?"

"How about love?" Ellen asked sensibly.

George hadn't meant for the conversation to stray toward love and marriage, and he didn't think it was a good idea. He was trying to think of a way to change the subject when there was a light tap on the door, and the psychiatrist walked in. He felt himself relax immediately.

After the customary pleasantries were exchanged, Dr. Ames got right to the point. "Ellen, your brother has something very important to discuss with you."

Ellen frowned slightly and turned to George, giving him her rapt attention.

"Yes, hon, I..." He had planned to ease into it gradually, but now that the time was at hand, he didn't know any way to say it but bluntly. "Steve's back."

Ellen tensed, but only slightly. Certainly her reaction wasn't as dramatic as George feared it would be. Her mouth set in a hard line and began working, and he saw her chest heave. "Is the woman with him?" she asked.

"Yes." He quickly glanced at Dr. Ames, who encouraged him to continue with a nod of her head. "That's the reason the girls and I are back here. Steve's threatened to charge me with kidnapping."

"That's... absurd! Ludicrous!" Ellen snapped. "He's doing that out of pure hatefulness."

"You know how he's always felt about me."

Ellen looked away, fastening her gaze on a potted plant her father had sent her when she'd first entered the hospital. "I think he was jealous of you."

This was news to George. He'd always thought his brother-in-law simply disliked him; that their personalities clashed. "Of me? Why on earth would he be jealous of me?"

"For one thing, he resented the girls' and my fondness for you."

"For pete's sake, I'm your brother! Were you supposed to hate me?"

"In many ways, Steve is an insecure man. He needs constant reassurance that he's the brightest, most handsome, most admired, etcetera. One of the reasons he married me, I think, was that he needed my undying devotion. It fed his ego. The sad thing is that I went along with it to the point that I lost my own identity."

Hope rose like a wellspring in George's heart. If Ellen had developed that much insight into the nature of her marriage, a great deal had been accomplished. He pressed ahead. "There was a hearing yesterday. I asked for custody of the girls until you were well, but Steve is fighting it. I—" he quickly crossed the room, sat beside his sister and took her hands in his "—I don't think they're going to give them to me, hon. I don't think I even have a fifty-fifty chance. The courts have this thing about natural parents, and I've got two strikes against me to begin with—my profession and my marital status. I just don't think I'm going to get them." A hint of panic crept into his voice even though he had vowed to remain calm at all costs. He searched Ellen's face, hoping for some sign that he was getting through to her. He saw nothing, and he was afraid that any minute Dr. Ames was going to tell him he'd said enough. "You're going to have to come home and take over. Otherwise, Steve and that woman are going to take Stacy and DeeAnn to South America.''

Ellen gasped, and her eyes widened. She flung George's hands aside, stood and walked to the window. For several long wordless minutes she simply stood there, leaving George to glance helplessly at Dr. Ames, wondering if he had gone too far. The doctor, however, looked completely unperturbed, and he had to remember that at this point in Ellen's life, Dr. Ames probably knew her far better than he did.

Finally, Ellen turned around and began speaking. "So, my darling husband and helpmate wants his daughters. Peculiar, since he never had much time for them before. George, have you ever wondered what psychotherapy does for a person? I'll tell you. It makes you dig down deep inside and take a good look at yourself. Believe me, I wasn't too crazy about what I saw. I could tell you about all the times I looked the other way when a more sensible woman would have suspected her husband of philandering. This new woman isn't the first, I'm sure of it. She's just the most serious. I always thought that as long as Steve didn't leave me, I was making a go of it, holding on, keeping things together. And, oh, that was so important to me. Anything was preferable to going home and telling my father that I'd failed."

"Hon, don't be hard on yourself," George said.

"Being hard on myself has been the best thing that ever happened to me. Putting my stupidity under a microscope has been very liberating. I allowed Steve to become the center of my life, and he bled me dry. I don't know why I fear being alone. I was always alone. I raised the girls alone because Steve was 'busy.' And I was too afraid to find out what he was busy doing. Well, no more. This time he's gone too far. Wanting to take my daughters to live with another woman in a foreign country, indeed! George, that son of a bitch gets those girls over my dead body! Dr. Ames, can you get me out of this place?''

"Of course I can, Ellen," the psychiatrist said calmly. "But first, we'll have a long talk. I want to be sure you're ready."

"And, darling brother, can you get me a good divorce lawyer?"

Ellen was shaking and close to tears. George stood and went to take her in his arms. He was smart enough to know that it wouldn't be this easy for long. The adrenaline was flowing now, and she was angry, but she'd calm down and be afraid again, many times. She had taken a step—more like a gigantic leap—forward. "That might not be necessary, hon. When Steve finds out you're back home, I imagine he'll agree to a no-fault divorce with you getting custody of the girls. No hassle and not much expense."

"Whatever you say," she whispered. "And you'll stay with me through it?"

There was a pause. Then he said, "Yes, if you need me."

"Thanks. If there's a Hall of Fame for brothers, I'm nominating you."

George didn't think any compliment had ever pleased him so much.

He didn't stay long after that. Now it was up to Ellen and Dr. Ames. The psychiatrist followed him out into the hall when he left the room. "She's doing very well," she said. "She's found something to take her mind off herself. This threat to her daughters might be just what she needed. I'll talk to her, and if I draw the conclusions I think I will, I imagine your sister will be home very soon."

"Thanks, Doctor. I hope Ellen realizes how fortunate she was to have you when she needed someone."

"Ah, Mr. Whittaker, I hope she realizes how fortunate she was to have you."

George wished he felt better than he did about the events swirling around him. No doubt Ellen would thwart Steve's attempt to take the girls to South America, which was good, but that still left one inescapable fact: they would be staying at the farm with their mother. And sometime soon he was going to have to tell them that.

He went in search of Laurie and the twins and found them sitting near the fountain in the atrium. "You two run on down and say good-bye to your mom. We'll wait for you here."

"Is Mom coming home?" Stacy asked.

"I think so, pretty soon."

The girls left, and George sat down beside Laurie. "Is that true, George?" she asked.

"Looks like it. She says Steve's not going to get those girls. She's right. He won't get them if she's well enough to fight him. The old lioness-with-her-cubs instinct came through."

"Well, that's...wonderful." Laurie looked away, lest her expression betray her innermost thought—that it was wonderful only to a degree. Things would never be the same again.

"Laurie, I..." George began hesitantly. "I'm afraid I let Ellen believe I'd stay with her as long as she needs me."

"Oh? What about your job?"

"I'd like to keep it, but if Cassie has to let me go, well ... I'll deal with that when the time comes. The point is, I know you must get awfully restless sometimes. I can't ask you to stay around here indefinitely."

I wish you would, she thought morosely. *I wish you'd beg me to stay by your side. I wish you would passionately declare that you couldn't survive fifteen minutes without me.* "There's not all that much that needs doing back home, and I'm not exactly itching to leave the girls, you know."

A rush of relief swept through George. If she'd said she needed to get on back he wasn't sure what he would have done. Only with Laurie was this going to be bearable. "Good. But you tell me when you want to leave, okay? I'll take you. I might have to come back—probably will—but I'll drive you home. I have to get my truck, anyway."

That was the time, she knew. She should tell him that she really needed to go home—get it over with. It wasn't going to get any easier. "Sure," was all she said.

Stacy and DeeAnn returned then, and the four of them drove back to the farm. It was a strangely silent drive. The girls could usually be counted on for conversation, even when it was about nothing much. But today they seemed deep in private thought.

When they turned off the main road onto the lane leading to the farmhouse George finally broke the silence. "Looks like we got a storm heading our way."

That was when Laurie noticed the angry clouds forming in the west. "Good grief, it's practically upon us. I'm glad we got home when we did."

"Naw, that baby's a good hour away."

She just couldn't get used to flat, flat country.

THE STORM BLEW UP just before they sat down to supper. Summer thunderstorms on the plains never meant gentle, life-giving moisture, but pounding sheets of water accompanied by 40 mile an hour winds and thunder rolls so vicious the entire farmhouse seemed to shake.

"Suppose we ought to go to the storm cellar?" Anna asked.

Jonas snorted. "I'll take my chances in here, if you don't mind. I don't like sharin' my quarters with all those crawlin' things that live in that cellar."

Stacy and DeeAnn exchanged anxious glances, and Laurie thought it would take the National Guard to get her into that cellar. "It's just a summer storm," George said calmly. "It'll blow over in no time."

He was right. The storm gave them a good drenching and moved east, leaving washed air and earth behind and a considerable drop in the temperature. "We all ought'a sleep good tonight," Jonas observed laconically. "Feel that breeze."

The evening passed in much the same way that all evenings at the farm passed. Anna shooed everyone out of the kitchen as soon as supper was over. Laurie had ceased feeling guilty about that since it was obvious that Anna disliked company in her kitchen. Then Jonas went into the living room to watch television. He chose the programs, and he didn't like any noise. For that reason, George and Laurie kept the girls occupied until bedtime. Except for the nights when they drove into town for one reason or another, the four of them usually simply sat on the front porch, talking and watching night come. Then everyone went to bed early. The routine was so repetitious and unvarying that it was stifling. Laurie couldn't imagine why there had always seemed to be so much to do back home, but that was the case. There had been more laughter and noise and activity.

Of course, that was when everyone was there, she thought. Who was going to supply the laughter and noise now?

Tonight the cooler air made the porch more inviting. The four of them played guessing games, which required nothing but imagination, until the girls started yawning. "Okay, off to bed with you," George said, and they acquiesced without a word. Laurie and George stayed outside a bit longer, talking about nothing in particular, thinking about everything in the world. Finally Laurie stood. "I guess I'll call it a day, too. Strange how hard it is to sleep once the sun comes up. The heat, I guess."

"Maybe it'll be better tomorrow." He looked at her longingly. "Good night."

The little bedroom where Laurie had been staying was, for once, cool and comfortable. Still, she couldn't sleep. After being in bed for a half hour or more, she wasn't even drowsy. She missed her own bed, her own house, her own kitchen. A part of her longed to go home, while another part reminded her that nothing would be the same when she did, so why not stay in Oklahoma as long as possible?

Lying there, wide awake, she heard the door to her room open. Raising herself up on her elbows, she saw George enter and close the door behind him. Then she heard the unmistakable click of the lock. Her heart raced wildly, then calmed as a warm glow seemed to spread through every cell and pore. He was only half dressed—barefoot, and wearing jeans and a shirt, but the shirt had been pulled free of the waistband and unbuttoned. Without a word he crossed the room, sat on the edge of the bed and touched the side of her face.

"Hi," he whispered.

"Hi. Do you . . . really think you should be in here?"

He shrugged. "I don't know. Maybe not, but I couldn't stay away, and it's much too muddy to try driving down to the pond."

Laurie smiled almost shyly. Stretching out her arms, she pulled his face down to hers. "Well, I'm very glad you came."

They kissed greedily. Then George quickly dispensed with his shirt and jeans. He wore nothing underneath. Before he could slip beneath the sheet, Laurie ran her fingertips along the length of his bare thigh. "You're a beautiful man, George."

"I've been called many things in my life, but never beautiful."

"Then you've known some disgracefully unobservant women."

Suddenly he was under the sheet, drawing her to him, nuzzling her neck. Then he was covering her face with quick kisses, fondling her breasts. Their lovemaking was at once hot and passionate, gentle and prolonged. Laurie had to bury her face against his chest to muffle her ecstatic cries. It was like a transfusion, a life support system, and what, she wondered, would she do when deprived of him? Wither and die? Live her life as a spinster schoolteacher? Move to some other place and begin that new life she'd been thinking about?

It doesn't necessarily have to be that way, Laurie. You've been special to George, you have to know that. He might stay.

Somehow she didn't agree with the small voice. No matter how wild and farfetched her fantasies about George had become, she'd never been able to picture the two of them wiling away their dotage in the mountains together, and

God knew she had tried. That scenario just didn't jibe with the man he inherently was. She recalled once telling Cassie that she could easily picture George sailing through life, blissfully alone. Unfortunately she still could, and it squeezed at her heart. Last time, he'd left with very little more than a "So long, Laurie." What would he say next time? Thanks for the memories?

"How long do you think it will be before Ellen comes home?" she finally asked.

"I can't think it will be very long. She's not in prison. I guess it's like anyone who's been sick. Once the doctor says you can go home, you can go home. Dr. Ames's talk with Ellen must have gone all right. I'm sure she would have called me if there were problems."

"It's going to be very difficult for her at first."

"Yes, I know. God, I hope Dad comes through."

A lump formed in Laurie's throat. She desperately wanted to ask him about his own plans, but she wouldn't. Sticking her head in the sand was something she had become adept at. "So many of the girls' things are still in the cottage."

George's voice sounded none too steady. "They'll have to be shipped."

"Yes." She rested her head in the comfortable curve of his shoulder. When she was in his arms she usually felt such peace and contentment, but his arms weren't working their usual magic now. She tried to think of what to say, then gave up. What she really wanted to say was *"I love you and I need you, not just sexually but in all the myriad ways a woman needs a man."* But this didn't seem the right time. Laurie wondered if there would ever be a right time for those words. In all the months they had spent together, she'd never seen even a faint sign that he would enjoy hearing them. And as for everything else—the girls, Ellen—there really wasn't anything left to be said. She supposed they each knew how the other felt.

George stirred. "I'd best not fall asleep here. I guess I ought to go to my own room."

"Yes. I wish you didn't have to."

"So do I, Laurie. So do I."

A few more minutes ticked by before he made himself rise and put on his clothes. At the door he turned and blew her a kiss, then let himself out and moved soundlessly down the hall. Once he was gone Laurie experienced a bleakness of spirit like none she'd ever felt before. How in the world had she allowed herself to grow so used to him in such a short time? she wondered. She placed her hand on the indentation in the pillow where his head had been. It was warm. She rolled over, buried her face in it, and after a while she was able to sleep at last.

CHAPTER SIXTEEN

ACTUALLY, everything moved pretty quickly after that. Ellen was home within three days. Her instructions from Dr. Ames were simple: she was to take her medication and continue to see the doctor once a month, more often if Ellen herself felt the need. Steve made only a token protest, reinforcing George's belief that he'd never wanted the girls to begin with. He also agreed to a no-fault divorce and to continuing the child support payments he'd been making. As long as George wasn't getting the girls, he appeared to be satisfied.

On the morning that George drove to the city to get Ellen, Laurie stayed behind with the girls. Even though the farmhouse was big, sleeping space was limited, so it had been decided that Laurie would move in with one of the twins, Ellen would share George's room with the other, and George would move to the small bedroom Laurie had been using. That meant there would be even less privacy than before, something that occurred to George almost immediately—something Laurie tried not to think about at all. Instead she spent the time George was gone making the room changes with the girls. And she gave Stacy and DeeAnn a little pep talk while they were doing it.

"Your mom is going to need lots of love and attention, you realize that, don't you?"

The twins nodded in uncertain unison.

"It's not easy spending so much time in a hospital. You get sort of out of touch with life, if you know what I mean. So your uncle and I are counting on you two to make this transition as smooth as possible. We want you to let her know how glad you are to have her home. Okay?"

More nods.

"You know, you've gotten awfully used to George and me telling you what to do, but now your mom will be around. You must remember to ask her what you can and can't do."

Stacy spoke up. "Laurie, how long are you going to stay here?"

Laurie tried to concentrate on the bedspread she was folding. "I don't know, sweetheart. Not much longer. I've been away from home a long time, and there are things that . . . need doing."

"Like what?" DeeAnn wanted to know. "What do you have to do now that no one's there?"

"Just . . . things."

"I . . . guess you have to go back."

"Well, of course. It's my home. It's where I live."

"Boy, I'll bet you're going to hate it with us gone," DeeAnn said.

Laurie had to look away. "Boy, I'll bet I am, too."

"Are you going to write to us?"

"Of course. But you have to promise to answer my letters."

"We will. Tell Jill if she'll write, we'll write to her, too."

Laurie's heart felt as though it were weighted down with lead. Talk about sharp points! When the time came for the final goodbye, she wasn't going to get through it graciously, of that she was sure. It was a relief to have George and Ellen arrive a few minutes later. The twins ran downstairs to greet their mother, which gave Laurie a short time alone to collect herself before joining them.

That first day was easy, as was the second. The girls had so much to tell Ellen, it seemed they talked nonstop from breakfast to bedtime. And once they were in bed, Ellen bent her brother's ear until the time even the adults had to call it a day.

Jonas was overly solicitous of his daughter in the beginning, which only embarrassed Ellen, but that not being his true nature, the solicitousness soon abated. Mostly he and Anna tried to stay out of the way and let the younger folks handle everything.

And only twice did the girls forget and run to Laurie with a "May we do this or that?" She simply said, "You'll have to ask your mother." All in all, Ellen's homecoming proved to be a happy one.

On the third day George made the first tentative mention of Ellen's looking for a job, but it seemed to unsettle his sister, so he quickly dropped the subject. That was when he realized that Ellen's integration into the mainstream might take longer than he'd hoped.

Then on the fourth day the phone call for Laurie came, and what he had privately feared became reality.

He answered the phone, then handed it to Laurie. "For you," he said tersely. "Jill."

Laurie grabbed the instrument and spoke anxiously. "Jill, honey? Is anything wrong? Where are you?"

Her sister laughed. "Why do you assume all phone calls are bad news? Everything's fine. We're at Tony's parents' house. But when in the devil are you going home?"

"Well, I'm . . . not sure. Why?"

"Laurie, look at a calendar, will you? We're leaving for Albuquerque next week, and I need to get all the wedding gifts ready for shipping. And so many of my things are still in my room. I don't have a key to the house. Did you leave one with anyone?"

Laurie bit her lip. "No, no, I didn't. Not too smart of me, but we left in such a rush."

"Well, I've got to get all of that stuff. I want to take some of it with me, and I was hoping I'd get to see you before leaving. No telling when I'll get the chance again."

"Lord, honey, I want to see you, too." She couldn't let Jill go off to Albuquerque without even seeing her again. "I didn't dream you were going to be in Oklahoma so long."

"Neither did I, but George's business took longer than expected. Well, I . . . just a minute. Let me talk to him."

He was only a step or two away and had been listening intently to Laurie's end of the conversation. He was almost sure he knew what was coming next. When she explained the problem to him, he heaved a sigh and said, "Okay. I'll take you home."

She looked at him, and her stomach churned. "Wh-when?"

He shrugged, feeling miserable. "Tomorrow, I guess. Why put it off?"

"Why, indeed?"

"Without the girls along, you and I can spell each other at the wheel and drive straight through. And . . . I can bring their things back with me."

Lifting the receiver to her ear again, Laurie said, "We'll leave tomorrow, Jill, and we'll drive straight through, so I guess you can come anytime after that."

"Good. How are the girls?"

"They're . . . fine."

"And George?"

"He's fine, too."

"Tell them all I said hi and that I miss them . . . sort of." Jill giggled.

"I take it married life is looking rosier."

"Ah, sure."

"That's good. Give Tony my love, and I'll see you in a few days."

Laurie hung up and stood staring at the phone a minute. *Well, maybe this is for the best,* she thought. What possible purpose would prolonging the departure serve?

Turning, she walked into the dining room where she encountered George and Ellen. They were in the middle of a conversation and didn't notice her for a minute.

"You're leaving?" Ellen was asking, her voice fearful, almost panic-stricken. "But you promised—"

George placed his hands on her shoulders. "It's just for a few days, hon. Just until I get Laurie back home and ge my truck. You know I'm not going to run out on you. I'll be back and stay as long as you need me."

And that, Laurie knew, could be a very long time—long enough for George to perhaps lose his job so there would be even less reason for him to return to the mountains. Long enough for his memories of what they had had together to fade. So tomorrow really could signal the beginning of the end.

She didn't know how she got through supper. Anna's good cooking seemed to stick in her throat, and every bite was an effort. Laurie could barely look at the girls; every time she did she had the worst feeling that she was going to burst into tears. The minute the meal had mercifully ended, she went upstairs to pack, sending up a silent prayer that the twins would get immersed in something on television and leave her to get through the rest of the day as best she could. She couldn't break down and get all weepy in front of them.

Of course her prayer wasn't granted. Stacy and DeeAnn were all too aware that this was the last night they would spend with Laurie, maybe forever, and they were drawn to her like a magnet. Tonight, instead of bursting in with their usual exuberance, they entered the room almost shyly.

"Hi," they chorused.

"Hi."

"Packing?" Stacy asked unnecessarily.

"Mm-hmm."

"Laurie, Uncle George says when we're a little older we can go visit you in the mountains if you're still there." The girl looked puzzled. "Where else would you be?"

That's a good question, Laurie thought. "Oh, there are these people who have been wanting to buy my land, and I've given some thought to selling. Nothing definite has been settled."

"Where would you go?"

"I don't know, sweetheart."

"You'll always let us know where you are, won't you?"

"Of course. You know I will." She was deeply moved by their concern over staying in touch with her, but that would change. Time would pass, they would acquire new interests, and some day when they thought of her, if they ever did, they would remember her simply as a nice lady they'd spent a few months with years ago.

The girls crossed the room and sat on the other bed, watching her with somber little faces. Laurie realized she had folded, unfolded and refolded the same blouse three times. She tossed it in the suitcase and reached for another. "You know, Stacy, maybe I can find you some new rocks for your collection. I'm not an expert like you and George, but I can try. I'll get them all polished up at the lapidary shop and send them to you. Would you like that?"

"Oh, boy, would you?"

"Sure. I'm not...going to be very busy now...that there's only me. And, DeeAnn, I want you to promise that the first chance you get to take a course in creative writing, you'll do it, okay?"

DeeAnn's face brightened momentarily, and she nodded enthusiastically. "And I'll send you some more stories, too."

"I'd love that, I really would."

"Will you tell Melissa we're sorry we couldn't say good-bye?"

"Of course."

"And give Princess a big hug for us?"

"Y-yes." Oh, how she wished they would go find something to do! She had never felt so blue, so powerless over her emotions.

A heavy pall of silence fell over the room. Laurie pretended rapt absorption in her packing; actually, she could barely see the garments she was carelessly piling into the suitcase for the damnable moisture collecting in her eyes. Finally she heard a rustling sound as the girls stood up. "Guess we'll go take our baths now."

"All right."

"We'll see you later. And in the morning before you leave."

Laurie looked up. "Oh, sweetheart, there's no need for that. George says we're going to leave very early, and—"

"But, Laurie," DeAnn said in a plaintive voice, "we have to."

"All . . . right." So tonight wouldn't be the end of it, after all. Every drop of misery was going to be wrung out of the farewell.

As soon as she knew they were gone, Laurie roughly brushed at her eyes, almost angry at the tears that now came so easily and frequently. God, she was going to miss them! How long would she have to feel this way before the ache dulled and the numbness came? If they really did get an unusually early start in the morning, this time tomorrow night she would be home, and after that what would break the sameness of her days? She would never see Stacy and DeAnn again; that seemed to be the way things were going. George would leave as soon as he was rested, and chances were good she'd never see him again, either. Jill would dash in for a day or two, then be off to Albuquerque, and her visits would be limited to two, possibly three a year. She'd never be able to so much as look at the cottage again without remembering the time George and the girls had lived there. She'd never be able to rent it to anyone else again. The picture in her mind was one of such absolute aloneness that she shuddered.

I'm going to sell that damned place! Before it was a place of permanence for Jill and Andy. Well, they're gone. Now it's just a place full of memories that need to be expunged. I'm going to take the money and run!

The decision should have been liberating; strangely, Laurie didn't feel much of anything. She was trying to decide whether to go downstairs and join the others, or to stay in the room when Ellen walked through the door. "I'm not interrupting you, am I?" George's sister asked quietly.

"No. I just finished packing."

"You've been a hair away from tears all evening," Ellen said sympathetically. "I know the feeling."

Laurie's lashes dipped briefly. "I'm afraid I let those little people get under my skin."

"I came up here to thank you."

"I really wish you wouldn't."

"All right, I won't," Ellen said with a small smile. "I wouldn't know how."

"I've made the girls promise to write, and I'd like it if you'd encourage that. Their interest will wane in time, but in the beginning it . . . would be nice. I'd love hearing from them."

"Of course."

"And you take care of yourself. Just take it a step at a time."

"Sometimes I get awfully nervous, thinking about meeting old friends again, wondering if they think I'm . . . crazy or something."

"Anyone who does wasn't much of a friend to begin with."

"I feel awfully guilty about keeping George here and away from you."

Laurie frowned. What an odd thing for her to say. "Ellen, if there's one thing I'm sure of it's that George will do what he wants to do."

"I . . . I wish there had been time for us to get to know each other better, to really become friends, Laurie."

"I wish so, too." Did she? she wondered. It seemed to her that knowing certain members of this family had brough her nothing but heartbreak.

IF THAT NIGHT was difficult, the following morning was a ordeal. It began shortly after the sun had cleared the hori zon, at which time Laurie woke and went into the bath room to shake off the vestiges of what little sleep she' gotten. Then she quietly dressed, stuffed her gown into th suitcase and shut it, trying all the while not to look at th sleeping DeeAnn in the other bed. She hoped George wa up and ready so they could get on the road. Only when she had left the farm would the healing process begin.

He was up and ready, but first, nothing would do but that they eat one of Anna's farm-sized breakfasts. Laurie wasn't hungry, but she forced herself to eat a respectable amount. And before they had finished the meal, Ellen joined them, looking better than Laurie had ever seen her look. Finally, George stood and announced that it was time they were going.

Laurie breathed a sigh of relief. She was going to be spared that one last goodbye to the girls. It was something to be grateful for, at least.

That wasn't to be, however. When they all walked to the foyer where George had put her suitcase, they saw two very sleepy-looking girls in shortie pajamas sitting on the bottom step, looking like two lost waifs. The minute they saw Laurie they rushed to her, one on either side, and began clinging to her like a lifeline. One of them was crying quietly. Maybe both were. Laurie closed her eyes, swallowed thickly and couldn't find her voice. Opening her eyes, she looked at George pleadingly. *Please help me.*

George read the message, and his heart went out to her. He quickly closed the gap between them and gently tugged each twin away from her. "Come on, you guys. You'll see Laurie again."

"Wh-when?"

Laurie didn't even know which one had asked the question. She hurried out of the house and got into the car, deliberately turning her back on the house. She simply hadn't been able to say good-bye one more time. By the time George got to the car, tossed her suitcase in the back seat and slid behind the steering wheel, her tears were falling in profusion.

Seeing her cry, really cry, tore at George. "Laurie, honey, don't cry. They'll come to visit you."

"It's... n-not th-the s-same."

He felt so helpless, and that was a feeling he despised above all others. "Look, tell you what. I'll stay down south a few days longer than I'd intended, until you have your visit with Jill. Then you can come back with me. How's that?''

"That w-would only b-be putting off the in-inevitable.''

"I'm sorry. I ... wish I could do something.''

"You can't. Please, George ... j-just go!''

"Okay, okay.'' He started the car, wheeled it around and pointed it toward the main road.

Laurie leaned her head on the back of the seat, letting her breath escape in a strangled sigh. Now that it really was over it seemed to her there was so much she could have done to avoid this miserable ending.

What, Laurie, what? her maddening inner voice taunted her. *This was out of your hands from day one. Your biggest mistake was getting so involved with George and the girls in the first place.*

I know, I know, but I couldn't help it.

The determining factors had nothing to do with you. The divorce, Ellen's illness, Steve's animosity toward George were what brought this to its inevitable conclusion. There's nothing you can do now.

There must be.

Fine time to be thinking that.

Then Laurie made another mistake. Drawn by some latent masochistic tendency to prolong her misery, she twisted in the seat and looked back at the house. Stacy and DeeAnn had come out onto the front porch and were sitting on the top step. They looked very forlorn. Laurie thought of all the nights the four of them had sat on the porch, watching the sunset and making up silly guessing games. She wondered who would do such nonsense with them now.

Suddenly an explosion occurred in her brain. Turning, her heart thumping like mad, she watched the main highway looming only a few yards ahead. "George, stop this car!''

"What?''

"Stop the car! Pull over! I ... I want to talk to you.''

"Laurie, we've got hours and hours ahead of us with nothing to do but talk," he groaned. Still, he did as she had ordered. He slowed and pulled over, then stopped the car.

"I've been thinking," she said.

"Couldn't we discuss it sometime during the next eight or nine hours?"

"No."

"Okay. So, what have you been thinking?"

The trouble was, she hadn't been thinking. This had all come to her in a flash, and her thoughts were a jumble in her head. She had to try to sort them out as she went along. "Well, Ellen seems fine, right? She's going to get a divorce, and she seems to have accepted it, right?"

"Right. Right." He reached for the key in the ignition. "Laurie, I'm really not looking forward to driving to the mountains and then turning around and coming back, all in a couple of days or so. Let's rehash this rehash as we go, okay?"

"No! Not okay. Just listen to me, please."

George settled back in the seat, a partly amused, partly bewildered expression on his face. "Okay. Talk away."

"The only thing that really seems to be bothering her is going back to face her old friends and trying to find a job, just starting all over and trying to make a brand new life for herself and the girls. I don't blame her, really. Job-hunting for the first time when you're in your mid-thirties, competing with all the fresh-faced young things right out of school... And her friends are probably married—not too good for her right now."

"I agree, but she's going to have to cope with a lot of things. It's just part of the recuperative process." George couldn't imagine what she was getting at.

Laurie wasn't too sure herself. She was letting her thoughts spill out as they formed. She wanted to be forceful and persuasive. "She'll probably have to take a low-paying job at first. And her old house is going on the market. She'll have to find someplace to live. Anything fit to live in that's adequate for her and the girls will be expensive. Stacy and DeeAnn will be latch-key children.''

George rubbed his eyes wearily. ''I know she has problems. She knows she has problems.''

''A load of them. Too many, really, for someone recuperating from a depression. So...'' She took a deep breath, then turned to him, her eyes bright and hopeful. ''George, there's so much room at home, with the house and the cottage—so much room and only me to live there.''

''Laurie, I—''

She hurried on quickly, not giving him the chance to say anything sensible that would destroy this fantasy of hers. ''The girls love it there. They've made friends. They like school. Stacy has her rock collection, and... I'll tell you something else. I've lived in the Davis Mountains all my life. I know so many people in Alpine and Fort Davis and Marfa, and not just a few of them owe me a favor or two. I know I could help Ellen get a job. Down there Ellen truly could make a brand new start in life, and there'd always be someone around to watch the girls, and...'' She paused to take a breath.

George smiled at her fondly. He reached out to finger a strand of her hair. ''What about your brand new start? What about the eighty-five grand? That's an awful lot of money.''

''I guess it is, but I've been thinking about that, too. The bank knows what I've been offered, right? Why wouldn't they loan me that much to buy livestock and feed and get the ranch going again? But if they won't, I'll go to the federal housing people. They'll loan me the money if the local banks turn me down. No one has a better credit rating than I do. I don't know if I ever told you this, but when my folks died they left a small mountain of debts. I paid every one of them off. It took years, but I did it, and everyone back home knows it. I swore then that I would never borrow so much as a dollar, but that's ridiculous. All ranchers have to borrow money occasionally. Cassie would give me the advice I need, tell me what to do and what not to do. Oh, it

would be so wonderful to see Tyler Ranch be a real working ranch again. And what a splendid life it would be for
the girls—animals all over the place. They would learn so
much."

George looked at her clearly and steadily, realizing what
she was offering. A kind of wild joy rose up in him, then
settled into quiet contentment. "Ah, Laurie, you amaze
me. What about Hawaii and Tahiti and Sydney and all
those places you've dreamed of?"

"They've been there a long time. I guess they'll still be
around years from now when—" she paused to smile as it
dawned on her that what had seemed preposterous only a
minute ago now seemed entirely possible "—when I'm a
cattle baron."

George slid across the seat and took her in his arms,
holding her loosely and propping his chin on the top of her
head. "You're going to need someone to help you run this
cattle empire of yours. Cassie can give you advice, but what
about the hands-on work?"

"I...don't suppose you know of some hardworking
cowhand who'd like the job, do you? Long, long hours and
almost nonexistent wages."

"Hmm, sounds like some other jobs I've had. I just
might be able to handle it. Would you really want me to
stay with you?"

"Of course," she said simply.

"Just like that?"

"Just like that."

George pulled back slightly and looked down at her
flushed, exhilarated face. "Tell me something. What if that
judge had called your bluff? What if he'd said I could have
the girls on the condition that I was getting married right
away? Would you have gone through with it?"

"Yes."

"You would have done that for me and the twins?"

Laurie's head went back, and she rolled her eyes. "Oh,
George, sometimes I wonder about you. No, you dense idiot, I would have done it for me! If all your brains weren't

in your roping hand you'd know I've been in love with you
for years."

"Laurie!"

"It seems to me I was disgustingly obvious, always
knocking myself out trying to be clever and charming and
attractive, anything to get you to notice me, but nothing
ever worked."

"This stuns me! You never said a word, never gave any
indication—"

"It wasn't my place!"

"Oh, for God's sake! Are you talking about all those
years I worked at the DO? I thought you barely knew I was
alive."

"I find it almost impossible to believe that a man could
live so long and never learn to see what's before his eyes.
Didn't you ever wonder why I was always hanging around
the DO?"

"Well, no. You and Cassie are friends."

Laurie laughed lightly and shook her head. "True, she's
my friend, and I like her, but come on! How fascinating can
two heterosexual women find each other? Didn't you ever
wonder why she asked you—or ordered you—to work for
me one day a week? That was her way of giving me some
time to impress the socks off you."

George took off his hat, raked his fingers through his
hair, then replaced the hat. "I don't believe any of this."

"I was such a lovesick creature in those days, and when
you left last November, I moped around for days mooning
over a lost love that I'd never even had. Oh, maybe it wasn't
love, not way back then. How can you be in love with
someone who never says more than 'Howdy' to you? But I
sure was interested, and I sure worked hard to get you interested. It was the most frustrating experience of my life,
believe me. I used to wonder why I didn't expend my efforts on something easy, like single-handedly bringing an
end to war and world hunger. You were so damned polite
I'd want to scream."

"I told you—you were too much of a lady. Coming on strong to you would have been like sidlin' up to the Queen Mother and saying, 'Hi'ya, honey, what's happenin'?'"

She touched his face gently. "But you know better now, don't you? You know I'm just flesh and blood—an ordinary woman."

"You're not ordinary, and you never will be." He drew her to him again, nestling her head in the curve of his shoulder. "Ah, Laurie, I don't have any idea how to be a husband."

"Who does until he becomes one? Does this mean…am I being proposed to?" Her heart seemed to spill from its bounds.

"I guess you are."

"You'd better think about this long and hard, George. I'll never let you go. If your feet start itching, too bad. You'll be roped, tied and branded—stuck with me until the day you die. You think you know something about responsibilities, but you ain't seen nothin' yet. You'll have a ranch to get on its feet, a wife who'll cling too much at times, and, hopefully, a couple of squalling kids. We'll never be rich, probably never even have much money. I'll teach for a year or so, just until we get going, but after that we'll be on our own. You'll probably never see Montana, and I'll never see Sydney. You had just better think about it."

"Somehow none of that scares me a bit." Again he held her away from him, looking at her with eyes that were alive and gentle and excited and loving. "I love you, Laurie. There! I don't know why that was so hard to say. I've thought it for months. During that time you taught me more about really living than I learned in thirty-three years. Looking back on all those rambling years, I think I was just looking for something or someone to tie myself to. I thought I was happy, but I was really just restless. These last months with you and the girls—now, that was happy. That gave me a reason to get out of bed in the morning and something to look forward to at the end of the day. Even a tumbleweed finally lodges itself against one particular fencepost eventually. Well, I'm lodging myself against you, and it feels damned good.''

Laurie's eyes filled up again, and her voice shook. ''Oh, George, I've been so lonely so many times. Years ago, when the folks died, there were so many worries I didn't know which way to turn. But I'd learned to live with that kind of loneliness. And then you and the girls came along and filled my life with such joy. Losing all of you promised to be more than I could cope with.''

''You were never in any danger of losing me.''

''I didn't know that. I was afraid that with the girls gone, you'd have no reason to stay.''

''I should have told you. The minute I felt it I should have told you.''

''Now I'm going to have all of you again, and, oh, God, I wonder if you can die from too much happiness.''

George frowned as something suddenly occurred to him. ''Laurie, Ellen is supposed to continue seeing Dr. Ames every month.''

''Please, there's no problem we can't work out a solution to. We'll find her a good therapist. So we'll have to drive to San Angelo or El Paso once a month. Big deal. It'll be fun for all of us to get away for a day or two. We'll do anything we have to do, just like we did with the girls. Okay?''

''Hey, lady, I just work here. You seem to be in charge.''

''I'm glad you realize that. Listen, this is the game plan. You need to give Ellen time to tie up all the loose ends, talk to Dr. Ames and get Steve's signature on some divorce papers. Say a week. Then they'll come back to stay with us for good. Agreed?''

''Suits me.''

''I wish we could take the girls back with us now.''

George rubbed his chin thoughtfully. ''Yeah, but we'd better not do that. It just might get Steve riled up, and they need to get used to their mom being in charge of them again. It's not going to be easy, but you and I are going to have to learn to be...just an aunt and uncle from now on.''

Laurie thought her insides had melted. "Yes, we are, aren't we? Let's go back and tell them. They'll want to do it, won't they?''

"Are you kidding? The girls will jump for joy, and the arrangement is a godsend for Ellen.'' George kissed her lovingly, once, twice, three times. Then he started the car, wheeled it around and headed for the house.

Stacy and DeeAnn were still sitting on the porch step. Seeing the car reverse its direction, they looked at each other and wiped their tears.

"Do you think they forgot something?'' DeeAnn asked.

"Yeah,'' Stacy said, an elated grin spreading across her face. "Us!''

Standing, they waved wildly, and with delighted whoops they ran down the steps to meet them.

CHAPTER SEVENTEEN

RAZE THIS HOUSE, INDEED! Laurie wandered through the rooms of the only home she'd ever known, seeing it through new eyes. No doubt she would live in it the rest of her life, but that suited her fine. She would probably never see any of the grand places she had envisioned, but that didn't seem very important, either. Once, many years ago, she had been so sure her life would be lived somewhere else, but now she couldn't imagine being anywhere but here.

It was late. The long drive was over, and they were safely home, both of them bone-tired but filled with excited anticipation. As Laurie unpacked, sorting the clothes that could be put in the closet from the ones that needed to go in the washer, she smiled, remembering Stacy's and DeeAnn's cries of glee when they had heard the plan she and George had devised for them. Ellen, hesitant at first, soon realized that they were offering her that rarest of all things—a fresh start in life. So, a week or ten days from now, their little family unit would be clustered together. It had been a long time since Laurie had felt so secure and unfettered.

She picked up her makeup case and carried it into the bathroom, setting it beside George's shaving kit. Seeing that kit served to remind her of the need for cleaning out drawers and closets to make room for him. It was going to be strange and wonderful sharing the house with a man.

Leaving the bathroom, she went to the bedroom window and peered out. Lights shone from the cottage's windows. George had gone in to check on things and gather some of his belongings. The cottage would belong to Ellen and the girls now, and it was certainly better than anything they could have afforded to rent. And coming back to it next week would give Stacy and DeeAnn a feeling of permanence. Laurie hoped that when they got older and life took them far away from the Tyler Ranch, it would be a place they'd want to return to again and again.

She saw the lights go out one by one; then George left the cottage. She hurried downstairs to meet him, entering the kitchen just as he walked through the back door. He was carrying a load of clothes, which he dumped on the kitchen table, and he was wearing a pleased-as-punch grin on his face.

"I called Ellen," he said.

"Oh?"

"I wanted to make sure she was getting things taken care of on that end. She told me something very interesting." He chuckled and shook his head.

"Well, do you mind letting me in on it?"

"She had a long telephone conversation with Dr. Ames this afternoon. Apparently the doctor thinks our plans are terrific. She said she knows I'll take good care of her. And Dr. Ames left a message for me." He paused and chuckled again. "Seems she was talking to Judge Benson. The judge told her he was glad everything had been resolved, but that if he'd had to hand down a decision, he was going to leave the girls with me. He said I seemed like a very reliable individual. Dr. Ames knew I'd get a charge out of that."

Laurie laughed delightedly. "Oh, George! See, didn't I tell you? You're a natural—a closet homebody. That judge was with you less than an hour, and he saw it."

"Me, of all people!"

Laurie closed the space between them, locked her hands behind his neck and kissed him soundly. "I'm very proud of you and of the way you handled yourself through all this. You're—" she tried to think of a good phrase "—a port in a storm."

He grinned. "I'm trying to stay humble as hell in the face of all this flattery. Lord, it's good to be home, isn't it?"

"Yes," Laurie said softly. "It's certainly that."

"The way I feel now, I'd just as soon never have to go further away than the county line. And we have a whole week, just the two of us."

"Ah . . . not quite, my love. Jill will be here tomorrow or the next day, remember?"

George sighed. "No, I'd forgotten, but I guess we can afford to give Jill a couple of days when we have the rest of our lives."

"The rest of our lives," Laurie murmured. "A lifetime ahead of us. I think we're going to need every second of it to do everything we want to do." She slipped her arms from around his neck and took him by the hand. "Turn out the lights, love. Let's go to bed."

"I'm right behind you."